'This is the third most ~~ ...~~ ...he Beano and 'Steve Brookstein - My ~~S...~~ *...also flipping funny* ...~~, it should come~~ with a free pair of socks because you'll laugh off your current ones.' Greg James, Radio 1 DJ

'A graphic and hilarious insight into what it's like to grow up to be a woman. It made me grateful that I'm a man.' Jon Holmes, comedian and Xfm DJ

'Thank you, Tash Desborough, for writing a book which has seen both of my teenagers disappear into their rooms for two days, only emerging every few hours to attempt to read me a line or two, but failing due to their fits of giggles . . . Please write another, immediately.' Liz Fraser, best-selling author and broadcaster

'I haven't put this book down since the I read the back cover and choked on my own spit, I laughed so much.' Emily (15), Liz Fraser's daughter

'It's so good, it made me envious; I wish I'd written it!' Andy Robb, author of *Geekhood: Close Encounters of the Girl Kind* and *Geekhood: Mission Improbable*

'People should read more books in general, and they should all start with this one. Only when they have finished *Weirdos vs. Quimboids* should they progress onto other literature eg, Dickens, Shakespeare.' Chris Smith, Radio 1 Newsbeat

'I LOVE it! I'm hooked...think Georgia Nicolson meets Adrian Mole. B.U.M. is my new literary heroine – sort of – a bloomin delightful read!' Nemone Metaxas, BBC 6 Music DJ

'It's laugh-out-loud funny, clever and quirkier than one of Paloma Faith's hats. I defy anyone to read this book and not laugh.' Wondrous Reads

'Georgia Nicolson has met her match . . . A brilliant read which will make you laugh like a loon.' The Overflowing Library

'Probably one of the funniest books with a female lead character I've ever read. *Weirdos vs. Quimboids* is a REAL teen girl's story and it's got laughs and cringes on every page.' Sister Spooky

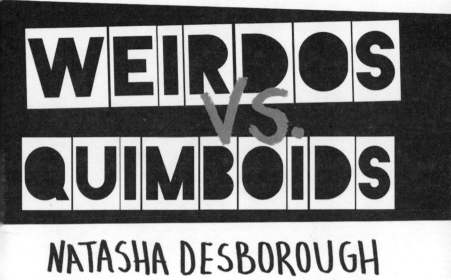

WEIRDOS VS. QUIMBOIDS

NATASHA DESBOROUGH

Catnip

CATNIP BOOKS
Published by Catnip Publishing Ltd
Quality Court
off Chancery Lane
London WC2A 1HR

First published 2013
1 3 5 7 9 10 8 6 4 2

Text © 2013 Natasha Desborough
Illustrations by Vicky Barker

A CIP catalogue record for this book is available from the British Library

ISBN 978-1-84647-171-1

Printed and bound by CPI Group (UK) Ltd, Croydon, CR0 4YY

www.catnippublishing.co.uk

For Louisa

UNDERSTANDING THE SCALE OF SHAME

LEVEL 1: THE BURDEN OF AN EMBARRASSING NAME
e.g. B.U.M., P.O.O., Lee King (Year 8), Rosie May Trump (Year 7), our History teacher Mr Longcock.

LEVEL 2: MINOR FACIAL BLEMISHES e.g. a massive SPOT on the end of your nose or a sexually transmitted cold sore.

LEVEL 3: EMBARRASSING PARENTS e.g. your mum wears a T-shirt in public bearing a cringeworthy slogan such as: END RACISM AND SEXISM NOW. KILL ALL WHITE MALES. (Thankfully this particular T-shirt died a death when dad 'accidentally' put it in the wash with his new black jumper.)

LEVEL 4: BOWEL ISSUES e.g. farting in an empty classroom just before someone comes in or doing a ginormous poo in the school toilet/friend's house when the loo won't flush.

LEVEL 5: AWKWARD PHYSICAL CONTACT e.g. accidentally touching a naked person in the changing room; kissing someone's ear or mouth when you were aiming for the cheek.

LEVEL 6: MAJOR PHYSICAL DEFECT *e.g. an obvious wart, an obvious erection (boys only of course), a gross fungal infection or a lady moustache.*

LEVEL 7: UNKNOWINGLY REVEALING UNDERWEAR *e.g. knickers getting caught in your skirt or accidentally pulling your T-shirt off along with your sweater and thus revealing your bra.*

LEVEL 8: FREUDIAN SLIPS *e.g. saying 'testicles' instead of tentacles, 'pubic' instead of public, 'orgasm' instead of organism or absentmindedly calling your art teacher 'Daddy' in front of the whole class (in my defence I was extremely sleep deprived after recovering from a nasty bout of Glandular).*

LEVEL 9: PERIOD ISSUES/NUDITY *e.g. tampons falling out of your school bag, someone walking into the toilet cubicle while you are 'sorting yourself out' or a stray nork popping out of your swimsuit in the communal changing area.*

LEVEL 10: WATCHING A SEX SCENE ON TV WITH YOUR PARENTS OR ACTUALLY CATCHING THEM AT IT. *AWFUL. AWFUL. AWFUL. Arrrrrrggghhhhhhhh!*

'Felix Winters looks so HOT in a tuxedo,' I whispered. *His bum cheeks are like two orbs of wonder.* 'Could a boy *be* any more perfect?'

'It would take a brave girl to attempt to prise him away from Fiona's claws,' Petrina replied from behind me. 'Look at her with her leg cocked up against his thigh. She's like a dog marking its territory on a lamp post.'

'One day he'll realise how shallow she really is,' I sighed, knowing that this would never really happen. 'Oooh look! Toby's undoing his shirt!'

Petrina shoved me roughly out of the way so that she could get a better look at the second hottest boy in the school. I shoved her back, not wanting to be separated from the vision of Felix for even one minute.

'You two are so pathetic,' a surly voice growled from the darkness.

I jumped about a foot in shock and smacked my face hard on the window. Luckily no one inside the party heard and they continued enjoying their über-cool lives. Walter removed his headphones and stepped into the light, his long fringe casting a shadow that shrouded his whole face.

I rubbed my freezing hands together and pushed them down into the warmth of my duffle coat pockets. I knew how Tiny Tim must have felt in *A Christmas Carol*, standing with my nose pressed up against the icy window, gazing in awe at a world beyond my reach. I watched in envy as the 'Winners' moved their lithe bodies in time to the thumping thud of the big-beat bass, their luminous faces expressing an ecstasy of which I could only dream. The velvet hum of ostentation lingered in the air and I breathed it in deeply. It smelled exotic and alluring.

'For God's sake, Blossom. Stop slobbering all over the window,' said Petrina sternly. 'We'll be even more uncool if you get spotted drooling like a leaky stopcock.'

Neither Petrina nor I have ever been invited to Fiona Tittledown's annual New Year's Eve Ball at her parents' golf club. It's the highlight of the Bridge Mount Secondary School social calendar and *everyone* gets invited. Well, everyone except us.

'I'm going home,' said Walter.

Petrina pushed her glasses back up on to the bridge of her nose. Her eyes are already massive, but behind those lenses it's like looking into two heavily kohl-lined, blue whirlpools. 'You can't spend New Year's Eve on your own. Don't you want to come back to Blossom's?'

Walter shrugged. 'Nah. New Year's Eve is overrated.'

I glanced down at my watch. 'We better get going, too. I said we'd be back by eight forty-five.'

Not only was it the biggest night of the school year, it was

12

also a Blue Moon and my parents had decided to celebrate this rare double occasion by holding a party for twenty guests in our back garden.

'Do you think the naked moon dancing will have finished by now?' asked Petrina, looking hopeful.

'Probably not,' I replied. 'The real fun begins at midnight when someone's crowned Lunar King or Queen. Then they welcome in the New Year by throwing Monopoly money onto a bonfire as they sing the National Anthem.'

'Sounds hideous,' scoffed Petrina. 'Is it supposed to be post-modern satire?'

'What's that then?' I asked, knowing it was likely to be yet another reminder of how utterly embarrassing my parents are.

'Pretentious political piss taking,' said Walter.

He may not say much but, when he does, Walter is usually spot on.

We arrived back at mine just as my parents' ceremonial naked dancing had finished (a small mercy that I was INCREDIBLY thankful for).

There had been talk of a naked group yoga session, but it had been vetoed by Mum due to the 'over-stimulating energy' caused by the Blue Moon. (Can you imagine? Bleurgh!) My sister, Breeze, was out at her boyfriend's club night, so she wasn't there to witness the sight of the guests all wrapped up in their smelly, organic, chunky knitwear singing around a bonfire.

It was Petrina who first noticed my dad standing at the end

of our garden, jabbing his finger aggressively at a man with a grey, pointy, wizard's beard. We both crept quietly towards them.

'Look it's all above board, my friend,' said The Wizard, his palms facing towards my father. 'Nothing dodgy.'

'Not in my house,' whispered my father slowly. 'Have some respect.'

'We're outside,' said The Wizard, calmly looking up at the night sky. 'Under Mother Nature's roof. And I go by *her* rules.'

My mum suddenly appeared between them. She looked directly at The Wizard.

'Are we all getting along nicely?' she said, before turning towards my dad. 'Like grown ups?'

Dad sheepishly walked towards the house, then stopped dead, looked over his shoulder and mumbled quietly, 'Idiot.'

The Wizard pretended to be mortally wounded, staggering around clutching at his chest.

'Ow, your words are like poison,' he mocked.

'INSIDE. NOW!' my mum yelled at the top of her voice. Mum rarely raises her voice when she's angry. Instead, she prefers to use her fierce yoga eyes to convey her displeasure. Like a deceptively serene Medusa, my mother can turn your insides to stone with one glance. It's terrifying and impressive in equal measure – a technique she has probably practised in front of the mirror for years. I'm hoping to perfect my 'sexy seduction stare' using the same training method.

MY NEW YEAR'S RESOLUTIONS

1. Find out who The Wizard is. (I can't stop thinking about him after his weird interaction with my parents.)

2. Get a boyfriend or, failing that, at least go on a date. (It's about time I got out of the starting blocks.)

3. Get invited to a proper party. (Naked moon dancing parties don't count. Neither do ones that include pass the parcel or musical bumps.)

4. Practise my guitar every day. (Dad bought me a metallic blue Yamaha Pacifica last summer for my birthday. I've called her 'Cassiopoeia' after the ancient Greek Queen who boasted about her beauty. I did wonder if the regular strumming of a female fret might mean I was subconsciously becoming a lesbian, but as I will probably name my next guitar 'Achilles' after the strong MANLY Greek warrior with dodgy heels, I think I can rule out the possibility for now.)

5. Stop squeezing my spots.

6. Cut down on Big Macs.

7. Form a band.

8. Meet Josh Raven.

9. Stop biting my fingernails. (Or at least stop biting nine of them. I will leave myself one nail to nibble on in case I get desperate. That way there will be no pressure.)

10. Start writing my Vampire series THE HARLOT MISTFANG CHRONICLES.

The following day when I quizzed Dad about his argument with The Wizard, he brushed me off by saying, 'Oh man, I can barely remember anything that happened after ten o'clock. The scrumpy almost knocked me unconscious.' But his anxious expression told me that his memory was as clear as glass.

Mum's response was similarly vague. 'What say you? A wizard? I know not what. Yon cider turned me fuddled.'

I wished I hadn't bothered.

It's not been easy having woolly, liberal-minded parents. My life was essentially doomed from the moment I was burdened with the name Blossom Uxley-Michaels. My mum always says that when I finally flopped out of her lady parts, a little bit of her brain fell out too. She says that tiny little fragments of her sanity were left lying on the blood-splattered hospital floor. What she doesn't realise is that tiny pieces of my dignity were left there too. Bridge Mount rules state that all pupils must have their initials embroidered on to their P.E. kit, but let's face it, even Fiona Tittledown, the (supposedly) coolest Winner to

16

walk the Earth, would struggle to hold on to any credibility with *B.U.M.* spelled out across their polo shirt collar. It's unfortunate that my best friend is called Petrina-Ola Olsen, as this makes us a double target. On the other hand, nothing cements a friendship quite like a constant stream of *Bumface* and *Poohead* taunts. Sometimes it helps to know there's someone else out there waking up with a Shame Level set at 1 (see *Understanding The Scale Of Shame* chart).

I really could have done without the stupid slangers, Fiona and her deputy prime-quimboid Lucy, sarcastically applauding as our family car broke down in a cloud of black smoke outside the school gates on the first day of term. It's bad enough being driven to school by your parents, but it's almost unbearable when your dad drives an ancient, multi-coloured VW camper van that lets off rhythmical engine farts and is decorated with hippie peace symbols.

'Maybe The Wizard was a drug dealer peddling his wares at your parents' New Year's Eve party?' Petrina pondered as we helped to bump start the van. 'Perhaps your dad was angry that drugs had been brought into your house.'

I shook my head, pointing at the graffiti cartoon of a Rastafarian smoking a big spliff carefully sprayed on one of the back doors.

'Dad's about as broad-minded as a person can get'.

Dad has a particularly humiliating anecdote that he likes to use as a warning against buying drugs from an untrustworthy source. A man claiming to be an African Voodoo King once sold him a dodgy Black Magic acid tab at the Glastonbury Festival. The next thing Dad remembers is trotting around on the Pyramid Stage three days later in front of 50,000 people, wearing only a tinfoil thong and claiming to be a donkey named Barbara. I've told him he doesn't need to repeat the story as I won't be buying drugs from anyone since I would never dream of taking anything to enhance my mood (apart from a responsible amount of alcohol and also Rescue Remedy, which I could possibly become addicted to if I'm not careful).

REASONS I DON'T EVER WANT TO TAKE MIND-ALTERING DRUGS

1. They can make you attempt to eat your own face.

2. They can make things look like they're melting and I hate all melting things. Those melting Salvador Dali clocks I saw in Walter's art book still give me nightmares.

3. They make you listen to Jazz and Jazz is AWFUL.

4. I don't want to run the risk of ending up like my parents. I'm sure drugs have a lot to do with their embarrassing behaviour. At least I hope it's drugs . . . God – what if it's genetic?

5. They are too expensive.

'The Wizard's probably just some idiot who got on your dad's nerves,' whispered Walter as we sat outside the hall waiting to go into our mock History exam. Walter and I have been friends since primary school when he rescued me from the apple tree to which I had been tied. In each other we recognised an outcast, someone who didn't fit in, who attracted sneers and unkind insults. So we stuck together like glue, our mutual misery a protective shield against the world.

On our first day at Bridge Mount Secondary School the lions identified the weakest gazelles and locked us both in the boiler room. After fifteen 'hilarious' minutes a Nordic nerd called Petrina-Ola Olsen released us and the perfect trio was formed.

'There's more to it than that,' I said quietly as Walter doodled in his sketchbook. 'I want to find out who The Wizard really is.'

Walter is an A grade artist. He's brilliant.

'Hey, is that supposed be Petrina?' I asked, leaning over his shoulder.

Walter slammed his exercise book shut. 'It's not finished yet,' he snapped.

It was a very good likeness. One day I might ask him to do a portrait of me. Not naked or anything. That would be like incest.

I'm not a vain person – I'm very much a no make-up (kohl eyeliner doesn't count, it's as essential to a woman as a bra), black jeans and T-shirt kind of girl, with dark, shaggy hair that looks a mess no matter what I try to do with it. I think I look kind of forgettable – the type of person who blends into the background at parties. (Not that I get invited to any parties, but I would imagine that had I ever been invited to one, I would have been swallowed up by the wallpaper.)

And while most girls our age like to show as much flesh as possible, Petrina can't seem to wear enough clothes. She always has black woolly tights under her skirt (even in the height of summer) and insists on 'doing the double'. (Petrina suffers from a saggy gusset so wears knickers under AND over her tights to prevent visible droopage. She is, quite frankly, a GENIUS.)

With her tiny frame, thick black-rimmed glasses and her blonde hair, Petrina resembles an intellectual Nordic elf. The slangers might call us 'Goths', but neither of us has the commitment or desire to conform to that particular label. It takes a certain devotion to get up every morning and apply the necessary amount of make-up to realise the full, magnificent potential of the Goth look and I am simply too lazy. If you really want to label us, I guess you could say that we're 'darker than average'.

So to say we were startled when a loud exclamation of 'BLOODY MINX!' echoed down the corridor would be a bit of an understatement.

It took a second for me to realise Mrs Finley wasn't talking about *me*, but the T-shirt I've been wearing under my school blouse (it's cold enough to freeze Jack Frost's snow balls at the moment). Bloody Minx are one of my favourite bands – I hadn't realised you could read the logo through my shirt.

I suspect Petrina and I remind Mrs Finley of herself at this age. It doesn't take a genius to work out that she was ridiculed at school on a daily basis (she's a large lady with a face like a pug dog's bum). It's her I have to blame for getting tricked into going to after-school trampoline club, which I intend to leave ASAP, especially after the horrible lesson last term where Mei Miyagi's sanitary towel shot out of her leotard whilst she was mid-straddle jump. Amazingly, Mei didn't seem at all embarrassed about the incident, not even when the sanitary towel slapped a stunned Kirsty Mackerby across the face. (Though, to be honest, I thought a seasoned lesbian such as Mei would be the last person to wear a brick in her pants. She must be very experienced in the knicker department and really ought to know that tampons are by far the most superior form of menstrual protection.)

'That does *not* comply with the school uniform regulations,' Mrs Finley growled, pointing at my *Bloody Minx* logo and steering us into an empty classroom.

'You can't suppress our right to personal expression,' said Petrina, instantly resorting to political rhetoric.

'I can if it's against school rules,' Mrs Finley replied firmly.

'Music transcends rules,' Petrina declared.

'Well, if music and freedom of expression mean so much to you, why don't you both volunteer for the school radio station?'

Petrina and I looked vacantly at each other.

'It would encourage you to interact with some of the more confident students,' explained Mrs Finley. 'This is a new exciting project and it would be good for you to participate.'

'But we've got exams coming up in June,' I said, knowing that Petrina would sail through her GCSEs while I would have to put in a lot of hard graft or fake a panic attack to get extra 'sympathy' time in the exams.

Mrs Finley laughed. 'School isn't *just* about academic study, you know. It's about developing social skills, communicating with other people and learning how to interact adaptively in our cultural environment. Good grades aren't a replacement for a social life.'

Thanks for reminding me that I have NEITHER!

'We just want to be singer/songwriters,' I said defensively. 'You don't need to be sociable to express yourself fully through the medium of music.'

Mrs Finley plonked one of her massive buttocks on the edge of her desk and folded her dimpled arms.

'Blossom, it's all very well articulating your emotions by being creative, but you can't go through life closing yourself off from society. As your teacher, I have pastoral responsibilities and I don't want to see you run the risk of labelling yourself as an outcast.'

'Not everyone feels the need to conform,' grumbled Petrina. 'It's good to be different and follow your own path. It takes courage.'

Mrs Finley pressed her triple chin back into her throat. 'Look, girls, you can take it or leave it. Toby Richmond and Felix Winters are running the station as part of the Young Enterprise scheme. They urgently need two assistants. I'd be grateful if you could let them know your decision by lunchtime.'

She lifted her colossal butt cheek from the desk and turned her back. I glanced at Petrina as we left the classroom, trying to gauge her opinion. Her serious expression gave away nothing.

'Wowzoids!!!' I said, collapsing against the cold corridor wall. 'Felix Winters!'

'Toby Richmond!' whispered Petrina breathlessly.

'We can't do it,' I said firmly. 'I've got enough on my plate already with trampoline club and starting a band.'

Why am I making lame excuses? I would do a 'Randy Ball-Out into Side Somersault' from the Eiffel Tower wearing a pink leopard-print bikini if it meant hanging out with Felix Winters.

'You're right,' agreed Petrina. 'It would be too much work and besides, we don't need to develop our "social skills" – hang on . . . you're starting a band?'

But oh my God Felix is proper sexy real-time HOT.

'Yeah, it's not like we're socially backward. And yes, I'm starting a band. With YOU. Didn't you get my email?'

I LOVE HIM, I LOVE HIM, I LOVE HIM.

'What email? Can I play my Roland synth? I've recorded some awesome hooks . . . Of course, if we did join the radio station, Felix and Toby might just invite us to a party,' Petrina said.

I looked at her earnestly. 'We *never* get invited to parties.'

Petrina's eyes were fixed with a thousand-mile stare, gazing into oblivion. 'But as their *close* assistants, it would be in their interest to keep us happy.'

'Petrina, nobody talks to us. Nobody likes us.' Harsh? Maybe, but true. Petrina needed to get a grip.

'What about Walter?'

'Walter doesn't count,' I explained. 'He's got an extensive collection of blunt record styluses that he keeps in his rucksack for God's sake. He's weirder than us!'

'Well I'm ready for a change,' Petrina declared. 'I'm fed up of being inaccurately classified as some kind of weirdo Goth. I say we climb that social beanstalk before someone chops it down.'

I swear Petrina will be Prime Minister one day.

'Only we'll climb it with our gussets bound up tightly against our groins,' she continued defiantly.

On second thoughts, perhaps she isn't cut out for the role of Prime Minister. But her speech was enough to get me back into the classroom to tell Mrs Finley that we were IN!

Petrina and I nervously approached Felix and Toby at break time to give them the news that we were now their new *aides*. (Petrina despises the term 'assistants'. She thinks it's degrading and sexist and has insisted that we are always to use the more empowering term 'aides'. In terms of radical feminists, her aspirations are right up there with my mum and Emmeline Pankhurst.) The boys were sitting in the small on-air studio in the music department, feet up on the mixing desk, listening to music and trying to work out some kind of playlist. The song was playing so loudly that the cheap speakers were distorting.

We knocked on the door. No reply. We waited politely then knocked again, louder. Still nothing. Unsure of the studio etiquette, we slowly opened the door and stepped in.

'Hi!' Petrina's soft voice was immediately lost amongst the thrash of a guitar riff.

'Hello?' I called a little louder. Still no response from the boys, who were vigorously air-guitaring.

We stood awkwardly by the door, gawping at this private show of HOTNESS played out just for our viewing pleasure. For a moment I felt like a bit of a perv, but I knew that any minute now, the two sexiest boys in our school would acknowledge our existence and the show would end.

'Hello!' I called again. 'Hello!' No response. I took a deep breath and braced myself to shout as loudly as I could.

'HELLO!' I yelled at the top of my lungs at the exact moment that Felix pulled down the fader to silent.

I startled Toby so much that he toppled backwards off of his seat onto the floor with a thud. Felix actually screamed, his sensual hands cupping his face the way a vampire victim does when the sexy, misunderstood bloodsucker pops out from behind a tree bearing his fangs. I was surprised to discover that an almost-adult-boy scream is exactly the same as an actual-adult-woman's scream – all shrill and soaring.

'Oh. Sorry. I didn't mean to frighten you.'

Toby quickly pulled himself up off the floor and Felix coughed. A deep, manly cough.

'You didn't frighten us,' said Felix making sure that his voice was deep and butch. 'You just caught us off guard.'

'What are you doing in here?' Toby eyed us suspiciously. Quite frankly I was positively delighted Toby and Felix knew we were alive. It felt like Petrina and I now officially existed.

Toby's dad is the one-time Jamaican Olympic bronze medallist, George Richmond (who, to be honest, is pretty sexy for an old man. Not that I fancy old men). Like his father, Toby is a lean six-foot three, with buns of steel and the (second) cutest smile you'll ever see. His best friend Felix looks as if he could be a charismatic singer in a rock band – except a zillion times cooler than any of the ones in existence. His ruffled, dirty blonde hair and intense blue eyes would look perfect on the front cover of any music magazine. Every girl and gay boy in the whole school fancies one if not both of them. (Well except for lesbians Kirsty Mackerby and Mei Miyagi. And also Paulette Dempsey because of her asexuality. Oh and Bonnie Parker from Year 10, who only goes out with 'on-the-cusp' Capricorns.)

Petrina stepped in. 'Mrs Finley sent us. She said you needed assistants.'

'Yeah, that's right,' said Felix. *GOD he's hotter than a three-testicled tom cat.*

'Know someone who's interested then?'

'Us,' said Petrina confidently.

Toby and Felix looked at each other. I saw Felix try to stifle a snigger. 'The Goth Girls?' he said.

'Yes,' I replied, thinking better of enlightening them with my 'darker than average' explanation. 'We're hardworking and both LOVE music more than anything in the world.'

'Oh yeah? Think you're music experts do you?' said Toby, winking at his friend. 'How about a little quiz?'

Petrina puffed out her chest. 'Bring it on!'

The studio plunges into darkness. Swirls of dry ice curl around our legs as Petrina and I sit side by side in big black leather chairs under a solitary bright spotlight. Felix and Toby stand before us: the slick, sequin-jacketed game show hosts. Felix flashes a dazzling white smile, 'Good evening. Your names please.'

'Blossom Uxley-Michaels.'

'Petrina-Ola Olsen.'

Toby spins around 360 degrees on the heel of one foot. 'Your occupation?'

'Students.'

Felix licks his finger and flattens an already immaculate eyebrow. 'And your chosen specialist subject?'

'Music trivia,' *I reply.*

Toby shuffles his question cards. 'OK, Bumface and Poohead, your time starts . . . now. What is the link between the bands The Innoculations and The Scares?'

Two of my favourite bands! 'The Gowan brothers.'

'Correct,' *says Felix.* 'Which successful UK band released The Green Room E.P. *before they became global superstars?*'

'Hotstop,' *says Petrina pushing her glasses back on to the bridge of her nose.*

'Correct. Susan Doff was the singer of which all-female rock band?'

'The Bracelets!' *Petrina leans across to give me a high five.*

'Correct. Who was the drummer of the grunge band Utopia?'

'Donkey Dave.' *Too easy.*

'Correct. What is the title of singer/songwriter Josh Raven's debut—'

But before Felix finishes the question I butt in with the answer.
'Moonlight Stalker.' Only my favourite song EVER.
'Correct. Well done, ladies. You've answered five out of five correctly. Which means you've won the fantastic prize of being our girlfriends for ever . . .'

OK, so Felix and Toby didn't actually leap out of their chairs to snog our faces off, but they were forced to admit that Petrina and I knew our stuff. A win for Team Weirdo!

A couple of days later during break, Paulette Dempsey convinced me to sign up to her new Young Enterprise venture: Dempsey Love. It cost 50p to join and all I have to do is fill out a form detailing my interests and the kind of person I'm looking for, then she will pair me up with my perfect match at Bridge Mount.

I'm secretly wondering if Paulette might have set up her new venture as a ruse to kick-start her own love life. She's a dumpy, freckled girl with thick, frizzy red hair, who's publicly declared herself to be 'asexual'. I'm suspicious. Anyway, apparently her lack of sexual orientation makes her perfectly qualified to provide a completely impartial matchmaking service. Not being prejudiced or anything, but I hope Paulette doesn't hook me up with a girl. I haven't yet come to any concrete conclusions on my sexuality, but I don't really think I'm currently on the lookout for lady-love.

I tried to persuade Petrina to sign up for a laugh, but she refused point blank, saying that true love should be natural and not forced. I disagree strongly: desperation leads to desperate measures. I am fifteen years old and have never even held hands with a boy (apart from the time Max Burcott challenged me to a game of Mercy Mercy and almost snapped my thumb off). Some of us need all the help we can get.

TOP 5 SEXY POP STARS WHO I WOULD LIKE TO MARRY ONE DAY

1. JOSH RAVEN singer/songwriter. Proper sexy, real-time HOT with a sublime voice.

2. ROBBIE BAXTER guitarist from Bloody Minx. Ticks all the boxes (e.g. doesn't use too much hair product, nice bum, isn't afraid to show his emotions, not too short). BUT he has had sex with a prostitute and that is disgusting.

3. LORENZO RICCOLI lead singer of The Barcodes. Beautiful with a sexy accent, but I suspect that he shaves his entire body. He definitely looks like a beaver-back to me.

4. JACOB WOOLFE brilliant singer and leading Hollywood actor as well. Really gorgeous looking, although he's a Scientologist and anyone who worships at the altar of an alien has got to be a bit mental.

5. CALEB WHITEHALL *the drummer in King Quiff. Gorgeous with a really cute smile, but perhaps a bit too small. If we got married, as I'm so short, we would run the risk of having dwarf babies. (Not that I am a size-ist or anything. I am actually very open-minded and would never harm a dwarf, even by accident.)*

In my new role as Guest Booker on Bridge Mount FM my job will be to hand-pick the studio guests. Top of my list is ex-Bridge Mount student Josh Raven. The way I see it, not only would I get the chance to meet a top, HOT superstar, it might also propel me to the dizzy heights of coolness that only a select few students even dream of. I sent an email to his management asking if he would like to come in for a chat:

From: Blossom Uxley-Michaels   7th Jan 16:45
To: info@poptasticmanagement.com
SUBJECT: Very important request for Josh Raven.

Dear Sir/Madam,

I am a huge, huge, huge fan of Josh Raven. I have bought both of his albums (which I LOVE) and have even learned to play Moonlight Stalker on guitar. I can't yet sing and strum at the same time (my hands and mouth just won't cooperate with each other – seriously, I'd make a rubbish ventriloquist), but with a bit of practice I soon will and may even release a cover version of it in a few years.

Anyway, that's all beside the point. I am aware that Josh is an ex-student of Bridge Mount Secondary School and wondered if he might like to come in as a guest on our new radio station. Fiona and Lucy's Breakfast Show would be best. Fiona and Lucy are prize quimboids and slangers of the highest order, but it's going to be our flagship show and they will have the most listeners. I understand that as an international megastar Josh needs maximum exposure, so this would be a great show for him to be on.

We can provide refreshments, but he'll have to sort out his own transport, although I'm guessing that he has more than enough money to cough up for a cab.

Let me know when is a good date for him. (Not Monday 31st January as I have an orthodontist appointment.)

Many thanks,

Blossom Uxley-Michaels

P.S. I'd love a signed guitar or photo if you have one going spare.

DEMPSEY LOVE QUESTIONNAIRE

The Easiest Way To Find Love In The Classroom

NAME: Blossom Uxley-Michaels   YEAR: 11   HEIGHT: 5ft 4in

LOOKING FOR:

male ☒   female ☐   (both) ☐

EITHER? I don't think we have any hermaphrodites at Bridge Mount.

RELATIONSHIP:

casual ☒   fun ☒   dating ☒   marriage ☐

HAIR:

dark ☐   blonde ☐   ginger ☐   don't mind ☒

HEIGHT:

over 6ft ☒   5ft 7"-6ft ☒   5ft-5ft 7" ☐   don't mind ☐

(I'm not being height-ist but it's a well-known scientific fact that short men have inferiority issues. I don't want to date anyone with emotional baggage.)

MUSIC:

pop ☐   rock ☐   dance ☐   classical ☐

WRONG, WRONG, WRONG!!! How can anyone give an insight into their musical tastes with just FOUR categories of musical genre? What about Hip hop, Future Garage, Grime, Reggae, Ska, Punk, New Wave, Grindcore, Tribal Dubstep, Indie, R&B, Liquid Funk, Afrobeat, Brostep, UK bass, Horrorcore, Zombie Rock

INTERESTS:

theatre ☒	parties ☒	sport ☐	animals ☒
reading ☐	music ☒	gigs ☒	arts & crafts ☐
cinema ☒	cookery ☐	gardening ☐	alcohol ☐

DISLIKES:

Narrow mindedness, people with bad B.O., pineapple, coconut, the word 'moist', Star Wars, drugs, cricket, golf, men who have sex with prostitutes, lateness, vajazzles, leather trousers, hairy backs, raisins (because they look like old ladies' nipples), people who slurp tea, needing to go to for a poo straight after having a shower and people who let their dogs French kiss them.

ADDITIONAL INFORMATION:

I am learning to play guitar and have just formed what will be an 'internationally acclaimed band' in the near future. I enjoy vampire films (especially the BITE ME series), reading Vampire novels and hope to write one of my own in my spare time when I'm not writing hit records. I would like to live in a house by the sea with my own private beach so that I can host über-cool beach parties every weekend. I am also double-jointed and once dislocated my elbow when I attempted to lick it.

or Screamo? You haven't even got a box for Jazz and, whilst nobody in their right mind would date someone who likes Jazz, you NEED that option just to filter out the wrong 'uns.

END OF WEEK TABLE OF ACHIEVEMENT

SHAME LEVEL PEAK	3 (the camper van breaking down outside school is always utterly humiliating)
GUITAR PRACTICE	3 hours and 29 minutes
SCHOOL WORK	I must try to spend more time revising for my exams and less time looking at funny cats on YouTube
PARTY INVITATIONS	0
SNOGS	0

With the station due to launch once the exams are over in a week's time, Bridge Mount FM's infrastructure was in place:

BRIDGE MOUNT FM KEY STAFF		
NAME	POSITION	JOB DESCRIPTION
Toby Richmond	Programme Controller / Presenter	The boss, in charge of all radio output and presents the drive time show
Felix Winters	Head of Music / Presenter	Compiles the music playlist and presents the lunchtime show
Fiona Tittledown	Presenter	Breakfast co-presenter
Lucy Perkins	Presenter	Breakfast co-presenter
Petrina-Ola Olsen	PR Manager & ~~Assistant~~ *AIDE*	Promotes the station and helps the hot PC and sexy Head of Music
Blossom Uxley-Michaels	Guest Booker & ~~Assistant~~ *AIDE*	Books interesting guests and helps the hot PC and sexy Head of Music
Walter Ecclestone	Producer	Produces the breakfast show
Paulette Dempsey	~~Assistant~~ *AIDE*	~~Assists~~ *AIDES* all areas of the station

35

We put Petrina's carefully designed posters all around the school and flyers were handed out to students and parents at the school gate.

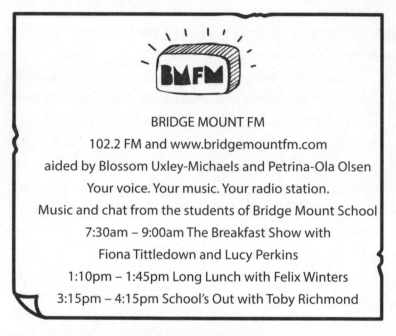

BRIDGE MOUNT FM
102.2 FM and www.bridgemountfm.com
aided by Blossom Uxley-Michaels and Petrina-Ola Olsen
Your voice. Your music. Your radio station.
Music and chat from the students of Bridge Mount School
7:30am – 9:00am The Breakfast Show with
Fiona Tittledown and Lucy Perkins
1:10pm – 1:45pm Long Lunch with Felix Winters
3:15pm – 4:15pm School's Out with Toby Richmond

'What are those two daylight dodgers doing here?' asked Fiona, looking up from her script as Petrina and I entered the studio.

'It's cool,' said Felix. 'They're helping on the station.'

Wowzoids! He just defended my honour. Not that I need defending of course, I'm a strong woman who can take care of herself, but it's brilliant to see that he has such good manners.

Lucy made a face. 'You're joking aren't you? Why don't you both clear off back to your coffins?'

Fiona laughed violently, banging the mixing desk with her hand to emphasise her approval. Petrina and I just shrugged.

Lucy Perkins is about as funny as chlamydia. (Which really isn't funny AT ALL. It can leave you infertile, so for that reason, then and there, I decided to *always* use a condom. Not that I needed one at that moment.)

'We're here for the long run,' said Petrina smugly. 'So you'd better get used to us being around.'

Fiona is the main presenter of the breakfast show with Lucy performing as her 'comedy' sidekick. They genuinely have no idea of the painful irony. Toby Richmond must find Lucy hilariously witty or had some bits of his brain removed as he's been dating her for almost two months and hasn't killed her. To make it a perfect vomit-y foursome, Felix has been going out with Fiona for one month and twenty-seven days (not that I'm counting or anything). What Felix sees in her, apart from her thick, luscious blonde hair, never-ending legs and enormous norks, is anyone's guess. With the personality of a doughnut, she clearly only got the presenter job because she's Felix's girlfriend.

Laughing together, with their almost identical bouncy, blonde hairdos, the slangers were like over-groomed, over-bred Afghan Hounds – except nowhere near as intelligent.

My parents were performing at a local music festival so Petrina and I went along to show our support. The name of their band is the fairly embarrassing Flying Rapunzel, but their sound is incredible.

They were billed as a folk-protest duo providing 'a blend of acoustic guitars and political vocal harmony', but the perfect musical accord was forgotten when a huge argument erupted, seemingly caused by Mum wanting to play a lute instead of her usual acoustic guitar. This simple request sent Dad into such a mood that he threatened to leave the band for ever. Obviously Dad's temper tantrum had no effect, since Mum stepped on to the stage, strumming away like an eco-minstrel of yore on her brand new, plinky plonky lute.

Flying Rapunzel had just begun singing their protest song *Fracking Is A Dirty Word*, when I spotted a tall man with a grey, pointy beard leaning against a wall at the back, arms folded, nodding in time to the acoustic rhythm. The Wizard! I grabbed Petrina by the arm, but when we looked again, the crowd had shifted and he was gone.

My sister turned up with her boyfriend Andreas, their positive energy causing our parents to forget their argument. Like Mum and Dad, Breeze is a strict vegan with a vast wardrobe of hemp-based fabrics. She looks like she's stepped straight out of the Woodstock festival 1969 – all willowy and floaty with long, silky hair and perfect skin.

Andreas, on the other hand, is dark, hairy and is very much NOT a vegan. He's a fiery Greek Cypriot who runs his own film-themed club night called 'Movie Nights'. Aesthetically, Andreas and Breeze are like ying and yang – poles apart, yet two halves of the same whole and living proof that opposites attract. There's hope for me and Felix yet . . .

The next day it was obvious that all was not well. I discovered Mum's lute smashed up in the recycling bin. Musical instruments are considered sacred objects in our house and to vandalise one would be as bad as murder. I was beginning to think that Dad might be on the verge of a psychopathic breakdown.

To distract myself from domestic worries, I focused my attention on getting to grips with my singing/strumming technique on Cassiopeia. She's an elegant guitar, but has the personality of a mischievous imp. I know for a FACT that had I been playing a more mature, well expensive, cherry-red, semi-acoustic Gibson ES-335, I would have mastered the guitar months ago. Singing and strumming simultaneously is bit like patting your head with one hand and rubbing your belly with the other and, now that Petrina and I had formed our band, I vowed to practise for at least an hour ever day. (The singing/strumming, NOT the head/belly rubbing.) We're an electro rock duo – Petrina on keyboard and me on guitar.

We spent an entire afternoon trying to think of a subversive-sounding band name – something headline-grabbing and topical that would get us noticed.

'How about The Violent Amputees?' I suggested.

'Too aggressive,' said Petrina. 'It sounds like a fascist movement. What about Walk Of Shame?'

'I think that would be sending out the wrong impression, Petrina. Don't you? We're not slangers.'

Petrina shrugged. 'Nina And The Norks?'

'Love it!' I said enthusiastically. 'I'll be Nina. You can be a Nork.'

'I am NOT being a Nork. My name sounds more like "Nina" than yours does. You should be the Nork.'

'NO WAY!' I protested. 'The band is my idea. You're the Nork.'

It was clear that neither of us was going to back down.

'OK, forget the Norks,' I said. 'How about The Mooncups?'

Petrina looked horrified. 'That's DISGUSTING.'

'What?' I protested. 'They're modern, safe AND environmentally friendly. Mum and Breeze swear by them.'

'Blossom, we are NOT naming our band after an eco menstrual cup.'

And so it continued for another couple of hours until Petrina finally came up with the perfect suggestion.

'Camel Toe,' she said, just a hint of desperation in her eyes.

Camel Toe? I know it's a euphemism for something but I can't remember what? A big nose? Builders bum?

'It's edgy,' she continued. 'Current *and* a serious social comment on the way music videos objectify and portray women as sexual objects. I mean, seriously, you can't look at YouTube or MTV without being visually assaulted by a stampede of camel toes.'

Of course! Nork cleavage. Or as scientific doctors call it, 'the intermammary cleft'. It's why push-up bras were invented – now you can't get away from them. YES! Petrina is a feminist GENIUS!

'Brilliant!' I declared. 'I'll be honest, I've always secretly wanted a camel toe as wide as the Grand Canyon but now those of us with a more modest frontal chasm will be able to feel proud. It's a name that states SIZE DOESN'T MATTER!'

I think Petrina must have been quite touched by my heartfelt passion as she was rendered speechless for a few moments.

✳ ✳ ✳

When I told my mum about our band name, she fell about in hysterics saying, 'That's brilliant! Just brilliant! Emily Davison will be cartwheeling in her grave.'

Frankly, I thought that was a very disrespectful way to speak of a dead suffragette who literally laid down her life in front of a horse.

'Grow up, Mum,' I snapped. 'This is post-modern satire. I thought you of all people would understand.'

In your face, MOTHER!

Mum began to laugh – a little too hysterically for my liking.

'Well, would you have preferred something more tacky,' I asked defensively. 'Like The Bawongas or something?'

Mum stopped laughing. 'Silly euphemisms. Breasts are breasts. A vulva is a vulva.'

ARRRRGGGGHHHH! My ears! My ears! They're burning.

'I could n-n-never be in a band called Vulva,' I stammered. 'Vulva is neither ironic, nor sexy. Unlike Camel Toe.'

More patronising, manic laughter from my mother. I felt angered beyond belief.

'I'm a woman, Mum,' I said proudly. 'In a world of twenty-four hour music channels, someone has to take a stand. A giant camel toe does not make a woman more sexually attractive. We don't need to have them surgically enhanced just because MTV says so. Whether you've got a big one or a small one, it's time for women all over the world to reclaim and embrace their camel toes.'

I clearly gave Mum food for thought as she stopped laughing and looked at me with an expression I'd never seen before. I might one day consider taking up public speaking professionally – I could be a natural.

Paulette Dempsey apologised sincerely for the delay in responding to my questionnaire, but so far I was the only person to join her dating agency. That made me feel JUST GREAT. Luckily, I wasn't relying on Dempsey Love alone to find my perfect match. I intended to explore every available avenue.

From: Blossom Uxley-Michaels   12th Jan 17:03
To: info@poptasticmanagement.com
SUBJECT: URGENT – Josh Raven needed VERY URGENTLY.

Dear Sir/Madam,

You will be pleased to know that I have been practising Moonlight Stalker every day on guitar and am getting rather good. I can play all the chords in sequence, but as yet can't quite manage to sing at the same time. According to Mr Callow the biology teacher, the left side of your brain controls the muscles on the right side of your body so I'm guessing that perhaps the left side of my brain is a bit on the lazy side or smaller.

I know you are very busy looking after Josh Raven's

glamorous life, but I hope that you will be able to let me know when he is available to visit Bridge Mount FM. He only left school five years ago, but so much has changed since then. He'd hardly recognise the place – Head Teacher Mr 'Titch' Blackmore has started wearing Cuban heels (some of the students are calling him 'ladyboy' behind his back), the vending machine now has a lock to stop pupils vandalising it (if legend is true then Josh almost got expelled for completely emptying the machine of Mars Bars and Monster Munch) and my bad skin outbreaks have begun to clear up (although obviously if Josh were to ask me out on a date it would be because he likes my personality, not because I have fewer spots. You only have to listen to Moonlight Stalker to know that he's not shallow).

Hope to hear from you soon with a firm date.

Many thanks,

Blossom Uxley-Michaels

P.S. Can I have one of his plectrums if you've got one going spare? One that he has touched of course. (If it's been in his mouth then that's even better.)

Since the Programme Controller and (hot) Head of Music were otherwise engaged (rumours were that Toby and Felix had food poisoning from eating a dodgy burger at Joe's Café), it was up to me, Petrina and Walter to prepare the station for its launch. This meant that poor Walter had to spend every lunchtime with the slangers. The difference between Petrina and I and Walter is that we secretly want to be popular. He doesn't. He's genuinely content with his position of King Weirdo, Ruler Of All That Is Odd. You might think it's a case of 'pot, kettle, black', but believe me, Walter's personal habits are strange even by my standards.

REASONS WHY WALTER IS KING WEIRDO

1. He insists on wearing odd socks. Matching socks are 'conformist and dull' according to Walter.

2. He eats live crickets and grasshoppers. (GROSS!) Apparently they taste like Twiglets.

3. Nobody knows the colour of his eyes. He keeps them stubbornly hidden away behind a curtain of fringe.

4. He collects blunt record styluses. I don't know why. He doesn't know why. He just likes them.

5. He doesn't hate Jazz (he thinks ALL musical genres have their merits).

For all his strangeness, Walter isn't actually bad looking. He's tall (perhaps a little gangly, although Petrina is certain he'll bulk out a bit in a year or two) with dark hair (although I'm not sure if that's his natural colour or if it's just blackened by unwashed grease) and a beautiful smile (which he doesn't flaunt that often). He looks nervous, yet when he talks, his voice is clear and confident.

Officially he has the position of Breakfast Show Producer, but since Lucy declared herself to be a comedian she's needed constant prepping and pandering. Poor Walter is effectively her dogsbody. The character Lucy has been spending most time on is 'Mrs Neacher The Rubbish Teacher' and the joke will be that students phone in with a question and she gives them a wrong, but funny, answer. I suppose potentially it could be really good, but with someone as talented as an amoeba writing the material, the outcome is destined to be appalling. Walter attempted to explain that perhaps the character wasn't working as well as it might, causing Lucy to have a total meltdown, screaming and throwing pens at the wall. Afterwards, rather than show any sign of embarrassment, Lucy said that comedians are highly strung and that it just goes with the job. I said she was a 'stupid, highly-strung slanger'. (Not to her face – I said it alone in my room afterwards.)

The news that another student has signed up to join Dempsey Love came as a relief. Fortunately the newest member is a boy and, while Paulette did warn me that he wasn't an 'exact' match, she said he ticked a few of my required boxes. A date has been arranged for us at Joe's Café next Tuesday. I tried not show too much excitement (I wanted to play it cool) but I'll confess that upon hearing the news, my stomach flipped over quite ferociously, causing a tiny amount of sick to come up into my mouth. (Which reminds me: avoid the burgers.)

I know it's unlikely, but what if there's a tiny, little chance that Felix is the mystery match? Perhaps he's had enough of his stupid girlfriend after spending quality time at the radio station with me and has realised that there's more to girls than just a tiny brain and humongous norks.

That said, with Felix and Toby off school sick, I was being forced to spend more time alone with Fiona and Lucy in the studio. This isn't what I volunteered for. I know they're the best looking girls in the school, but really, what else do they have going for them? They are shallow, senseless, uncultured and I know for a fact that Lucy has a lazy eyelid that flickers when she gets tired. Perhaps this rapid eye movement had somehow hypnotised Toby into falling for her because, quite frankly, most sane people would rather wash their face with a cheese grater than go out with Lucy Perkins.

I was missing Felix. Just before he got ill, he'd got a new haircut which made him look hotter than a Sonoran Desert Toad's bum. My grand plan is that when he sees me perform with Camel Toe he will be mesmerised by my immense talent and glittering charisma. Guitarists in rock bands are irresistible to the opposite sex and that is a scientific FACT. In a perfect scenario Felix and Josh Raven would watch me headline a gig, fall madly in love with me and then have to settle their dispute of passion with a duel at dawn. Prime ministers, captains, poets, lords and Bonobo Monkeys have all engaged in consensual combat with matched weapons (Bonobos actually use their winkies as swords – GROSS WOWZOIDS!) to settle arguments, so I didn't see why it wouldn't be perfectly acceptable for two hot boys to fight for my heart (and loins).

I stand watching barefoot on the grass, my white, floaty nightie damp with the early morning dew. Felix and Josh are back-to-back, muskets held tightly by their sides, one of them a mere twelve paces away from certain death.

'I love you, my darling.' Felix gazes passionately into my eyes, his hot new hairdo clinging to his glistening forehead.

'Blossom, my love. I will fight for you to the very end.' Josh is wearing the sexy pirate costume that he wore when he had a cameo role in the blockbuster movie Skull And Bones VI.

I flutter my eyelashes as fast as I can in a ladylike, demure way.

My lovers begin to walk the path of Fate.

A shot rings out through the air, sending startled rabbits hopping across the meadow. As one beautiful man slumps to the ground in a bloody heap, the other with runs to me with open arms, kissing me wildly and declaring his undying love.

'For ever, my sweet. You and me for ever. I love you.'

Felix or Josh? Josh or Felix? Hotness abounds. Which will it be?

I re-ran this scene through my mind a few times with different outcomes (e.g. where Josh ripped off his damp shirt and carried me, pressed tightly against his rock solid pecs, back to his massive mansion or where Felix took hold of both my hands as we spun round and round until we collapsed laughing in a sweaty heap on the dewy grass). While both were obviously amazing kissers, I'm ashamed to say that the money situation put Josh ever-so-slightly ahead of Felix. Which is a shame as it's definitely *not* Josh who has signed up to Dempsey Love.

Mum's still behaving strangely. I found her this morning standing by the kitchen window in her long towelling robe staring up at the sky.

''Tis plungy methinks,' she said.

'Eh?'

'The air. 'Tis plungy.'

'I haven't a clue what you're on about, Mum.'

'What say you?'

'Can you pass me the kettle please?'

'Aye. 'Tis a nimble crimble warlock thou doth declare.' Then she handed me the kettle, kissed me on the cheek and walked out of the kitchen on tiptoes, saying, 'Adieu, my good lady.'

All parents are weird. But being hippies, mine are probably weirder than most. My dad says that he and Mum fell in love at first sight when they met twenty-three years ago at a demonstration. They were protesting against a proposed bypass that would involve chopping down a vast number of trees to build a new road. Apparently Dad spotted Mum perched on the branch of an oak tree, strumming on her guitar, and, as he listened to her sing her self-written angry protest song, he knew that he wanted to spend the rest of his life with her. Mum says that she was 'high on life' when dad climbed the tree to chat her up, but since she thought he was quite handsome, she allowed him to 'share her branch'.

The two of them had a passionate romance that seemed to consist mainly of peaceful protesting, going to music festivals, forming a folk band, growing dreadlocks and smoking lots of marijuana. After a couple of years (of what I reckon most people would call 'bumming around'), Mum fell pregnant with Breeze. Now, all these years later they have (thankfully) lost the dreadlocks and got proper jobs. Mum became a yoga instructor and personal fitness trainer and Dad is the manager in a music shop, although I'm afraid they haven't stopped singing daft political songs and dressing like teenagers (ones even less cool than me, Petrina and Walter).

Sometimes I wished my mum and dad were a bit more ordinary, like Petrina's parents. Her dad is a businessman from Norway and her mum is a Human Resources Consultant from Croydon. They wear suits to work and look completely normal. Petrina says they are so wrapped up in their own lives that they barely know she's there, but at least they don't wear sandals with socks in the winter and have matching marijuana leaf tattoos on their left buttocks like my parents. (The fact that I know this is also NOT COOL.)

Breeze doesn't seem to find our parents anywhere near as embarrassing as I do, I mean, she didn't even flinch when our parents used to go out in public linked together by a chain that was fastened to each of their separate nose rings. (Thankfully they have outgrown that particularly mortifying kind of behaviour.) But then, Breeze is twenty, so she's had five extra years to get used to them. The mere thought of such a visible display of sexual bondage just caused my standard level of shame to rise a few notches.

I was lying on my bed, watching Josh Raven clips on YouTube, when my phone rang.

'Hello?' The number that had come up wasn't one of my ten contacts, so naturally I was suspicious.

'All right?' came a strange, yet half-familiar deep voice. 'Is that Blossom?'

'Yeah. Who's this?'

'Er . . . it's Felix Winters.'

OK, Blossom. The hottest boy in the school is on your phone. Play it cool. Play it really cool.

'Oh, hi, honeypie! What's cooking?'

Honeypie? HONEY FRICKING PIE? Where in the name of hideous terms of endearment, did that come from? And 'what's cooking'? When did I become such a giant quimboid?

'Um . . .' Felix went very quiet for a couple of seconds, allowing me a moment to shove my fist into my mouth and hit myself over the head several times with Boris, my beloved pink cuddly rabbit.

'I hear you've done me and Toby a huge favour.'

That's an understatement! While you've been off ill, Petrina, Walter and I have been working our backsides off to ensure Bridge

50

Mount FM can start with a bang on Monday. And we've had to deal with your stupid, dumb girlfriends. But I don't mind at all because I love you. I LOVE YOU.

'It was no trouble at all.'

'Uh-huh, well thanks anyway.'

God your voice is sooooooo sexy.

'Well, actually Petrina and Walter should take some of the credit too,' I said nobly, before changing tactics. 'Although I did spend most of yesterday working exceptionally hard. I didn't go to bed until well after midnight.' Perhaps Felix might feel guilty and fall madly in love with me due to my extraordinary kindness and dedication to the cause.

'Yeah, well, whatever . . . I just wanted to say . . . you know . . . thank you.'

'Hey, don't worry about it. Any time. What are friends for?' In my head I knew I should probably shut up (right now), but I just couldn't prevent the words from gushing out of my mouth.

'You can rely on me Felix . . . always and for ever . . . I'll be here . . . your eternal buddy.'

Shut up, Blossom. Shut your big face right NOW!

'Right,' muttered Felix. 'See you around.'

Oh my God, oh my God, oh my God, oh my God, oh my God, oh my God.

OH. MY. GOD!!!

And then he was gone.

This may have been the best day of my life so far. (Apart from the time I came second in my primary school Biggest Courgette competition. I won a trowel. That was pretty brilliant.)

51

END OF WEEK TABLE OF ACHIEVEMENT

SHAME LEVEL PEAK	3 (memories of my parents' public display of sexual bondage PLUS Mum said 'Vulva' out loud.)
GUITAR PRACTICE	2 hours and 56 minutes
SCHOOL WORK	8 hours. I wish had a photographic memory like Petrina, then I could have done much less. I'm exhausted.
PARTY INVITATIONS	0
SNOGS	0

On the morning of the station launch, Fiona and Lucy flapped around the studio in an excited frenzy, their adrenaline-fuelled shrieks piercing my ears like shards of glass. Naturally neither of them expressed any kind of gratitude for the scripts that we had prepared for them. In fact, they pretty much disregarded all our hard work, leaving Walter to patch together a shoddy first show by generating features and engaging phone-in topics.

The on-air studio is about the size of a broom cupboard, with a tiny mixing desk so basic that even someone as clueless as Fiona can operate it and three broadcast microphones. Walter was squeezed in at the back while Petrina and I sat in the adjoining production room, separated from the studio by a pane of glass. Toby and Felix casually flounced around looking important and beautiful, but offered very little in the way of productive input. Paulette Dempsey complained that she'd taken on too much work as she scurried back and forth from the vending machines collecting continuous tea, coffee and confectionary orders from the presenters.

My first guest booking was our Headmaster, Mr Blackmore, a man we're all a little afraid of and who suffers from an acute case of Napoleonic Syndrome due to his small stature. He's proper tiny, yet has the aura and presence of a MASSIVE giant.

Lucy and Fiona were in position around the mixing desk with Mr Blackmore seated opposite and Walter nervously handing out scripted questions. The rest of us sat in the production studio watching through the glass. Toby was operating the talkback button so Fiona could hear in him her headphones. This way he could move the conversation on if a link became too lengthy, or feed information to the presenters as and when it was required. He could also rein a presenter in if the topic was felt to be getting out of hand.

'Hi, people! You're listening to Bridge Mount FM. The best radio station EVER! I'm Fiona Tittledown and this is Lucy Perkins.'

'Hiya!' Lucy trilled in her annoying sing-song voice.

'So it's time to welcome our first guest into the studio. Our very own diddy Headmaster, Mr Blackmore. Better known to you and I as "Titch".'

Mr Blackmore scowled. If looks could kill, Fiona's vital organs would have melted into an icky pool on the studio floor, but it appeared that a few microphones and a set of cans were akin to a shield of steel. The slangers were fearless.

'Can I remind you, Sir,' smirked Fiona. 'Our listeners can't see you throwing evils at me. You have to verbalise your emotions.'

Fiona sat back smugly, clearly delighted by her own use of such a big word.

'Is that eyeliner you're wearing Miss Tittledown?' The irritation was clearly audible in Mr Blackmore's voice.

Fiona tossed her blonde mane about. 'It's radio, Sir. I have to look good.'

'Yeah,' agreed Lucy as she joined in with the mane tossing. 'The whole school is listening. We've got to think of our image.'

Mr Blackmore frowned. 'Have you ever heard the phrase "radio is the theatre of the mind"?'

I'm guessing most of the listeners used that phrase to fill the five-second silence that followed with a clear image of Fiona and Lucy's gormless expressions.

Walter signalled for Fiona to continue.

'How do you like your fudge packed, Sir?' she asked confidently.

Lucy put her hand over her mouth to contain her snigger.

There was a long, drawn pause as everyone in the production room held their breath. Mr Blackmore didn't flinch.

'I've heard you like gardening,' Fiona continued. 'Uphill?'

Surely a step too far . . .

Lucy giggled nervously, but Mr Blackmore replied in a deadpan voice. 'I have been known to get my hands dirty once in a while.'

'Have you ever had a beard?' sniggered Lucy.

'That's out of order,' said Toby frowning at Felix in the production room.

'Yeah,' said his utterly gorgeous friend. 'Well out of order. Tell her to shut up.'

Toby pressed the talkback button. 'Shut up, Lucy,' he commanded. 'Now!'

Lucy made a very rude gesture at us through the glass.

'I find facial hair rather uncomfortable,' Mr Blackmore replied calmly.

'Do you like our little studio? It's so small – we call it a closet.' Fiona pushed her luck. 'I guess you'll be coming out of it soon?'

Lucy was desperately trying to stifle her giggles while poor Walter had his face and fringe buried in his hands.

But Mr Blackmore was unfazed. 'Ladies, it sounds to me like you are having trouble expressing your questions in a comprehensible manner. If there is a sexual issue or dilemma that you wish to discuss, then I suggest you speak to your form teacher. The number for the student gay and lesbian helpline is up on the notice board.'

Felix and Toby fell about the floor laughing as the fluorescent humiliation radiated from Lucy and Fiona's cheeks. I couldn't help but notice that Felix had a really sexy laugh.

God he really is hotter than a rock star's leather trousers.

The interview may have been a personal disaster for Fiona and Lucy, but it suddenly propelled them to celebrity status amongst the Bridge Mount students, who thought their show was the best thing they'd ever heard. Lucy's abysmal comedy character Mrs Neacher The Rubbish Teacher was a particularly huge hit with the listeners. Sometimes there's just no accounting for taste.

So my first official date was with stocky, thumb-snapping (God it hurt), rugby prop, Max Burcott – a boy whose neck is as wide as my waist. Paulette Dempsey was right, he does indeed match three of the boxes that I had ticked on my questionnaire: male, over five foot seven inches and he likes parties. Other than that we have exactly zero in common – I mean I'm certainly not interested in 'Super League Rugby Heroes' or 'Big Budget Violent Slasher Movies', both of which were mentioned in the Additional Information section of his Dempsey Love questionnaire.

As arranged, we met in Joe's Café straight after school.

Don't look disappointed, Blossom. Give the poor boy a chance.

'All right?' he grunted as he slumped down into the chair opposite me. 'I bought you these.'

He pulled a box of Ferrero Rochers out of his school bag and threw them across the table. I caught them before they whizzed past onto the floor.

YUM! My favourite. At least he's made an effort.

'Thanks,' I said. 'That's very thoughtful of you.'

'Hey, watch this,' said Max snatching back the box, ripping it open and pulling out one of the gold-foil-wrapped chocolates.

Hey! Don't eat my Ferrero Rochers, you fat-necked pig. They're mine. ALL MINE.

He held the chocolate up for all to see. 'You will not believe your pretty little eyes!' he announced loudly, before placing the wrapped Ferrero Rocher on his tongue, complete with its decorative, brown case, and then closed his mouth.

If he takes another one I'm going to Karate chop his face.

A couple of builders enjoying a greasy fry-up turned round to see what all the fuss was about. I shifted uneasily in my seat, beginning to feel quite embarrassed (not to mention annoyed that he was EATING MY CHOCOLATES), so I tried to make light of the situation.

'Monsieur, wiz ziz Rocher you are rrrraarely spoilink us!'

But Max was deep in concentration and making some very strange faces. His eyes were bulging, cheeks puffed out into perfect spheres, which made him look like an ugly bullfrog having the life lovingly squeezed out of him by an over-eager toddler. Then all of a sudden he stopped. He put his fingers dramatically into his mouth and pulled out the gold wrapper followed by the petit fours case – both rather soggy, yet nevertheless still intact – *but* the chocolate miraculously was nowhere to be seen. The builders were genuinely impressed and gave him an enthusiastic round of applause. I clapped half-heartedly, relieved that Max's shoddy party trick was over. Except, apparently, it wasn't. He held his finger aloft as if to say '*Hold on – there's more!*' and the builders looked on expectantly. Max began sucking furiously, as though he might suck his whole face inside out. (Now that *would* have been a party trick.) Finally, after what seemed about a hundred years, he stopped and spat out a whole hazelnut into the palm of his hand.

'Eh? How about that?' he boasted, triumphantly holding it above his head.

OH. MY. GOD. Revolting.

'Yeah,' I tried to sound vaguely impressed. 'That's brilliant.'

'I've got a triple-jointed tongue,' he said winking at me suggestively. 'And that's not the only thing that's triple-jointed.'

Get the vision out of your mind, Blossom. Erase the image. Erase. ERASE!

I guess I could have mentioned my double-jointed elbow so that we might have bonded over our mutual hypermobility, but that didn't seem like a sensible option.

Max leaned across the table looked into my eyes. 'I'm a great kisser,' he said sincerely.

Time to implement the exit strategy I'd discussed with Petrina.

'Oh no,' I exclaimed in mock horror. 'I think I've just got my period. Gotta go.'

Poor Max. He really didn't know where to look. What is it with boys and periods? It's part of the circle of life. Just like love, death and trapped wind. Periods happen. GET OVER IT. Still, it was an effective excuse, allowing me to flee the scene without any questions. (It would have been more slick if I hadn't forgotten my Ferrero Rochers and crept back to retrieve them.)

I jogged the three-mile journey home, in the hope of burning off some calories from the WHOLE box of chocolates that I had stuffed into my mouth. Arriving back (and feeling rather queasy), I noticed a black Land Rover outside our house. The door opened and a man stepped out. The Wizard! I watched him open the boot of his car and remove a large holdall that he carried towards my front door. Mum answered and invited him inside. I hid behind a tree and waited for him to return, which he did about three minutes later. The holdall looked lighter, as if he had taken something out. The Wizard kissed Mum's hand (the way people did in the olden days when kissing on the face was considered a filthy pastime) and bowed down before her. This seemed to be source of great amusement as Mum's raucous laughter echoed all the way down to the end of our street. Yet, as comical as she found it, I definitely wasn't laughing.

***

So far I have only learned to play four chords on the guitar, which meant Petrina and I had to write our first song as Camel Toe using only C, G, A minor and E minor. *Poncerama* is a comment on what it's like to be a social outcast in a world where everyone wants to fit in. We're dead proud of the lyrics.

PONCERAMA
(by Uxley-Michaels and OLSEN)

VERSE 1
Poncerama, everybody thinks you're weird,
With your bowl-cut hair and your silly bum-fluff beard,
You'll never fit in and you're freakishly tall,
~~You've only got one eye and you've only got one ball.~~
AND YOUR MOUTH IS TOO BIG FOR YOUR TINY TEETH SO SMALL.

CHORUS
Poncerama oooh, Poncerama oooh, Poncerama oooh,
Poncerama ooo-ooh, Poncerama oooh,
It's no wonder that nobody really likes you.

VERSE 2
Poncerama, you only want to be a star,
~~But you won't make many friends if you wear a woman's bra~~
BUT YOUR TINY SAUSAGE FINGERS MEAN YOU WON'T GET VERY FAR.
You'll always be a loner; you'll never find a wife,

Confined to solitude for the rest of your life.

CHORUS
Poncerama oooh, Poncerama oooh, Poncerama oooh,
Poncerama ooo-ooh, Poncerama oooh,
It's no wonder that nobody really likes you.

BRIDGE X 2
No friends, no friends, no friends.
Weirdo, freaky, freaky, freaky, weirdo.

CHORUS X 2
Poncerama oooh, Poncerama oooh, Poncerama oooh,
Poncerama ooo-ooh, Poncerama oooh,
It's no wonder that nobody really likes you.

I decided to confront Mum as she practised her Downward Facing Dog yoga pose in the sitting room.

'Mum?'

'Now isn't a great time, Blossom. I'm doing a Sun Salutation.'

'I just need to ask you something.'

Mum began to move smoothly into her next posture, lying on her belly, arching her lower back, her face tilted up towards the ceiling.

'What?' she said serenely.

'Who was the man with the grey beard who was here the other day?'

Mum moved swiftly back into Downward Facing Dog.

'Do you mean Merlin?' she asked calmly. 'He's just a friend who was passing by. That's all.' And with that she continued to work through her series of yoga postures.

I had absolutely no idea what to say so I left her to it and wandered off into the kitchen where I watched some Josh Raven videos on YouTube. I've noticed that in every single one Josh is portrayed as a caring, sensitive SEX GOD whose heart gets broken by his stunning female co-star. (Usually a brunette with blue eyes, which gives me hope.) They all end in the same way – with Josh passionately kissing the girl in the pouring rain then falling to his knees, with black guy-liner running down his wet cheeks, as she leaves his life for ever. I'm going to add *passionately kissing in the pouring rain* to my list of things to do before I die.

From: Blossom Uxley-Michaels   21st Jan 8:10
To: info@poptasticmanagement.com
SUBJECT: Requesting Josh Raven's presence

Dear Sir/Madam,

I have had to stop practising Moonlight Stalker so that I can focus on writing my own material. I have had an idea for a song that I fully intend to write exclusively for Josh. It is a romantic ballad that will be called The Raven Lies In Blossom. It may take a while for me to figure out the lyrics as I can only think of one word to rhyme with Blossom. I'm not sure 'possum' will sit very well in a love song.

So I was hoping that you might be able to tell me when Josh will be available to visit Bridge Mount FM. We will of course play his new single and ask him questions that are not rude or inappropriate in any way. (By the way – in the first line of Moonlight Stalker when Josh sings 'I watch you moving on the screen' is he referring to a pornographic film?)

Hope to hear from you soon with a date.

Blossom Uxley-Michaels

P.S. If there's a hankie or tissue lying around your office that Josh has kissed or wiped his mouth on, please could you send it to me? I'd be very grateful.

END OF WEEK TABLE OF ACHIEVEMENT

SHAME LEVEL PEAK	5 (crawling back into Joe's Café on my hands and knees to retrieve my Ferrero Rochers)
GUITAR PRACTICE	6 hours and 13 minutes
SCHOOL WORK	0 (mocks have finished!!!)
PARTY INVITATIONS	0
SNOGS	$\frac{1}{2}$ (I didn't actually snog Max but I could've if I'd wanted to. BLEURGH!)

WEEK 4
NECK BRACE

Fiona and Lucy discovered that Max Burcott and I were the only members of Dempsey Love and that we had a date together. Their phone-in topic this morning was consequently entitled 'How Desperate For Love Are You?'

On the plus side, after getting such a huge amount of on-air exposure, Dempsey Love now has over 120 members. Paulette was absolutely delighted that so many people seem this desperate for love – it meant that by home time, she had pocketed sixty pounds!!! As a way of saying thank you, she promised to make finding me a perfect match her top priority. I realise that there is almost no chance of Felix signing up, but I am keeping my fingers crossed all the same.

Love and making music are the food of life (FACT) and now that I'm actively seeking a soul mate, music has never been more important to me. Petrina's parents very kindly let us set up our kit in their front room for our first Camel Toe rehearsal. It started so well. Poncerama sounded really good with a cool drum sample and Petrina's killer keyboard hook. All my guitar practice seemed to have paid off and our vocal harmonies were *tight*.

The only problem came when I got a bit carried away

during the middle eight and helicoptered my hair too vigorously, breaking an expensive, antique Chinese vase. Not only that, but Petrina's mum had to drive me to A&E with mild whiplash and I was instructed to wear a stupid neck brace for a whole week.

Mum came to collect me from hospital in a blind panic. She'd been out 'somewhere with terrible reception' when Petrina's mum had called say that I'd had an accident but that it wasn't serious. All Mum heard was: 'Blossom . . . accident . . . serious . . . A&E,' so I think she expected to find me in a coma or something. Actually, a coma might have been preferable, seeing as I'm having teeth braces fitted next Monday as well. That's going to look *really* attractive. I might well get a pair of trouser braces and go the whole hog.

Carefully lowering myself into the camper van passenger seat, I sat on something hard and cold. Mum quickly pulled it from under me and threw it on to the back seat before I could turn to get a proper look at what it was. My neck was stuck rigid, but I'm pretty sure I caught a glimpse of a flying golden chalice in the rear view mirror.

When I asked what it was Mum seemed flustered and muttered, 'Nothing. Nothing at all.'

It's possible I was hallucinating as I was off my face on painkillers, but a golden chalice would fit in well with all the other weird things that have been occurring at home over the past month.

✳ ✳ ✳

When the doorbell rang, I assumed it was a charity mugger. It's not like anyone ever calls for me, so you can imagine my surprise when I opened the front door to find Paulette Dempsey standing in the porch. Her scarf was wrapped so tightly around her face that I could only just see her green eyes and freckled nose poking out.

'Paulette!' I said. 'Do you want to come in?'

'No thanks,' came the muffled reply. 'I can't stop, I just wanted to tell you the good news in person.'

Paulette lives on the other side of town. She would have had to catch two buses to get to my place. I wondered what on Earth could be so important. 'What's that, then?'

'I've found a near-enough perfect match for you.'

'Really?' I'll admit, I began to feel excited. 'Who is it?'

'It's a surprise,' she said. 'But he's ticked every box that you've ticked, so you'll have loads to talk about. This could be a match made in heaven.'

Excitement overwhelmed me and I tried to shrug my shoulders – NOT a good idea when you are wearing a stupid neck brace.

'Can we wait until I don't have to wear this, please? It'll come off next week.'

'I think it makes you look quite regal,' said Paulette. 'Like Queen Elizabeth I or Shakespeare. Very stylish.'

'I gave myself whiplash by helicoptering my hair too vigorously,' I said. 'Hardly the height of sophistication.'

'I'm sure even the Virgin Queen liked to let herself go once in a while,' she said, with a smile. 'I'll sort something out for next week. I don't usually arrange the venue after your first session, but for you I'll make an exception. I owe you one.'

She undid her coat buttons to reveal a revolting purple top, covered in pink-sequinned butterflies.

'I bought this with the money I've made,' she said proudly. 'I've been eyeing it up for weeks. And it's all thanks to you.'

'Mmm, it's lovely,' I lied. (Well, what could I say? The fate of my love life lay in her hands.)

'Anyway, I've got to go now,' she said. 'I've had an influx of interest from the first years. Young love is fast, passionate and often short-lived. This is a prime opportunity for me to rake in the cash, so I have to ensure that Cupid's aim is perfect.'

Paulette holds in her hand a jewel-encrusted golden bow with a quiver full of arrows slung elegantly across her shoulder. Her delicate white wings flutter softly behind her.

'Blossom and Felix sitting in a tree. K-I-S-S-I-N-G.' She carefully fires an arrow, aimed directly at my heart. It passes through my skin as softly as a feather, leaving me tingling all over.

'First comes love, then comes marriage, then comes the baby in a golden carriage.'

Felix shudders, then smiles dreamily as the next arrow embeds itself firmly in his chest. To me he is a vision of perfection; a boy so chiselled he could slice bread with his jawline. He looks over and sees me with fresh eyes.

'I want you,' he says.

'You can have me, honeypie,' I reply. 'Always and for ever . . . I'll be here.'

As we kiss (a proper real-time HOT kiss), Cupid dances in the sky above us, thrilled that she has once again created true love.

The doctors advised me to get plenty of rest while I recovered from my neck injury, so I spent three whole days off school watching vampire films on the sofa. HEAVEN! I can totally relate to these mysterious, dark creatures of the night. In fact, I'd go so far as to say that the similarities between us are uncanny.

UNCANNY PARALLELS BETWEEN ME AND VAMPIRES

UNWILLING PHYSICAL CHANGES
My body is always doing weird things. My feet are getting massive and my face is constantly sprouting new spots.

IMMORTALITY
I know I will eventually get old and die one day, but right now that seems like a million years in the future. I mean, I don't even think my norks have reached their maximum peak yet.

ABLE TO SEE AURAS
If I stare hard without blinking at a bright light for thirty seconds and then look at someone, I can see their aura glowing around them. It's a psychic skill I may develop further in the future.

SOCIAL MISUNDERSTANDING
NOBODY GETS ME. (Apart from Petrina and Walter.)

LOYALTY
I would kill for my two best friends, but only in self-defence, obviously. I'm not prepared to go to prison for GBH or murder or anything.

DRINKING BLOOD
I am quite partial to black pudding which is effectively the same as eating a giant, congealed scab. So I guess if human blood was served up alongside a fried egg, a sausage and some baked beans then I may well give it a try.

Walter thinks that Petrina is even more vampire-like than me. I think he's got a point – she's a dedicated sun-dodger with more than a touch of the albino about her. I sometimes get the urge to sit her down and feed her a bloody steak just to boost her iron levels.

'Her mood swings are unrelenting,' said Walter as he lay slumped next to me on the sofa ready to watch *Bite Me – Dusky Dark Part 1*. 'She's paler than any vampire I've ever seen on film, she's totally nocturnal – always studying through the night – and she's way stronger than a girl of her size ought to be.'

Walter had stopped by on his way home from school to give me the (BORING) history notes that I'd missed that day. We watched the screen as Nigel, the sexy vampire leaned in to kiss the pretty, unsuspecting, mortal girl at the party.

'Do you think vampires can catch AIDS?' I pondered.

'Don't be daft,' said Walter.

'Why not? They drink gallons of unprotected blood.'

'Yeah, but they're dead.'

'So?'

'The blood doesn't actually go into their system. They just pee it straight out.'

'Vampires pee?'

'Definitely.'

'I never knew.'

END OF WEEK TABLE OF ACHIEVEMENT

SHAME LEVEL PEAK	6 (neck brace)
GUITAR PRACTICE	52 minutes (it was tricky with my whiplash disability)
EXAM RESULTS	All Bs (THANK GOD!!!) Petrina obviously got all A*s. She is such a brainbox.
PARTY INVITATIONS	0
SNOGS	0

WOLF MOON

ALSO KNOWN AS: QUITE MOON, ICE MOON,
MOON OF THE TERRIBLE, OLD MOON

It was strange. Mum only danced under the full moon for about five minutes before coming back through the kitchen where I was making a cup of tea, leaving Dad to make his ceremonial body shapes in the garden alone. Although revolting, their naked moon dance is as much part of our monthly family routine as paying the council tax and winding the 'eco-recycled tide clock' (even thought we live 36 miles from the nearest beach). Mum regularly consults her moon calendar to determine which yoga postures she teaches during lessons. Dad uses the biodynamic method of gardening, planting seeds and tending vegetables according to the lunar cycle. In fact, their lives are so governed by the moon that it even dictates their sexual activity. (This is unwanted information shared by my parents that try as I might, I just CANNOT get out of my mind.)

According to superstition, a male child is more likely to be conceived at a full moon, so naturally my parents were quite annoyed when I popped out of the womb instead of the anticipated bouncing baby boy (who I'm told would have been named Thoth, after the Egyptian God of The Moon). Sometimes I find myself really longing for a penis when I think of how much easier my life would have been if I'd been given the initials T.U.M. instead of B.U.M. Although . . . 'Thoth' – not the easiest name to pull off.

The thought of Dad dancing alone to the moon's rhythmic pull resonated right through my body. It wasn't embarrassment that I felt so much as fear. I'm not really superstitious, but I desperately hoped this wasn't in some way a symbolic indication of things to come.

From the moment I arrived at school wearing double braces my day was destined to be hellish. Thank God I was able to seek sanctuary at the radio station, where Toby's reaction to my stupid orthopaedic collar and new tramline brace was simply to look me up and down and mutter, 'Intense.'

To be honest, I'm not entirely sure if Felix actually noticed anything different about me – if he did, he certainly didn't show it. He was probably just being tactful, sensitive and gentle. Fiona and Lucy, on the other hand, have been leading the taunts of:

'Hey! Here comes Braceface Bumface!' and 'Brace yourself . . . it's Robo-Bumface!' etc, etc.

Aside from Walter and Petrina, only Mei Miyagi made the effort to make me feel better, 'Your tramlines work well with your cheekbones,' she commented. 'I like it.'

After school, I was so emotionally exhausted that I went up to my bedroom and wrote a song on my guitar. This was quite an achievement seeing as I was unable to look down at the fret board. I found pouring out my raw emotions was very therapeutic, enabling me to strum and sing simultaneously without effort. Emotional pain makes a person a better musician – FACT. Just look at Nick Drake, Kurt Cobain, Ian Curtis and Amy Winehouse. They demonstrate perfectly how you can turn a negative experience into something positive. (If you forget about the fact that they all got depressed and died.)

I never thought I'd say this, but from now on I will always carry a mirror in my school bag. It's not like I'm self-obsessed, but this lunchtime Felix pointed out that I had something stuck in my brace. When I went to the girls' toilets to inspect it I discovered a long piece of dental floss hanging there. Obviously I was mortified as, not only had it been there all morning, but of all the people to tell me about it, it had to be Felix. *ARRRRRRRRGHH KILL ME!!!*

Petrina had come into school late after a doctor's appointment and Walter said that he hadn't noticed it. (Which makes sense – I'm surprised he can see anything with that fringe obscuring his vision.) Still, it wasn't all bad news as my orthopaedic collar was removed after school. Without it I felt how I imagine those wealthy African women with super long necks would feel should they fall on hard times and be forced to sell their gold neck rings. My head was lolling and flopping all over the shop.

Now that I can see the fret board again, Dad is giving me more guitar lessons. He sat at the end of my bed this evening playing the most depressing, maudlin tunes that, even if I was a hugely successful singer-songwriter happily married to Josh Raven, would still have caused me to consider suicide.

When he finally left the room I had to put the radio on and listen to some cheesy pop just to lift my spirits. I asked Breeze if she'd noticed Dad's mood, but she put it down to a mid-life crisis. Trust Breeze to be flippant. She was a bit preoccupied after her latest argument with Andreas, who just spent over three-hundred-thousand pounds on a replica James Bond Aston Martin DB5 for the launch of his *Movie Nights* club night in London. Breeze thought that spending so much on a non-eco-friendly car was nothing short of obscene.

'Have you no respect for the environment?' she bellowed as he got out of the car outside our house.

'It's just a bit of fume,' yelled Andreas.

'It's dirty fume,' screamed my sister.

'It's PR.'

'It's pollution.'

'Think of the money.'

'Think of the heart disease and lung cancer you will be causing. Can you live with that?'

'Yes I can,' growled Andreas. 'So what do you say to that?'

'I say you are an inconsiderate, furry oaf.'

'HA! You think I am so sexy.'

'Frack off.'

Their arguments are far more entertaining than any of the rubbish on TV. Someone should give them their own reality show. Mr Parkin from number 34 would be delighted.

Breeze has always told me that my love for Josh Raven is 'unhealthy' and 'stalkery'. She remembers him from her year at school and says he was a 'flashy idiot who would do anything to be the centre of attention', which included him streaking across the playing field during the summer fête. (I have scoured YouTube to find the evidence but ANNOYINGLY it does not seem to exist.) She told me to focus instead on my upcoming 'realistic' date that Paulette Dempsey has arranged for Saturday, twelve-thirty at the cinema.

As it happens, Poptastic Management still haven't replied to my emails. I know they must be busy, but there is no need for rudeness. All they have to do is check Josh Raven's diary and find a free hour for him to pop in to the school. He was on TV the other night performing his new single *Blinded By Your Beauty*. The way his nose crinkled up when he sang the word 'baby' was mesmerising.

'He looks like something from *Lord Of The Rings* – all googly eyes and huge teeth,' said Breeze, breaking the enchanted spell.

I ignored her, throwing a cushion at her stupid face instead.

'And look at his hands,' she continued, clearly enjoying herself. 'He's got old lady fingers, all long and spindly. And you know what they say about a man's fingers, eh?'

'Shut up, Breeze.'

Breeze is a Winner. At school she was so cool and gorgeous that she was in an elite group of her very own. She didn't want friends and hangers on – she was her own best friend.

'Didn't you feel lonely at school?' I asked her, changing the subject.

Breeze was annoyed. 'NO,' she retorted. 'I was an individual. BIG difference. I'm no sheep.'

'Your initials are the same as mine,' I pointed out. 'How come you didn't get called Bumface?'

Breeze laughed. 'Seriously,' she said, framing her flawless cheeks with her hands. 'Do I look like an arse?'

I scrutinised her for a few moments, searching for any facial feature that might be even vaguely bum-like. Annoyingly there weren't any. Yet.

Yeah, but you still didn't fit in.'

'No,' she shrugged. 'But I didn't want to fit in.'

My sister's arrogance is unrivalled.

'Anyway,' she continued. 'The biggest misfit in my class was Creepy Dave and *he* attracted all the bullies.'

'Creepy Dave?' I was probing for information.

Breeze yawned. 'Yeah. He was a really strange kid. I'd sometimes catch him staring at me with his beady eyes before scuttling off into a dark corner somewhere. He freaked me out a bit.'

She physically shuddered at the recollection. I wondered just how creepy a boy called Dave could be – but then, how much does my face *really* resemble a bum . . . ?

Breeze and I are different in many ways, but none more so than in our eating habits. As young children our parents always included meat in our diets. They might have believed that meat was murder, but they wanted us to make our own choices in life when we were older. As a result I'm the only meat-eater left in my family. Breeze is now a strict vegan, having first become a vegetarian at the age of thirteen. I remember the exact conversation she had with us at the kitchen table when she told us her decision.

'I can't eat this.'

'Why not, Breeze?' asked Dad.

'Because it tastes of pig.'

God my sister was dumb. Time for me to step in. 'That's because it's pork.'

'Yes, I *know* that, Blossom. It just tastes really piggy. It's all pink and oinky.'

'Pink and oinky? Like pork?'

'No, like a pig. All piggy.'

'So does beef taste "cowy"?'

'Don't be stupid. Beef tastes like beef. But I don't want to eat meat any more. It's cruel and unnecessary. I want to be a vegetarian.'

'OK, your loss.'

And that was that.

Mum and Dad don't actually buy meat any more when they do the weekly shop, but I can buy it whenever I fancy. Thing is, although I totally agree with the vegan ethical reasoning, I just LOVE the taste of beef burgers. And bacon. And chicken. Cowy, piggy and . . . er . . . chickery. Yum.

END OF WEEK TABLE OF ACHIEVEMENT

SHAME LEVEL PEAK	12 (Level 6 for teeth brace + Level 6 for neck brace)
GUITAR PRACTICE	30 minutes
SCHOOL WORK	Not much as I've been physically deformed all week
PARTY INVITATIONS	0
SNOGS	1 (potential snog on the near horizon)

The day of my second Dempsey Love date arrived with much anticipation. To my annoyance, having taken hours to *not* look like I'd made much effort, in my eagerness to meet the man of my dreams I'd arrived at the cinema a good thirty minutes before the arranged time. Which wouldn't have been so bad had my date not been half an hour late, meaning that I was left standing in the FREEZING cold for a whole hour. By one o'clock my toes had gone numb and were LITERALLY about to snap off due to severe frostbite when a familiar figure rushed up to me looking a little panicked.

'Oh God, I'm so sorry,' he said, his gingery bum-fluff stubble tickling my cheek as he kissed me. 'I had to wait ages for a bus.' He glanced at his watch. 'Looks like we've missed the film, so how about we grab some lunch in Frankie's Diner?'

Matthew Ludlow is the Year 11 joker. If there's trouble or disruption in class, you can guarantee that Matthew will be involved at some level. He's one of those people who have learned to use their natural comedic talent as a decoy to veer all attention away from their deep insecurities. He's an average-looking guy, with strawberry blonde hair and pale skin, prone to nasty outbreaks of spots – but who am I to talk? He's no Felix

Winters, but he was male, breathing (and not Max Burcott), so I didn't feel too disappointed. And he was over five-foot-seven.

'Sounds good to me,' I replied, fluttering my eyelashes in my very best attempt at being flirtatious. But then I got an eyelash in my left eye and had to get Matthew to help me fish it out, which ruined the effect a bit.

We sat opposite each other in Frankie's Diner and ordered burgers and fries. When the waitress brought our drinks, Matthew pulled a metal hip flask out of his pocket and waggled it in my face.

'Fancy a cheeky vodka?'

Oh my God. That's what homeless people drink out of.

I wondered if I was on a date with a tramp in training.

'Erm, no thanks,' I replied.

Matthew laughed a bit too loudly, 'You're not a lightweight are you?'

'Most certainly not,' I retorted. 'I just don't like to drink in the day time.'

I'm not entirely sure why I was being defensive when a) we're both too young to drink b) Matthew shouldn't have brought alcohol into the restaurant and c) vodka is revolting.

Matthew poured a big slug of vodka into his glass of Coke and took a huge sip.

'Yee har!!!' he yelped.

This was turning into potentially one of the most embarrassing moments of my life. I was on a date with a fifteen-year-old alcoholic.

'So, apparently our Dempsey Love questionnaires say that we have similar taste in music,' I said, trying to find our common ground. 'What bands are you into?'

'I'm not really,' he replied, belching quietly into his fist.

That is GROSS. A waft of burpy fumes floated up my nostrils. And it's not true what they say – you CAN smell vodka.

'But Paulette said you ticked all the boxes that I'd ticked.'

'Yeah, I ticked every box cos I thought it'd give me a better chance of finding a love match,' he grinned. 'You know – cover all bases.'

Oh.

'But you're having a good time right?' Matthew looked genuinely concerned, brow furrowed, as he looked me straight in the eye.

'Erm, yes,' I fibbed. *To be honest, Matthew, I would rather be chewing on glass.* 'I'm having a ball.'

'Great!'

When we finally emerged from Frankie's Diner an hour and a quarter later, Matthew was noticeably merry.

'Wanna go for a ride?' he asked. Before I could answer, he'd thrown me over his shoulder in a fireman's lift and started running down the busy high street. We must have looked a sorry sight: Matthew struggling to hold on to me as he staggered into the road, walked into bins and fell into bushes and me hanging down his back, looking utterly petrified and hoping that I wasn't going to end up in A&E. Again.

'STOP!' I shouted at the top of my voice.

Matthew ground to a halt immediately and put me down

on the pavement so that I could gain a sense of gravity and calm my spinning head and churning stomach.

'OK?' he asked kindly.

'I think so,' I replied, still waiting for the ground to steady beneath my feet, but before it did Matthew scooped me once again into his arms, as though he was carrying his new bride over the threshold, and began sprinting back along the high street. I screamed my head off, my hands clinging round his neck for dear life. He turned a sharp left into Queens' Walk then legged it through the gate into the park. Thankfully, being February, it was empty and silent. He kept on running right until the end of my road, when he stopped and gently put me down on my feet again.

'Do you have some kind of weird mental condition that makes you want to carry people all over the place?' I asked wearily.

'Yes, I think I do.' He was a bit out of breath.

Surely this is not the man of my dreams?

Of course, when Petrina and Walter met me in McDonalds later they wanted the full low down from my *hot* date.

'Did he kiss you?' asked Petrina.

'Nope.'

'Did you want him to?'

'Nope.'

'Are you going to see him again?' enquired Walter.

'Only at school,' I replied as I bit into my Big Mac.

Afterwards at the bus stop I thought I saw The Wizard

coming out of the Yoga Centre where Mum teaches. Neither Petrina nor Walter saw him as by the time they'd turned round he'd disappeared back into the crowd. Maybe he really was Merlin the magical Wizard. One wave of his wand and *poof*, he vanishes into thin air.

So it turned out there had been a big party this weekend at Kirsty Mackerby's house and on Monday morning the school was literally buzzing with the sordid details. Fiona and Lucy's breakfast show consisted of all the juiciest bits of gossip from the birthday bash that took place while Kirsty's parents were away in Paris. Petrina and I had never been invited to a party, and wouldn't normally expect to be, but since taking on credible roles at the radio station (and since Matthew Ludlow went and could easily have asked me to be his date), we were both extremely disappointed not to have been invited to this one. Apparently Matthew spiked the fruit punch with tequila that he stole from Kirsty's parents' drinks cabinet. The result was forty-three squiffy teenagers doing the conga down the street. Other highlights Fiona and Lucy revealed on-air include:

✳ Kirsty and Mei having a lovers' tiff after Kirsty accused Mei of flirting with Max Burcott.
✳ A game of strip poker.
✳ An unidentified couple getting caught together in Kirsty's parents' bed.
✳ Miffy, the pet cat, being forced to crowd surf.
✳ Matthew Ludlow being sick in the garden pond.

At the end of the breakfast show Mrs Finley waddled into the studio requesting an immediate emergency meeting.

'You need to have stricter editorial guidelines in place. The content this morning was simply not appropriate,' she said. 'Who produces this show?'

Fiona and Lucy pointed at Walter.

'You try and get them to stop, Miss,' Walter spoke from under his curtain of hair.

'It's what the listeners want to hear,' said Lucy arrogantly. 'And it's our duty to tell them.'

'She does have a point, Mrs Finley,' I said.

Hang on – am I really defending these quimboid slangers?

'The content of this morning's show was topical and spontaneous following on from an event that was relevant to most of our listeners,' I continued.

Oh my God. I AM! Quick call a therapist. I'm mentally ill.

'What you discuss in private or in your own time is one thing. But what you broadcast on-air needs to be monitored,' said Mrs Finley firmly, her big fleshy chin wobbling about like a cockerel's wattle.

'You can't censor us,' said Petrina angrily.

'I'm not trying to censor you, Petrina. But I *would* like an editorial and compliance policy drawn up immediately.' Mrs Finley looked directly at Felix and Toby. 'Is that understood?'

Felix and Toby looked confused.

'Um . . . I don't really know . . . um . . . er,' said Toby.

'Yeah . . . er . . . compliance . . . yeah . . . cool,' said Felix.

Mrs Finley leaned right into Toby's face. 'Super,' she said, spitting directly in his eye. 'I'll expect to see the policy first thing in the morning.' She galumphed out of the room, closing the door loudly behind her.

'Anyone have a clue what she was on about?' asked Felix.

'She's trying to strip us of our creative freedom,' exclaimed Petrina dramatically.

I felt a surprising wave of outrage building up inside me. 'We can't be expected to make engaging, innovative radio if we have to worry about restrictive red tape compliance rules.'

'Yeah,' said Fiona. 'If I want to tell the world that Mei Miyagi and Max Burcott were caught together in Kirsty Mackerby's parents' bed, then that's what I'm going to do.'

Petrina and I were gobsmacked.

'Mei and Max?' whispered Petrina in disbelief. 'In *Kirsty's* parents' bed? Noooo!'

'I wonder if it had anything to do with Max's triple-jointed tongue?' I pondered quietly to Petrina.

'Didn't he suggest that he had another triple-jointed body part?' she whispered.

I nodded. We both paused for a few moments of slightly disturbing thought.

'Mei's straight? Wow!' said Walter. 'What will Kirsty do?'

Silence struck the studio as we all wondered what we'd do if the one person we most desired didn't want us.

Poor Kirsty. Mei is the only other lesbian in school.

As I gazed thoughtfully into space, my eyes accidentally made direct contact with Paulette's. She frowned.

'Well I'm asexual,' she said proudly. 'So don't look at me.'

'Don't flatter yourself,' sneered Lucy. 'Just cos Kirsty's the last lesbian, doesn't mean she's desperate.'

Lucy turned and high fived Fiona.

But Felix looked shocked. 'Asexual? So let me get this right – you don't find me even a little bit attractive?'

Paulette shook her head. 'Nope.'

Felix looked at her intensely with his gorgeous sexy eyes.

'Really?'

'Nope.'

He walked slowly towards her.

'Not even,' he murmured softly. 'When I do . . . this?' He leaned forwards and kissed Paulette on the lips.

Paulette closed her eyes and for a brief moment she looked as though she might float up off the floor.

'Nope,' she said firmly. 'Nothing.'

Fiona was looking annoyed, but Toby and Lucy were laughing their heads off.

I lie back on the crisp bed linen, surrounded by a hundred beautiful lesbians all wearing pure white robes. They stroke my hair, rub my feet and feed me beef burgers on a silver tray. A single white dove sits on the oak beam above me. It does not poo on my head. I am content. This is paradise. Suddenly, the door bursts open.

'Is this what you really want?' A young man enters the room. He is wearing a tight black T-shirt and tight black trousers. He is FIT. He is Felix.

'I do not need you,' I say firmly. 'I have all that I desire right here.'

'Are you sure?' Felix steps towards me.

'Yes,' I say. 'Quite sure.'

A beautiful lesbian takes a single grape from the dish she is holding. She puts it in my mouth, but I am not aroused.

'You cannot resist me.' Felix looks at me longingly with his delicious eyes.

I look away for a brief moment. Then I look at his tight trousers again. He is proper, sexy real-time HOT.

'Look at my loveliness,' he says, as he puckers his luscious lips.

'Take your loveliness away,' I demand. 'Leave me alone with my beautiful lesbians.'

'Do you like what you see?' he asks taking off his T-shirt and showing me his LOVELY chest.

'No.'

'Do you want me?'

'No.'

He is now mere inches away from my face. He smells sexy.

'Not even when I do this?' He kisses me passionately on the lips.

'No, not even when— oh, all right then.' He has worn me down. I can't fight it any more. 'If you insist.'

The beautiful lesbians all look extremely disappointed, but they know they mean nothing to me. They sadly slink out of the room leaving me to do some SERIOUS kissing.

Being a lesbian would have provided me with an excellent excuse when Matthew Ludow asked me to go ice-skating with him next weekend. I instead panicked and told him I was allergic to ice. I'm rubbish when put on the spot.

* * *

Mrs Finley wanted an editorial policy for the radio station, so Petrina and I presented her with one.

BRIDGE MOUNT FM
EDITORIAL GUIDELINES

1. *No on-air violence*
2. *No dive bombing*
3. *No heavy petting*
4. *No nudity*
5. *No ball games*
6. *No Jazz music*
7. *No flashing images*
8. *No exorcisms*
9. *No rioting*
10. *No on-air drinking*

Mrs Finley handed it straight back to us and told us that this was not a joking matter. We told her that we weren't joking.

'Then I'm afraid I'm going to have to take the matter to the top,' she said sternly, before summoning us to a crisis meeting with Mr Blackmore. The radio team argued our case for complete freedom of speech, but the teachers stood firm, meaning that an agreement couldn't be reached.

That was on Wednesday. By Thursday we were on strike in the school playground chanting:

'What do we want?'

'Creative freedom.'

'When do we want it?'

'Now!'

Petrina made placards bearing the slogan *Don't Take Away Our Creative Freedom*. Fiona and Lucy made ones saying *If I want to say 'sh*t' then I'm gonna say 'sh*t'*. It was so dumb, it was clever. By censoring themselves they'd added their own irony. Only they were too stupid to even realise.

It was quite exhilarating (and a bit scary) taking such strong action against the teachers, but we had the support of the whole school. Mr Longcock was protesting with us, saying that 'freedom of speech is our democratic right'. Contrary to the slangers' placards, we didn't want to shout swear words all over the airwaves. We simply wanted to be allowed to speak directly to our fellow students about the things they wanted to hear.

In the absence of any breakfast show presenters, Mr Blackmore stepped in to host the show. I don't know why he bothered as nobody was listening. Who in their right mind would want to listen to our head teacher harping on about the paradoxical representation of love in Shakespeare's sonnets? I mean, I like a bit of The Bard, but not rammed down my ears first thing in the morning against a soundtrack of Jazz – TOTALLY breaking Rule 6 of the proposed manifesto. Anyway, most of the students were out in the playground chanting along with the Bridge Mount FM team.

*** * *

By Friday, the local press had got wind of the story and sent a reporter down to find out more. Fiona and Lucy had disappeared into the girls' toilets to apply bucket loads of lip gloss ready for the press shots, so it was up to Petrina to act as spokesperson.

'We won't back down on this,' she said firmly into the reporter's audio recorder. 'We're not going to be bound up by out-of-touch editorial guidelines that will affect our creative output.'

Right at that moment, Toby arrived in the playground all sweaty and out of breath having just been for an early morning run. As the son of a one-time Jamaican Olympic medallist, it's no wonder he is following in his father's footsteps. Must be in the genes. He's a member of a local athletics club and is in serious training for the 400m sprint. For an instant Petrina looked as if she was having a stroke – her arms dropped by her side, her tongue lolled out and her speech became incoherent.

'Va, va, va, va . . .' she mumbled. I was on the verge of calling an ambulance when I noticed her eyes were fixed on Toby who had jogged up alongside her wearing shorts that were so teeny tiny they really ought to have been illegal.

'So what are you hoping to achieve with this protest?' asked the reporter.

But Petrina's thoughts were now somewhere else entirely.

'Lovely legs,' she purred. 'Long, dark, muscular, sweaty, sexy . . . edible legs.'

The reporter looked a bit baffled but carried on regardless.

92

'Right. And you think you can achieve this by going on strike?'

I'm ashamed to say that Petrina was actually salivating. Like a rabid dog.

'Yes. Thighs like a Trojan Warrior,' she burbled. I knew I should step in, but Petrina's the one who's supposed to be good with the press. All I could do was pray she regained her senses.

The reporter sensed a scoop. 'So all this is really about image?' he probed. 'Are you just looking for cheap publicity to raise the profile of Bridge Mount FM?'

Petrina began slowly swaying her hips from side to side. 'Caribbean hotness, la la la,' she sang.

'What she means,' interrupted Walter, realising that Petrina had TOTALLY LOST HER MIND, 'is that tightening editorial regulations will shackle the programme makers and on-air talent.'

The reporter seemed satisfied with this comment and continued the interview with Walter, while I led Petrina away to get a drink of water. Toby's legs were clearly a health and safety issue that needed to be discussed at the next school council meeting.

After the reporter incident Walter became very subdued. He doesn't say a lot, so the two-minute interview probably used up his entire monthly quota of words. Doing such a brilliant rescue job drained him so much that his head hung low for the rest of the day.

Still, by the end of that afternoon, we were all on the homepage of the *Evening Gazette*'s website alongside Walter's interview. Well, I say 'we', but it was really just Fiona, Felix, Lucy and Toby all pouting like models with Petrina, Walter, Paulette and me lurking behind. The top of my face had been chopped off so all you could see of me was my metal mouth and the spot on my chin that had sprouted overnight. Walter just looked like an extension of Paulette's hair and Petrina's face was all scrunched up like a wrinkly old lady because she was photographed mid-sneeze. But we were stating the case for our cause and we were defiant.

My parents were deliriously proud that their youngest daughter was leading a peaceful protest. Mum said that now I was a freedom fighter for creative rights, I was a true member of the family. I know they've always been secretly disappointed with my love of beef burgers, so I suppose I'd redeemed myself by partaking in a bit of political crusading. Dad hinted that he'd like to see Camel Toe pick up the muso-political baton, but I'm afraid that isn't going to happen. Petrina and I will continue to write songs about the simple trials and tribulations of life and love. Our band name alone is enough of a political statement to be getting on with.

END OF WEEK TABLE OF ACHIEVEMENT

SHAME LEVEL PEAK	6 (Combination of my brace and big chin spot appearing on the Evening Gazette's homepage)
GUITAR PRACTICE	4 hours 13 minutes (I'm definitely improving)
SCHOOL WORK	Roughly 4 hours. Petrina let me copy some of her maths homework. She really is the best friend ever.
PARTY INVITATIONS	0 (NOT THAT I'M BITTER!!!)
SNOGS	0 (But Matthew Ludlow was so drunk on our date, I probably could have snogged him loads)

WEEK 7
WEIRD PARENTS

Events at home were still weighing on my mind, so I met Petrina on the opposite side of the road to the yoga centre where Mum taught. I planned to follow her to see if I could figure out what she was up to. I'd laughed at Petrina when she pulled on a tatty old pair of black fingerless gloves and a thick, woollen balaclava, but after half an hour in the bitter cold I was laughing on the other side of my blue frozen face.

'You still look like a pervert,' I said blowing on my hands.

'Look,' Petrina said, ignoring my jealousy, as the yoga centre door opened. 'Someone's coming.'

A stream of people, presumably the participants of Mum's yoga class, came spilling out. We waited another five minutes or so until the door opened again. This time my mum stepped outside, followed by The Wizard.

'He's giving her something,' said Petrina.

'An envelope' I said.

'Money,' said Petrina. 'Drug money.'

'Petrina, will you *please* get over the drugs?'

'Sorry,' she mumbled, looking disappointed. I have a suspicion that Petrina would secretly enjoy the scandal of my mum being a heroin addict – her parents are so normal that a bit of family excitement, however awful, would be a relief from the boredom.

Mum and The Wizard wandered off down the road together. We tippy toed behind in pursuit, trailing them for about three minutes before they both disappeared inside a dry cleaning shop. We hid behind a bus stop.

'What are they doing?' whispered Petrina.

I made a face at her. 'That's what we're trying to find out, you big quimboid!'

A few seconds later, Mum and The Wizard re-emerged, each carrying a large item of clothing, safely zipped inside two white polythene bags.

'Maybe they've had their High Priest robes dry-cleaned,' said Petrina. 'To wash off the blood from the sacrificial offerings to the Voodoo Lord.'

'Thanks, Petrina,' I said sarcastically. 'You're making me feel so much better.'

'Look, they're going again,' she said pointing.

We followed them to a car park, where they paid for a parking ticket then climbed into The Wizard's black Land Rover and drove off, leaving us none the wiser.

February 14th. A date that usually hangs over the year, casting a shadow of angst and disappointment. But this year a whole pile of cards fell through the letterbox. Dad had one, Mum had two, Breeze had four and I received my first EVER Valentine's Day Card. It was a Dempsey Love design (£1.50 per card according to the printed price on the back – Paulette's surely going to be a millionaire by the end of the year), with a picture of two lovebirds kissing. The anonymous handwritten note inside read:

ROSES ARE RED.
VIOLETS ARE BLUE.
I'M A SCHIZOPHRENIC,
AND SO AM I.

I knew immediately it was from Matthew Ludlow, but I was thrilled to have finally received a card. Petrina texted to say she'd received an anonymous card too – you can tell she hopes it was from Toby.

My feeling of euphoria continued throughout the day after it was announced that Bridge Mount FM had won! The strike was over. We held an early morning discussion with Mrs Finley and Mr Blackmore where we basically promised not to be unnecessarily provocative on-air and to 'think carefully before we speak'. This of course will be a mammoth challenge for Lucy and Fiona – I'm not convinced that either of them actually know how to think. When Mr Blackmore declared that an agreement had been reached we all jumped out of our seats, roaring as if an England striker had just scored the winning goal, then embarked on a round of emotional victory hugs. But when I went to embrace Fiona Tittledown she physically recoiled, as if I was covered from head to foot in gunky snot. You'd think that something like this would break down the walls of faction; that the Winners and the Weirdos could stand together, shoulder to shoulder, united in our triumph. Alas no. It would probably always be Them and Us.

Felix did, however, give me a small peck on the cheek. I decided not to wash my face and to attempt to spend the whole night sleeping on my right side so that the kiss didn't rub off. His lips were as soft as I had imagined. I think he uses kiwi lip balm.

Later I was watching TV with Mum when her phone rang. As she went to answer her it, a five-pointed star necklace that I'd never seen before fell out of her handbag. Before I could get a proper look, she quickly stuffed it back inside and moved her bag closer.

'Is that a new necklace?' I asked once she was off the phone.

'What?' said Mum, almost pushing her bag down the side of the sofa.

'Can I see it? It looks pretty.'

'Oh, it's nothing – just a silly keyring that I got free in a magazine,' she replied casually.

She stood up, clutching her bag tightly at her side. 'Doth thou require a cupeth of rosehip tea? I be gasping methinks.'

'Er . . .yes please, Mum.'

'Fare thee well.'

And with that she left the room. She didn't even come back with my tea either.

I was making my own hot drink when Andreas rolled up dressed as James Bond in his new Aston Martin to take Breeze to the Valentine's Day launch of Movie Nights at its newest

London venue. My sister might have kicked up a fuss about the car's fuel consumption and devastating effect on the environment, but she's quite happy to be driven about in it. Not that I blame her – her Bellatrix Lestrange oufit from *Harry Potter* featured sky-high black stiletto boots, which would have given her terrible trouble if she'd had to walk to the bus stop. I've come to the conclusion that my own feet are far too fat to walk gracefully in heels. On the few occasions that I've borrowed a pair I've galumphed round like a drunken man in drag, resulting in excruciating blisters and/or a twisted ankle.

Sadly, although the club launch was a huge success, Andreas and Breeze had another huge a row, which ended with them splitting up.

'He accused me of gawping at another man in a "totally sexy way"', she explained the next morning over a bowl of revolting muesli. 'Can you believe it?'

'Were you gawping?' I asked in a very sympathetic, but also VERY curious kind of way.

'No!' she snapped. 'I was squinting to see if it was who I thought it was.'

'And who was it?'

'Creepy Dave,' she said.

'The freaky guy from school?'

Breeze nodded. 'I'd recognise his spindly features anywhere. Can you believe he called me a harlot?'

'Creepy Dave?'

'No! Andreas.'

'So what did you say?'

'I called him a "coughed-up furball" and then stormed out of the club.'

Just then Breeze's phone rang for the umpteenth time. I could tell she was still seething as each time Andreas's name flashed up her nostrils flared rapidly. No matter how much she internalises her vexation, those oscillating snout-holes are always a dead giveaway. I hope the split isn't for good, not least because I want Breeze's bedroom when she finally moves in with Andreas. Plus, he might be hairier than a racoon's armpit but I'm really quite fond of him.

END OF WEEK TABLE OF ACHIEVEMENT

SHAME LEVEL PEAK	2 (I don't care so much about the brace now. I'm trying to think of it as just a really big spot)
GUITAR PRACTICE	4 hours 13 minutes
SCHOOL WORK	Enough
PARTY INVITATIONS	0
SNOGS	0 (Although I did have a really great dream where I snogged Josh Raven during the after-school trampoline club. He touched my bottom briefly as he helped me up from the crash mat. Best. Dream. Ever.)

WEEK 8
BESPECTACLED BEARS

With eight original songs ready to appear on the Camel Toe demo album, Petrina and I wanted to spend as much of half term as possible tweaking the lyrics and perfecting the music. Dad told us that he was owed a favour from an old friend who would help us record and produce it at the beginning of March. Last time Dad called in a favour from an 'old friend' it was so that Mum could fulfil her lifelong ambition of lying naked across the altar stone at Stonehenge (where his 'old friend' worked) on the Winter Solstice. My parents indulge in far too much naked activity for my liking. If we were meant to run around starkers all day, God wouldn't have invented clothes. FACT.

CAMEL TOE DEMO ALBUM:
'PONCERAMA'S REVENGE'

1. LUTRAPHOBIA This is a meaningful song all about Petrina's genuine fear of otters. Once at a wildlife centre an otter gave her an evil stare causing Petrina to have a panic attack. She had to breathe into a brown paper bag and everything. We think it's important to create awareness of this serious condition.

2. QUEASY QUIMBOID This is essentially a track about a loser who drinks too much and does revolting burps that smell of vodka. (N.B. Matthew Ludlow was the INSPIRATION, but this song is absolutely NOT about him.)

3. PONCERAMA The title track. An up-tempo but poignant song explaining how tough it is to be considered a weirdo.

4. THE MAN WITH AN EGGY BEARD Once when I was in a café with Dad, a man at another table was eating a full-English breakfast and had a piece of fried egg trapped in his beard. It was one of the most disgusting things I have ever seen and I felt compelled to write an angry rock song about it.

5. BREAKING ME GENTLY This is a love song about a spineless man who stays with his girlfriend even though he doesn't love her. She knows that he doesn't love her, but he doesn't know that she knows. (Although she knows that he doesn't know that she knows that he doesn't love her.) It's pretty deep.

6. TOUCH ME ANYWHERE AND EVERYWHERE (BUT DON'T TOUCH ME THERE) This is a feminist song for the sisterhood.

7. SLANGER HOTEL *Inspired by Fiona Tittledown and Lucy Perkins. This is all about an exclusive hotel where the Winners gather to bitch and gossip. The song is told from the perspective of a hotel porter, who gets bullied by the stupid slangers.*

8. THE WIZARD *A haunting song about a mysterious magician who casts love spells over the women he desires, then lures them to their deaths.*

We gave an exclusive live run through of our songs to Walter, whose opinion we always value. His views are usually concise and honest – possibly because of his limited daily word allowance. No point wasting words on lying is there?

'So what do you think?' I asked expectantly as the final chord of *The Wizard* came to an end.

'Perceptive,' came Walter's brief reply.

This was inadequate. An angry wave of irritation flooded over me, which indicated that I was probably a bit premenstrual.

'Which is your favourite song?' asked Petrina.

'*Poncerama*.'

Silence. We waited for him to expand. Walter thinks A LOT.

Come on, then. What are you thinking about, Walter? Fringes? Tasty grasshopper sandwiches? Your extensive blunt stylus collection? COME ON.

'Catchy, simple melody,' he finally continued. 'Lyrics I can relate to.'

'And is there anything you didn't like?' Petrina always likes to bring in an element of negativity for balance.

Walter thought for a moment. '*The Man With An Eggy Beard* needs to be more aggressive. An angry guitar solo or something.'

WHAT? I'm not Matt Bellamy, you know. I've only just managed to master singing and strumming along to four chords.

I was definitely premenstrual.

'Shredding is really difficult,' I said defensively. 'I can't do a fancy, fiddly guitar solo.'

'Get someone else to do it,' Walter suggested.

'Who?' I snapped. *OK, so have you got Jimi Hendrix's number? Oh no, you haven't. Because Jimi Hendrix is DEAD.* 'We don't know anyone who plays fancy, fiddly guitar.'

I was trying not to get into a mood but . . .

'Look, you asked for my opinion. I gave it.'

'Yeah well, I wish we hadn't bothered.'

I am in a MASSIVE, menstrual, mardy mood.

Kirsty and Mei's separation didn't last long, which I'm pleased about as they are definitely the cutest couple in the school. They've always been very open in their displays of togetherness and, true to form, they publicly announced their reconciliation in an on-air phone-in on Toby's afternoon show. (Seeing as the school is open for staff, Mr Blackmore has agreed that we can continue to broadcast throughout half-term.) Apparently Mei was 'just experimenting' with Max Burcott, but now knows that her heart and loins will always be with the ladies.

The announcement triggered a flurry of phone calls from anonymous students listening at home who were seeking advice on their own sexuality. Toby was completely out of his depth when it came to dealing with the callers (he only really likes to talk about sport and music), but Mei really came into her own, offering sound words of wisdom and comfort from her mobile phone. As a result, Toby decided to give Mei her own ten-minute strand as the Bridge Mount FM agony aunt. Felix and Toby wanted to call it 'Mei's Big Slot', but Petrina, Walter and I vetoed that. We might not have editorial guidelines, but we do have taste.

By all accounts Kirsty had kept Mei on a very short lead at the Year 11 party that had taken place over the weekend. Yes, that's right, yet another party we'd been excluded from. Kelly Bowyer (from Fiona's gang of cronies) held a Bad Taste fancy dress party in a church hall on Saturday night. From the snatches of gossip that I'd heard, I knew that Felix went as a pimp, Toby wore a mankini (just the mere thought of which sent Petrina dangerously close to passing out), Fiona went as a pregnant nun, Lucy was a run-over dead cat and winner of the bad taste award went to (surprise, surprise) Matthew Ludlow, who was dressed as a used sanitary towel. He managed to sneak in a bottle of Vanilla Vodka Cream Liqueur that he swigged throughout the evening, until he threw up all down his costume. Someone then posted a video of it on YouTube. It's disgusting. The government should use it as an anti-drinking advert for wayward teenagers. I'm so glad I didn't leap into a full-on relationship with him. A vomit-covered, life-size sanitary towel has mollified any remotely romantic feelings that I might have had. I immediately took his Valentine's Day card down from my windowsill and put it straight into the recycling bin.

It's difficult to imagine how many hoops Petrina and I might have to jump through to get invited to a party. We thought that Bridge Mount FM would be our ticket to the cool parties, especially as we've been working so closely with Felix and Toby, but we were wrong. Neither of us want to change who we *are* to climb the school social ladder, but I suppose we might be prepared to change what we *do*, *think* and *say*.

REALISTIC WAYS FOR PETRINA AND I TO CLIMB THE SCHOOL SOCIAL LADDER:

1. Felix dumps Fiona to go out with me (unlikely)

2. Toby dumps Lucy to go out with Petrina (unlikely)

3. I become Josh Raven's girlfriend (unlikely)

4. Camel Toe become the coolest band EVER (possible)

5. Matthew Ludlow asks me out (possible, but being associated with him at the moment would probably LOWER my social status rather than improve it)

Obviously Walter didn't go to the party either, but he didn't seem bothered. In fact he said he'd rather be anywhere else than at a Winner's party.

'But, Walter,' said Petrina, when we were talking about it at lunchtime in McDonalds. 'Aren't you even a little bit intrigued to experience the cool things that happen at a party?'

Walter shrugged.

'God I'd love that,' I said dreamily. 'Champagne fountains, über-cool DJs, swimming pools –' (not that I'd every wear a swimsuit in public, of course – especially after the time Walter pointed out that my new white swimming costume became see-through as soon as it got wet) – 'proper sexy real-time HOT boys and loads of snogging at the end of the garden.'

'I'd rather be at a gig,' said Walter.

'Don't you want to be liked?' asked Petrina.

'You like me, don't you?'

'Well, yes, but don't you want to be more . . . more, hmm . . . *widely* liked?'

'Na,' said Walter casually. 'Knowing that you two are my friends is good enough for me.'

'We need to stick together,' I said wisely (if I do say so myself). 'Like spectacled bears.'

'Like what?' asked Walter, looking puzzled.

'Spectacled bears,' I repeated.

'Never heard of them.'

'That's because they're almost extinct. Which is why they stick together, just like we should.' A bit of trivia I remembered from Geography lessons. I wonder if there will ever be a time when my knowledge of ox-bow rivers will come in handy?

'But how come,' said Petrina, 'when Lucy Perkins farts in front of the class it's charming, but if Blossom or I were to let one go in a lesson we'd be laughed out of school?'

'Face it,' said Walter. 'We're destined to be outcasts for ever.'

'Oh yeah?' I said defiantly. 'We'll see about that.'

Dad has really come up trumps. He's arranged for Camel Toe to record *Poncerama's Revenge* at a proper recording studio. (So there was no need for me to staple my duvet to the wardrobe for makeshift soundproofing.) He's a good friend of Pete Hartley, the legendary record producer who has worked with some of the biggest names in rock and pop. They've known each other since before Breeze was born, when Pete dabbled in political activism in between producing award-winning albums. Dad even played guitar as a session musician for him on a few projects. So as a favour Pete has very kindly agreed that Camel Toe can record at his plush home studio and have his invaluable expertise for ONE WHOLE DAY. When I rang Petrina to tell her the news she responded by continuously screaming down the phone for 53 seconds. For a few moments I actually thought she was going to die of excitement.

Felix was definitely impressed when I told him our news. Apparently he intends to become a record producer himself one day. I think he was hinting that he wanted to come along to the recording, but it is for band members only. No groupies allowed. (Apart from Walter, but he doesn't count.)

The famous, über-cool, record producer Felix Winters sits at the huge 48-channel mixing desk, waiting eagerly for the biggest band in the world to join him.

The heavy, soundproof door opens and Camel Toe enter the room.

'Hey, Felix,' I say, lifting my Prada shades to reveal sensual, smoky eye make-up. 'What's happening?'

'Hey, babe,' says Felix, clearly noticing my hotness.

'All right?' says Petrina, the fake fur on her black, designer coat ruffling under the cold blast from the air conditioning.

'Yeah. You guys ready?'

'We're always ready to make music,' I say in a sexy, husky voice. 'It's what we were born to do.'

We get ourselves ready in the luxurious recording booth. We put on our custom-made headphones. I pick up the well-expensive, cherry red, semi-acoustic Gibson ES-335 guitar. It feels so comfortable in my hands, like a hairbrush or a Bic biro. Petrina warms up by running through some scales on her keyboard. Her hair is so sleek and shiny under the studio lights and the REAL diamonds in her designer glasses twinkle like stars.

Felix speaks to us through the talkback. 'OK, guys, let's just get some vocals.'

Through our headphones we hear the intro to our track Touch Me Anywhere And Everywhere (But Don't Touch Me There). *We begin singing. Our vocal harmonies are incredible. We are so professional. Felix gives us the thumbs up.*

Suddenly the control room door bursts open. Felix looks shocked as Josh Raven rushes in.

'Oh God, I'm so sorry I'm late,' he says, pushing his sexy hair out of his sexy eyes with his sexy fingers. 'I was having lunch with a very important music industry person, but I wanted to be here so badly. I ignored the expensive Champagne, caviar and white truffles set before me in the exclusive restaurant and ran all the way to you.'

'Hey, Josh,' I say casually. 'No worries, dude. Come and lay down your vocals.'

Josh enters the vocal booth and positions himself in between me and Petrina. He smiles at me, mouthing, 'I love you.'

I mouth back, 'I know.' Petrina winks at me approvingly.

Felix mouths, 'I love you, Blossom,' through the window.

I mouth back, 'Of course you do.'

He mouths back, 'What?'

I am simply oozing star charisma and sexy oestrogen.

We record the track. It sounds amazing and we know it will go straight to number one in the charts. I leave with Josh Raven because Felix has to stay behind to work on the track. Josh takes me to the penthouse suite of the posh hotel that he is staying in. It has a Jacuzzi and everything.

Fiona and Lucy's latest disagreement began on-air during their breakfast show when Lucy got mad at Fiona for not laughing out loud during her school-themed stand-up routine.

'Hey, Religious Education is really boring isn't it? I mean we all know who designed Noah's ark don't we?' Lucy paused. 'An ark- itect!'

Silence in the studio as Fiona stared blankly at her friend

and Walter scrunched his face up under his fringe.

'I was shocked when Mr Graham told me about the Dead Sea,' Lucy continued. 'I didn't even know it was sick!'

Silence in the production room. Toby was busy inspecting random objects, trying to pretend that his girlfriend wasn't about as funny as A DYING KITTEN.

Undeterred, Lucy went on. 'Mr Blackmore rolled his eyes at me this morning. I picked them up and rolled them straight back to him.'

Walter's head was in his hands. Behind the glass in the next room, Felix squirmed while Toby lay on the floor having actually slid right off his chair.

'Mrs Finley told me that my homework was a piece of cake . . . so I ate it.'

'ENOUGH!' shouted Toby from the floor. 'This is unbearable. Someone please shut her up.'

Felix pressed the talkback button so that Fiona was able to hear him in her headphones. 'Stop her, Fiona. It's painful. People will be turning off their radios.'

Fiona looked at Walter who shrugged. Lucy was still in full comedic flow.

'So the ghost teacher said to his class, "Right, look at the board. I'll go through it again"'

Fiona coughed. 'Ahem.'

But Lucy carried on. 'Why did the students study in the aeroplane? Because . . .'

Fiona began to clap. 'Yay! Brilliant!' she said, cutting her best friend off in her prime (if you could call it that). 'That was Lucy

Perkins – comedy genius on Bridge Mount FM. And here's the new single from our very own ex-student, Josh Raven.'

Lucy's expression was like thunder. 'I was just getting to the punchline. Why did you talk over me?'

Fiona searched for a viable reason. 'Er . . . ummm . . . we were running late and needed to get a song on. Felix was hurrying me.'

'But you didn't even laugh,' said Lucy angrily. 'That was some of my best material.'

'Really?' said Fiona looking genuinely shocked.

'Call yourself a friend?'

'I can't make myself laugh, Lucy. I only LOL if something is really funny.'

'So what? You're saying that I'm not funny?'

'No, I was laughing on the inside. I just wasn't outwardly laughing,' said Fiona, clearly in a bit of a panic. 'You know what I mean don't you, Walter?'

Walter shook his head. 'Lucy. You have no comedic timing, no expression and your jokes are rubbish.'

Fiona and Lucy were clearly taken aback.

'Oh, I'm sorry!' said Lucy with a sarcastic laugh. 'The school freak is criticising *me*? Why don't you go back to your coffin, you lanky-haired streak of piss.'

Petrina's furious expression echoed how I felt. We both stormed into the studio.

'Don't speak to Walter like that,' she said defensively.

Lucy looked at Fiona. 'Poohead to the rescue!'

Fiona laughed, then her over-eye-linered eyes narrowed

evilly on me. 'And her loyal sidekick Bumface is always close behind.'

'Hey!' I exclaimed. 'It's not my fault that Lucy's about as funny as a motorway pile up.'

'I'll have you know,' growled Lucy. 'That for the past few weeks, I've been studying comedy in great detail.'

She grabbed a large book from the desk entitled: *THE ESSENTIAL COMEDY BIBLE: A Guide To Being Hysterically Funny.* 'I know the differences between the comedy genres,' she continued. 'Scatological, observational, improvisational, satirical – I KNOW THEM! Plus I've learned over two-hundred one-liner jokes. I intend to become the best female gag-smith in the world.'

'Thing is though, Lucy,' I retorted. 'You just don't have funny bones.'

'Obviously my talents are wasted on this tin-pot station,' said Lucy, snapping into highly strung mode once more. 'I'm out of here.'

'I'll see you later at the shopping mall?' Fiona said hopefully.

Lucy threw her a filthy look. 'Not if I see you first,' she sneered, before storming out of the studio. And then coming back to get her book. And then storming off again.

Lucy remained sulking for the rest of the morning until Fiona confronted her during Felix's lunchtime show. They ended up having a proper, full-on, real-time, claws-out, hair-pulling, scrap on the floor. Felix and Toby were delighted to see their girlfriends bitch-fighting at their feet. Pathetic, moronic, intellectually-challenged slangers.

It had been a week since they split, but Andreas isn't the kind of man to give up without a fight. He loves my sister and wanted her back on his hairy arm, so he staged his own little protest outside our house in his Aston Martin. He vowed to stay in his car with the engine running until Breeze came out to speak to him. I overheard Mum telling Dad that it was the most romantic gesture she'd ever seen in her whole life, which for some reason sent Dad into an enormous sulk. Breeze spied moodily from her bedroom window, with a face like a smacked arse, until Andreas unzipped his jacket to reveal a T-shirt bearing the slogan *Individually unique. Together complete.* (A quote from Breeze's favourite cult film *My Lover Was A Vegan Virgin*.) This clearly did the trick. Breeze rushed downstairs and out of the front door, where she literally threw herself on to him, knocking him flying into the gutter. They kissed for ages in front of the gaping neighbours, until Dad yelled out of the window, 'For God's sake you two, get a room!'

Yuck.

Of course my parents don't mind Andreas staying the night in Breeze's room at weekends when she's not studying for her teacher training degree, so, after dry humping in the middle of the road, they disappeared upstairs. If I had a boyfriend, I'm not sure I'd feel comfortable bringing him home for shenanigans. It's one thing having a nice time on your own, but it might be different as a double act. What if I was a screamer? What if he was? With parents in the next room. Can you imagine? AWFUL.

QUESTIONS TO ASK MY FUTURE FIRST HUSBAND ON OUR FIRST DATE

1. WILL YOUR PARENTS MIND IF WE STAY AT YOUR PLACE WHEN THE TIME COMES? I don't want to run the risk of having loud sex when my parents are present. (Actually, do I want his parents to hear either? Hmm. I think I'll put off the whole sex thing for as long as possible.)

2. ARE YOU INFERTILE? I intend to have children one day when I am over the age of thirty. If we are not on the same life path then we best split up now to save wasting time.

3. DO YOU HAVE A SEXUALLY TRANSMITTED STI? If you do not know then please could you have some tests at the clinic?

4. IF BALDNESS RUNS IN YOUR FAMILY GENES, WHAT PATTERN OF HAIR LOSS WILL YOU FOLLOW? If it's the one where you get the little bald circle on the back of your head like the Royals please can you guarantee that you will shave your hair?

5. ARE YOU INTO VAJAZZLES? I am NOT. It's au naturel with me. Best prepare yourself.

If in the future it turns out that I'm a lesbian or bisexual the same questions will apply to my wife. (Except number 2 – and the baldness one.)

When I discovered a white dress splashed with dark red stains slung on the top of the dirty linen basket I decided to take a closer look. I'd never seen the dress before. It looked like something that a princess would wear in a fairy tale when waiting for the Prince to rescue her from the tower.

'Mum!' I called from upstairs. 'What's this in the washing basket?'

'What's what?' she called back.

'There's a white dress covered in blood or something.'

'Errrrrr . . .' Long pause. 'I had a bit of a tomato ketchup explosion accident. Too vigorous with the shaking. That's all.'

'Shame it ruined your new dress.'

Another long pause. 'Ahhh. Alas, forsooth the pretty lay in the privy. Fare thee well, nonny nonny and a hey nonny nonny noo.'

Why does my mother speak in gobbledegook when she has to answer an awkward question?

When I looked again later that day the dress was gone.

From: Blossom Uxley-Michaels   25th Feb 12:54
To: info@poptasticmanagement.com
SUBJECT: JOSH RAVEN WANTED NOW

Dear Sir/Madam,

It is a month since I last emailed you and still you haven't replied. I think this is bad form and, quite frankly, rather rude.

So I suppose you would like to know what's been going on in my world. Well, my band Camel Toe now have eight original and brilliant tracks, which we will record in a proper studio soon. I wrote one of the songs – Touch Me Anywhere And Everywhere (But Don't Touch Me There) – with Josh in mind, so I think it would be really great if he could collaborate with us. We could release it as our first single: Camel Toe featuring Josh Raven. He wouldn't even have to come to the studio with us – he could just pop round to my house for an hour or so as I have a digital recorder and a microphone in my bedroom. I could soundproof my wardrobe with some duvets and blankets and nobody would ever know the difference.

I am also waiting for you to confirm a date for Josh's visit to Bridge Mount FM. He could come round to my house afterwards to record his vocals and then we could visit his mum's grave together as the church where she's buried is at the end of my road.

Hope to hear from you soon.

Many thanks,

Blossom Uxley-Michaels

P.S. I'm not a crazy stalker type or anything, but if there is a spare lock of Josh's hair lying about on a hairbrush or a desk or his pillow could you please send it to me?

END OF WEEK TABLE OF ACHIEVEMENT

SHAME LEVEL PEAK	1 (a good week)
GUITAR PRACTICE	3 hours 33 minutes (I am just getting to the stage where I can not only strum and sing simultaneously, I can also close my eyes at the same time. I want to look passionate and meaningful when I sing. Not just cool.)
SCHOOL WORK	3 hours (spent most of the week downloading David Bowie's back catalogue. He's made about a million albums and it almost broke my laptop.)
PARTY INVITATIONS	0
SNOGS	0

STORM MOON

ALSO KNOWN AS: MOON OF ICE, SNOW MOON,
MOON OF THE RACCOON, HUNGER MOON

February is the month of the Storm Moon – Mum's favourite for naked moon dancing. (Dad has always preferred the enormous autumn Equinox Harvest Moon.) Mum finds it to be an exhilarating way of preparing for the forthcoming spring, both mentally and physically. But when I looked out of my bedroom window, all I saw was my father's lone silhouette, dancing a duet with nature under the Storm Moon, shining full and bright in the starlit sky. As long as I can remember neither of them has missed a single moon dance. It's something they both look forward to, come rain, shine, hail, thunder or snow. This morning when I asked Mum about her absence she replied simply that she was 'desperately needed elsewhere'. I racked my brains, but I honestly couldn't think of anything that had ever been – or could ever be – more important to her than this spiritual, monthly ritual.

My journey to school in the camper van was accompanied by a mortifying soundtrack of backfiring and explosions, which climaxed with the exhaust pipe falling off right outside the school gate. Thankfully nobody seemed to notice as they were all stood around the school 'Miscellaneous' notice board, clambering to sign a form. The notice read:

DEMPSEY LOVE PRESENTS...

SUPER SPEED DATE AFTERNOON

Cut The Crap And Get Straight To The Point
(The Fastest Way To Find True Love)

SUNDAY MARCH 13th

St James's Church Hall

2pm – 4pm

ENTRY

£4

(Snacks And Squash Included)

Paulette was standing next to the crowd dishing out flyers. She looked different. She spotted me as I collected my hot chocolate from the vending machine and waved me over.

'Hey, Blossom!' she called. 'Could you ask Felix to plug this on his show when you see him, please?'

Why does Paulette look weird?

She thrust a flyer into my hand.

OH MY GOD. She's wearing shoulder pads under her jumper.

'Yeah sure,' I replied staring at her shoulders.

'Thanks. Over a hundred people have signed up already and I only pinned the notice to the board half an hour ago.'

No, Blossom. You must resist the urge to rest your hot chocolate on Paulette's enormous shoulder pad.

'Who'd have thought so many people were looking for love?' I smiled, desperately trying to avoid looking at her shoulders.

Paulette's expression was deadly serious. 'Love is the second most important thing in the world.'

'What's the first?' I wondered.

Life itself is probably the first. Without life there is no love.

'Money,' she replied firmly.

She has no heart? A heartless Cupid. So sad...

'I'll do mates' rates for you, seeing as you're my best customer,' she continued.

Do I look that desperate?

'Brilliant, thanks! I owe you one – BIG TIME,' I said.

OK, I am that desperate.

'I could give you a group discount if Petrina and Walter come too?'

125

'I wouldn't hold my breath,' I said. 'Petrina doesn't like what she calls "forced love".'

'It's not "forced" love,' Paulette explained. 'Just concise. Why spend hours trying to work out if you've found The One when you can figure it out in three minutes?'

As Paulette disappeared back into the crowd to distribute more of her flyers, I spotted Fiona and Lucy giggling as they wrote their names up on the speed dating list. And right below they added Felix and Toby.

'This is going to be hilarious,' I heard Fiona say. 'Just think of all the losers we'll get to humiliate.'

Stupid, senseless, shallow slangers. I'll show you. I'll woo Felix until he falls dead at my feet. Just you wait and see.

Yesterday I arrived at school only to be overwhelmed by a strange atmosphere – a kind of noxious expectation that sent chills up my spine. My unease was fuelled when Paulette asked me what I intended to have for my 'final meal' when I got home after school. When I enquired as to what on Earth she was on about, she said that she had decided that she would be having a quick-fix meal (to save time) of steak, chips and baked beans with Ben And Jerry's Cookie Dough ice cream for pudding, washed down with a can of Diet Coke.

I had no idea what Paulette meant, but the weirdness continued. Whispers in the corridors, dramatic emotional embraces in the classrooms, solemn knowing looks in the assembly hall – something was going on, but I didn't have a clue what it was. I ran to find Petrina who explained that a prophet called Bambo Biggins had predicted that the whole world would end at 4.45pm the next day. She dismissed the whole furore with a flippant brush of the hand. She doesn't believe in anything unless there is scientific evidence to back it up. Not God, not ghosts or even fate. She says she is a 'natural born cynic' and had it all sussed at the age of two when she pulled the beard off Santa Claus at the Christmas fair to reveal the fat female vicar from the local church.

Everyone knows that rumours are common place in schools. It is also true that eighty-five per cent of them are false (which is actually a figure I just made up, but I'm excellent at probability so this is probably a guaranteed mathematical FACT). But this was one particular rumour that freaked me RIGHT OUT.

Fiona Tittledown and Lucy Perkins, on the other hand, found it all very exciting. Their squeals and giggles could be heard all over the school as they plotted their predictably explicit activities with Felix and Toby at the exact moment that the world ended. I wish I could be as jovial, but I'll be honest – I was absolutely petrified. There was a big clenched fist inside my chest that tightened each time I thought about it. How could everyone be so trivial about something so catastrophic?

That evening (possibly my last) Mum tried to make me feel better by explaining that a similar apocalyptic prediction was made when she was at school and that they all survived and lived to tell the tale. But that was about a million years ago when there were only a handful of TV channels, computers were completely rubbish and people were so poor that they had to eat coal. Of course now we have proper technology so

I figured that the likelihood of scientists knowing that the end of the world was about to happen was pretty high. I felt the need to at least *try* to prepare for my impending DOOM.

THINGS I WANT TO DO BEFORE I DIE IN THE APOCALYPSE (AMENDED)

1. Kiss Felix Winters (possible)

2. Have sex (impossible seeing as I'm not prepared to do it with Matthew Ludlow)

3. Have a hit single (impossible)

4. Marry Josh Raven (impossible)

5. Climb a mountain (impossible)

6. Go on a romantic weekend to Paris (impossible)

7. Passionately kiss a boy in the pouring rain (possible – depending on the weather forecast)

8. Write a best-selling vampire novel series (impossible)

9. Dance naked under the full moon (possible)

10. Get tipsy on expensive Champagne (possible-ish)

With only a few hours of my life remaining, I endeavoured to achieve whatever I could. My parents aren't very posh so we had no Champagne in the house, but I did manage to sneak a glass of Tia Maria up to my bedroom. It was quite nice in a sickly kind of way. Next was *dancing naked under the full moon*, which my parents say is the most liberating experience a person can have. Quite frankly the vision of Mum and Dad's naked parts flapping about in the open air always makes me feel physically queasy, but I was intrigued to find out what all the fuss was about. As a) there was no full moon and b) it was teeming outside (good for point 7 – *if* there had been a boy around), I turned off my bedroom light, took off all my clothes and threw some serious shapes on the rug under the dazzling light of my clip-on LED reading lamp. It was indeed a very liberating experience. I felt free and at one with my bedroom. That is until the door opened, the ceiling light was switched on and Breeze walked in to tell me that I was playing my music too loudly.

Oh. My. God.

In a naked panic, I quickly grabbed Boris The Rabbit to cover my modesty, while Breeze let out a scream, spun 180 degrees on her heels and spluttered, 'Turn it down. We can hear your muff downstairs. MUSIC. We can hear your *music* downstairs.'

Later, she claimed that the scream she emitted was due to the shock of my poor taste in music, not because of my nakedness. Nudity is supposed to be no big deal in this house. Anyway, my embarrassment was irrelevant as we were all about to die.

On Armageddon day, there was a definite air of rebellion wafting about the school. Detentions were dealt out left, right and centre, as most Bridge Mount pupils believed that their unruly actions would have no repercussions. Even Walter got a detention for spending the entire art lesson drawing an Apocalyptic scene of zombie Bridge Mount students, blood, guts and desecration when he should have been sketching the contents of a fruit bowl. But WORST OF ALL the end of the world was scheduled to take place at four forty-five, during my after-school trampoline club. In spite of my crippling fear, I did not want to die mid-straddle jump, wearing a leotard that was a size too small and wedged up in between my bum cheeks.

'Why is everyone buying into this "end of world" gubbins?' Petrina asked me after lunch.

'Because it was all over the radio yesterday.'

'No it wasn't, Blossom. One TV presenter mentioned it.' Petrina gently touched my arm. 'Look, I'm going to walk Walter home after school so that his warped imagination doesn't swallow his brain. Do you want me to walk you home too?'

'No, it's OK thanks. I'm going to die energetically in trampoline club.'

When Fiona caught me taking a last look at Felix as he was striking a pose by the lockers, she threw me the filthiest of looks before grabbing him by the tie and sticking her tongue down his throat. It's not my fault he possesses a magnetic aura that draws the compass of my loins towards him. But my ambition of kissing him before I died was looking unlikely.

A violet hue begins to slowly swallow up the cloudless blue sky, followed by an angry shadow of red. Soon everything around becomes a glowing furnace of flames. The panicked students of Bridge Mount Secondary School flee the burning building, their terrified screams ringing through the air.

With make-up smeared all over her tear-stained face, Fiona Tittledown runs around the playing field looking REALLY ugly and shouting, 'Felix? Felix? Where are you?'

My heart pounds in my chest. I can't see him anywhere in the crowds of students. Surely Felix isn't dead?

I begin to feel my hot skin bubbling. I know I will soon be nothing more than a pool of boiling mush.

A loud explosion rings out across the sky. The school is collapsing. The world is breaking. I look over at Fiona. She is melting. It's gross.

And then a tall, dark, figure slowly emerges from the inferno burning in front of me

'I've been looking for you, my love,' says Felix.

He glances over my shoulder and sees Fiona all floppy in a big wet puddle of herself.

'Urrgggh,' he says. 'That is so disgusting.'

He pulls me towards him. We stand face to face, our lips almost touching. He is very hot and sweaty, but does not have bad B.O.

'I love you, Blossom Uxley-Michaels,' he murmurs, before kissing me passionately.

Then, as our world is engulfed in flames and planet Earth implodes, Felix and I melt together and became one happy, bloody swamp of human remains.

Needless to say the world didn't end, but when Mum arrived to pick me up at five o'clock I was an emotional wreck, relieved to have survived Armageddon, yet utterly traumatised by the ordeal. I have also told the instructor that I will not be attending trampoline club any more, following another embarrassingly public sporting wardrobe malfunction. Life is just too short to worry about losing your leotard up your bum.

All week Petrina has stubbornly refused to sign up for the Dempsey Love speed date afternoon.

Let's put our names down for speed dating. x

NO WAY.

Oh go on. It'll be LOL city :D

No.

Lucy's entered Toby 'for a laugh'...

Really? When can I sign up?

YAY! I'll shag you up in the morning ;)

Erm...I love you and all that but REALLY?!

OMG. 'SIGN' you up. I HATE autocorrect.

END OF WEEK TABLE OF ACHIEVEMENT

SHAME LEVEL PEAK	7 ("I can hear your muff")
GUITAR PRACTICE	46 minutes (practising the guitar didn't seem important when faced with the prospect of the end of the world)
SCHOOL WORK	0 (again, the impending Armageddon cancelled any need to do homework)
PARTY INVITATIONS	0
SNOGS	0

WEEK 10
SCOOBY DOO

Pete Hartley's recording studio is set in the plush grounds of his enormous mansion, where he strolls around like a king, making fabulous music with some of the world's biggest stars. Dad dropped us off with Walter at ten-thirty. We couldn't believe our eyes. Pete's lavish amenities include swimming pools (one indoor, two outdoors), tennis courts and a MASSIVE hot tub. As he showed us round his swanky home – dressed in flip-flops, Speedos, wraparound shades and an XL pink Hawaiian shirt, with a fat Cuban cigar in one hand and a Pina Colada in the other – I found it hard to believe that Pete (who was really friendly) could have ever been an angry political activist. He took us to one of his indoor pools, where a hairy rock band were drinking cocktails with twenty beautiful groupies. I began to panic a little in case an orgy was about to take place.

'Guys, this is Steel Dragon.' Pete gestured towards the long-haired, lanky-limbed rockers. 'You've probably heard of them.'

Amongst the sea of tangled hair, I suddenly recognised the HUGE afro of lead singer Billy Hawkins, who stood up to reveal the tightest trousers I have EVER seen on a man.

'Hi,' he said in his chilled Californian accent. 'Great to meet ya. Do ya wanna beer?'

'No thanks,' said Walter. 'We're only fift—'

'Only dropping by.' I butted in, trying to be cool. We didn't want to look like nerdy school kids in front of an iconic rock band. 'And it's a bit too early for us, if you know what I mean?'

Billy laughed and held up his turquoise cocktail. 'Yeah, man. I get it. Maybe later, huh?'

'Yeah, man,' said Petrina in her coolest voice.

'What *are* you doing?' whispered Walter.

Petrina's cheeks turned pink. 'Shut up,' she hissed back.

I was feeling quite cool, chewing the *phat* with an international rock star. 'We've got some tracks to cut, dude,' I explained.

Billy nodded. 'Ever the pro, huh?'

'You know what I'm sayin', bro,' I said, not actually understanding what either of us was on about, but I don't think he noticed.

Walter looked at us as if we were completely deranged. Petrina and I ignored him.

'We're recording our seventh album,' said Billy proudly. '*Long Legs On Fire*. It's gonna be awesome.'

'This is our demo album,' said Petrina. 'It's called *Poncerama's Revenge*.'

Billy clearly approved. 'Far-out title, man.'

The recording studio was huge, swanky and a bit intimidating. Every wall was covered in commemorative gold discs and photographs of Pete hanging out with some of the world's most famous rock stars. One signed photo stuck out like a hedgehog in custard. Josh Raven standing casually next to Pete who was doing a really cheesey, double thumbs-up pose.

'Wowzoids!' I said. 'Josh Raven was here?'

'Yeah,' said Pete, sitting down at the ridiculously enormous mixing desk. 'He recorded his first album here a couple of years ago. Great kid. He dropped by last week just to say hi.'

'What?' I couldn't believe it.

Petrina grabbed my arm. 'Calm down, Blossom. Take it easy.'

'He was *here*. Just down the road from us? Why didn't he come into school? I've been asking him for months.'

Pete shrugged. 'He's a busy man. Places to be, people to see. I'm sure there are a million places he'd rather be than school.'

Josh Raven might as well have taken his mic stand and stabbed it deep into my heart. I felt utterly betrayed.

Pete spent the whole day with us in the studio. He's so knowledgeable, suggesting things that we'd never even thought of. An extra hook here, a key change there, a horn-peppered groove on one track, a stripped-back acoustic sound on another. He made us sound AMAZING. The icing on the cake, though, had to be Billy Hawkins barging into the studio (clearly quite drunk, even though it was only two-thirty in the afternoon) and demanding to sing backing vocals on *Poncerama*. It was so brilliant to hear him sing the lyrics that Petrina and I had written. I think Billy could really relate to the words – he's a strange, but kind, man who would probably never have got a girlfriend if he hadn't become a world famous rock star.

Walter and Steel Dragon's notoriously reclusive lead guitarist Wazzock looked as though they'd been separated at birth as they sat mumbling at each other through their protective fringes. They got on so well, in fact, that Walter persuaded Wazzock to make up a fiddly guitar solo that Pete then slotted into the middle eight section of *The Man With An Eggy Beard*. It was always supposed to be an angry song but now it sounds FURIOUS!

And so it transpired that Camel Toe recorded an original demo, produced by the legendary Pete Hartley, with guest appearances from Steel Dragon's Billy Hawkins and Wazzock. Quite frankly, if that doesn't make us cool, then nothing will.

From: Blossom Uxley-Michaels   8th Mar 18:12
To: info@poptasticmanagement.com
SUBJECT: ANNOYED!!!

Dear Sir/Madam,

I know for a fact that Josh Raven was in the close vicinity of my school just two weeks ago. I'm not a weird stalker type, but I have it on good authority that he was at Pete Hartley's recording studio. So, I am asking myself, why did he not take the time to pop into my school for a quick interview? Was he really that busy? Well, I can answer that question myself: no. He was not. He just dropped into Pete's studio to say 'hi'. He wasn't recording an album or anything. He could have used that precious 'hi' time to speak to the students of his old school. Students who buy his albums and concert tickets and help to make Josh Raven the megastar that he is today.

To say that I am disappointed is an understatement. I am hurt, saddened and actually very cross.

So, by way of compensation, I hope that you will be able to find a date in Josh's diary for him to visit the school ASAP.

Hope to hear from you soon.

Many thanks,

Blossom Uxley-Michaels

P.S. I have just recorded a duet with Billy Hawkins from Steel Dragon, so I don't need Josh to appear as a guest on Camel Toe's demo. If he apologises to me personally then I will consider him as a guest artist on my next album.

Of course, nobody believed that Camel Toe has recorded a demo with Steel Dragon so we had to live down the shame of being branded liars live on-air by Fiona and Lucy. But luckily Paulette Dempsey became a convenient distraction when she guested on the Breakfast Show.

'So, how exactly does speed dating work?' asked Fiona, yawning as she filed her nails on a pink, spotty emery board.

'Well, basically,' explained Paulette. 'When you arrive you'll be checked in and given a number. Those with badge number one will start at table number one, those with badge number two at table number two and so on.'

She leaned back for a brief moment, so that Walter could adjust her microphone. 'Then you have three minutes,' she continued, 'to find out if you and your date are compatible. When the three minutes are up, I blow my whistle. The girls stay seated and the boys move round one table. This continues until you have met everyone there. At the end of the session there is a board where you tick the boxes of the dates you'd like to see again. If there is a match, then you might just have found true love.'

'Sounds interesting,' smirked Lucy. 'So how about you, Paulette? As Bridge Mount's official matchmaker, have you found true love?'

'Don't be silly,' scoffed Paulette. 'I'm asexual.'

'So I've heard,' said Fiona tapping her biro against the mixing desk. 'But you're telling me that you don't fancy anybody?'

'Nope.'

'What, you've never even had a crush on a popstar?' queried Lucy. 'Or a comedian?'

Lucy gazed down lovingly at the unofficial Ricky Gervais biography sitting on the desk. Everyone in the room grimaced.

'Never,' said Paulette shaking her head.

'Are you sure you're not a lesbian?' asked Fiona. 'Kirsty Mackerby might be available at the moment.'

'No,' replied Paulette firmly. 'The only thing that butters my muffin is a great big, sexy pile of cash.'

She held up her wrist to reveal a brand new (disgusting), crystal-studded Swisha watch.

'Do you think the man of my dreams bought this?' she asked. 'Of course not. I bought it with my own entrepreneurial skills.'

'Wow,' said Fiona admiring the hideous watch. 'I've got to wait until my birthday before I'll get one of those.'

'That is so cool,' said Lucy gazing in awe.

You could see Fiona and Lucy were thinking about how much they could make if they traded Felix and Toby in.

Go ahead, girls, I won't stand in your way!

Last night was a bit manic. The four of us went out for a family meal at a pizza restaurant. Breeze was in a filthy mood having just seen Creepy Dave lurking outside the house. (Although nobody else saw him, so it might have just been a ruse to hide the fact that she is a grumpy mare when she has PMS.) I think I was passively expressing some angry emotions when I ordered a meat feast pizza for no other reason than to annoy everybody. My parents didn't comment, but Breeze flew into a rage, threatening to sit at another table if I didn't change my order. Dad asked her to be 'more accepting' and to 'respect people's choices'. She spent the rest of the evening scowling at me.

Then on the way home the camper van broke down (again) and we had to wait for almost three hours to be towed back home. Breeze refused to sit next to me, saying that my breath stank of dead farmyard animals. She really is unbearable sometimes. By the time we got home it was almost midnight and I was exhausted, so I just threw my clothes in a pile on the floor by my bed and crawled under the covers.

I totally slept through my alarm and only woke up when I got Petrina's text reminding me that it was mufti day at school. With Dad yelling up the stairs, I grabbed some clean underwear and then put on the skinny jeans, The Cure retro T-shirt and baseball boots that were still lying on the floor from last night. I have paid my pound, I *will* wear my own clothes. When I arrived at the radio station Paulette was fussing about getting the tea and coffee, Felix and Toby were sorting out the music for the show playlist, Petrina and Walter were editing some student vox pops and Fiona and Lucy were trowelling on even more make-up. Mufti day is effectively a fashion show for the Winners, who strut up and down the corridors like glamour models flaunting their low-cut, prozzie outfits on a catwalk. Amongst the understated and unassuming students, Fiona and Lucy looked like a couple of pimped-up turds in a trifle.

'Hey, Bumface,' said Fiona, without actually looking at me. 'Who've you booked on the show today?'

Whilst tempted to say *I've hired a hit man to blow your stupid face off*, I opted for: 'Kirsty Mackerby's mum is coming in to talk about astrology. Didn't you get the info and questions that I emailed you yesterday?'

'I haven't had time to look,' replied Fiona. 'Busy social life. Just not enough hours in the day.'

'Never mind.' *Well I guess it must take up a lot of precious time perfecting your dumbness.* 'I'll print it all out for you in a minute.'

'Hey, Blossom,' called Felix. 'Cool T-shirt.'

Look at him. He's so perfect. White T-shirt, bum-hugging jeans. If I die of an undiagnosed sudden heart defect right now, I want to be immediately reincarnated as those jeans.

'Are you kidding?' sneered Fiona. '*That* skanky old thing?'

I'll happily covert to Hinduism.

'It looks like something my Grandad would have worn,' giggled Lucy.

Although I'm not sure if I could give up beef burgers.

'I like it,' said Felix.

I would so become a vegetarian for Felix Winters.

'You don't get much cooler than The Cure,' said Petrina, without looking up from her computer screen.

'Oh yeah?' scoffed Lucy. 'And what would *you* know?'

Petrina casually made a rude gesture with her fingers.

'I bet you two have never even heard of The Cure,' said Toby to the slangers as he walked into the studio wearing tight, Lycra CYCLING SHORTS. 'Best band ever.'

Petrina and Walter looked up at the sound of his voice. Walter immediately turned away as if he may be blinded by the sight before him. Petrina's eyes however, were immediately drawn towards Toby's hypnotically bulging crotch. She used all her strength to try and avert her eyes, but failed. Toby's groin was like Kryptonite to Petrina's immense Superwoman-like force of will and determination.

Fiona broke the spell. 'What's that?' she asked, pointing down at my left foot.

'What's what?' I wondered, looking down.

'Something on your foot.'

She was right. There was something poking out from the leg of my jeans. I reached down to grab it and gave it a yank, but oh, how I wished I hadn't bothered, as I now held in my hand yesterday's brown, baggy Scooby Doo knickers.

When I got dressed this morning they must have still been inside the trouser leg (I was very, *very* tired when I got undressed) and slowly worked their way out as I journeyed into school. *ARRRRRRRGGGGHHHH.*

I felt my cheeks burning up.

Fiona and Lucy took a moment to realise what I was holding, before breaking into uncontrollable hysterics.

'Scooby Doo!'

'Those are the most revolting pants I have ever seen!'

Felix and Toby were laughing too.

Dear baby Jesus or any Hindu god. Please use your power to kill me from my undetected heart defect RIGHT NOW.

'Wow,' said Felix. 'Sexy undies.'

Feeling mortified, I went to sit with Petrina and Walter, while the laughter continued behind me. I still didn't know what to do with my pants – I just held them scrunched up in my hand until Walter unzipped the pocket on my bag, allowing me to push them out of sight.

'Don't worry about it, Blossom,' said Petrina reassuringly. 'It could have been worse.'

I was unconvinced. 'How? How could it possibly have been any worse?'

'It could have been that awful tiger-print, velour thong that you were wearing that time you got your dress caught in your pants at the Christmas Ball.'

She was right. Those knickers were hideous. Really, really hideous. One must remember to be thankful for small mercies.

Obviously, the slangers showed no mercy, broadcasting the story to the entire school. The rest of the day was set against a soundtrack of:

'Here comes Scooby Poopy Poo.'

'Look there's Bumface Ploppy pants.'

'Hey Bumface! Is that a Scooby Doo in your pants or are you just pleased to see me?'

That doesn't even MAKE SENSE.

END OF WEEK TABLE OF ACHIEVEMENT

SHAME LEVEL PEAK	7 (Scooby. Doo.)
GUITAR PRACTICE	3 hours 41 minutes
SCHOOL WORK	2 hours (gentle revision to begin with)
PARTY INVITATIONS	Does a ticket to a Speed Date Afternoon count?
SNOGS	0

The kitchen table is traditionally the family gathering place for meals, discussion and problem solving. Ours was no different, made of chunky, rustic oak and affectionately tattooed with the blemishes and scars of our family life. Coffee cup rings, burns, biro and felt-tip pen marks all decorated this well-loved piece of wood. In one corner you could very clearly read the words *I love Big Macs*, that I scratched into the surface with my compass point when I was twelve. A big, blotchy, purple stain right in the centre of the table was evidence of when Dad demonstrated that pickled beetroot was an excellent makeshift lipstick. Oh, and there were some tiny, rock hard 'bits' that clung to the underside of the table in one corner, like miniature stalactites. This was Breeze's ancient secret bogey collection that she started when she was about nine. She used to carefully pick them out of her nose and stick them under the table when she thought nobody was looking. In recent years I have occasionally caught her sitting underneath admiring her rather large stash of fossilized nose truffles. She might be drop-dead pretty, but Breeze has GIANT blowholes.

Mum didn't come home on Friday evening and I found

Dad sitting at the table in the darkness, staring into his camomile tea looking sadder than I have ever known. He always encourages us to be open and share problems, yet his distant, liquid eyes told me at that precise moment he would prefer to be left alone. Things aren't right between Mum and Dad.

The next day, with a fuggy head and a heavy heart, I caught a bus into town to satisfy my fierce burger craving. Petrina found me sitting alone with my mouth wrapped around a Big Mac.

'You OK?'

'No,' I said, with a gob full of meat. 'But it's better than being at home. I've never seen my dad look so miserable.'

'Do you think perhaps he's having a mid-life crisis?'

'I reckon my mum is having one. She's been behaving very strangely.'

Petrina raised her eyebrows. '*My* mum's been acting strangely for years. Isn't that just how parents are?'

I shook my head. 'She's started talking in a strange way.'

'What, like she's speaking in Tongues or something?' said Petrina, trying to be helpful.

'No. Like Old English. You know – all "thee", "thy" and "hey nonny nonny".'

'Maybe she's trying to be more sophisticated.'

'Remember The Wizard?'

'How could I forget?' said Petrina.

'And then there's the golden chalice and pentagram star necklace that she didn't want me to see.'

'Yeah. That really *was* a bit odd.'

'I know. *And* she didn't come home to dance under the Storm Moon.'

I could tell by her expression that Petrina finally realised the seriousness of the situation.

'I told you it was bad,' I said, taking a bite from my deliciously meaty burger. 'And then there's the mysterious long white dress that I found in the linen basket, covered in what could have been . . . blood.'

'You sure it wasn't just tomato ketchup?'

'That's what Mum said. But then she *would* wouldn't she –' I changed my voice to a low whisper in case anyone was listening – '. . . if she needed to cover her tracks?'

Petrina reached across the table and took hold of my hand as she looked directly into my eyes (which had become a bit bleary).

'It'll be OK,' she said in a reassuring voice. 'It's just parents being parents. They say that teenagers are another species, when in actual fact it's mums and dads who are the strangest of all.'

St James's church hall was festooned in pink, white and red, with hundreds of helium-filled, heart-shaped balloons tied to just about every grounded object. Paulette really had pulled out all the stops to make the room look as romantic as possible. She was wearing a small pair of angel wings over a T-shirt bearing the slogan *I'M CUPID'S BOSS* and holding a large, heart-shaped stopwatch in her raised hand. The dating was already underway, with couples sitting opposite each other at the separate tables arranged in a circle around the hall.

'I think I'm going to be sick,' said Petrina, as we paid our entrance fee. 'This looks dreadful.'

Lucy and Fiona were largely ignoring their dates, instead making indiscreet signals at each other by sticking their fingers down their throats and gesturing signs of boredom.

'Oh my God,' I whispered, pointing over at a table in the far corner where, to our surprise, Walter was sitting with his chin resting in his hands as a pretty-looking Year 10 girl babbled at him. He wearily raised his hand in acknowledgment.

'What the . . . ?' mouthed Petrina.

Walter shrugged as if to say, *well I had nothing better to do*.

'What's he doing here?' she asked me.

'How would I know?' Seriously, I might have known him for ever, but Walter's a mystery to me most of the time.

Paulette blew loudly into her whistle to mark the end of the current dates. The boys obeyed, rising from their chairs to move one table to the left. Max Burcott was now sitting opposite Fiona Tittledown. (I wish I could have eavesdropped on *that* date.) Matthew Ludlow was 'dating' the girl in Year 12 who is rumoured to have three nipples and lucky old Walter had been joined by Lucy Perkins.

At that moment, Felix and Toby walked into the hall and were immediately ushered by Paulette towards some vacant tables. Toby had come straight from training, judging by the small bum-skimming shorts he was wearing. I gently put the palm of my hand under Petrina's chin to close her mouth, which had suddenly dropped open.

'The hottest boy in the school,' she drooled.

'Second hottest,' I reminded her. 'Look at Felix's bum cheeks in those jeans. Like two denim doughnuts.'

I would love to sink my teeth into them. I hope this is not the early signs of a future sexual fetish that will eventually classify me as a pervert.

I launched myself into mid-air, diving head first onto the empty seat opposite Felix. Fetishes be damned.

Play it cool, Blossom. Play it cool.

'All right?' he asked, looking bemused as the chair skidded into the next table while I clung on as if I was body-boarding a big wave.

'Erm, yes,' I replied casually. I repositioned the chair and sat down.

Paulette blew her whistle.

I had three minutes to win him over.

We sat quietly avoiding eye contact for about twenty long seconds.

I was first to attempt the icebreaker. 'So,' I said in my very best sultry, sexy voice. 'What shall we talk about?'

Felix looked at me blankly.

He could easily be a model. Easily!

'Dunno,' he said.

I lowered my chin to maximise the effect of my seductive eyelash fluttering. 'Tell me about your passions.'

'Eh?'

'What stokes your fire? Gets you hot under the collar?'

I reckon I could probably get a job one day as a voiceover artist on one of those sexy tampon adverts.

'*Star Wars*,' said Felix scratching his armpit.

I have never got past the first five minutes of any of the Star Wars *films. Mind numbingly dull. Lie, Blossom, lie.*

'Wowzoids, that's such a coincidence. I LOVE the *Star Wars* series,' I pretended.

Felix looked genuinely excited, leaning in towards me, his beautiful eyes all keen and hopeful. 'Really? It's so cool to find a girl who understands my obsession. Fiona thinks the films are boring. She's got no taste.'

Your voice is like the sound of a million nightingales singing in the trees.

'Mmm,' I nodded.

'I've recently acquired a genuine production, fur, Ewok lower body component from *Return of the Jedi*. Of course, Fiona thinks it's nothing more than a brown furry nappy. I mean can you believe it?'

I shook my head, not knowing what on earth he was talking about.

'How can she not understand that it's an integral part of the Ewok costume with hand-stitched, velcro fastenings at the side and an elastic gusset. It's worth over three hundred and fifty pounds.'

Oh my God. He said 'gusset'. So sexy.

'Petrina wears her knickers under AND over the gusset of her tights,' I chirped gleefully, leaping upon a topic of mutual accord.

Felix was silent for a few moments (*possibly sexually*

150

aroused?) before he continued. 'Right . . . So which of the films is your favourite?'

Eek! Keep it generic. Bluff your way through it Blossom.

'Oh . . . I love the one with . . . the man . . . who, er . . . saves the . . . umm . . . girl.'

Felix nodded sagely. 'Yeah, I guess you can't beat the original. None of the prequels quite match up, but personally I'd say that *Return Of The Jedi* is my favourite.'

'Well, that would obviously be my second choice,' I said.

Over on the next table Petrina was pouting and tossing her hair, spouting a fountain of nonsense and saliva while Toby sat opposite picking bits of dirt from his fingernails. At the back of the hall Walter stared vacantly in Petrina's direction, quietly ignoring the animated gestures made by Lucy Perkins, as she used their 'date' to try out some of her best one-liners.

'So what do you think of the theory that Ben Kenobi is the clone of Obi-Wan the Jedi with clone designation of OB-1?' asked Felix.

'Yep,' I responded confidently. 'It's a brilliant theory.'

I am so wooing him.

'Really?' he said looking rather surprised. 'In what way?'

Uh-oh!

'Erm . . . in the way that Ben . . . Occhio . . . is a clone of erm . . . the little robot that looks like a pedal bin.'

Felix's face began to turn red. 'Are you really a fan of *Star Wars*?' he asked.

Do NOT panic.

'Oh God, yes. Absolutely. The biggest fan.'

Felix clearly didn't believe me. 'How many *Star Wars* films have there been?'

Take a logical guess Blossom. There have been loads of them. More than three, less than twenty. Life's a gamble. Fingers crossed.

'Fifteen?' I asked hopefully.

Felix stood up just as Paulette blew the whistle.

Well, I think that went well.

At the end of the afternoon I had ticked the boxes of the three boys I would like to see again. (Felix OBVIOUSLY and then two back-ups – one of which was Walter. The other was Matthew Ludlow. He might be an alcoholic, but he's still a sweet guy.) However, I received zero ticks in my box, meaning that I was dateless. A speed date reject. I should have had at least one tick as Walter, Petrina and I had promised each other a platonic condolence tick in case that exact situation occurred. I noticed that Walter had remembered to tick Petrina's box (although she had forgotten to tick his), but he hadn't ticked mine. Having kept my side of the bargain – making sure Walter didn't look like an unattractive quimboid – I was (understandably) annoyed that he had let me down.

Felix hadn't said a single word to me since the weekend and I was convinced I'd totally blown any smidgen of a chance that I might have had. But then, on Tuesday, in the debrief after the Breakfast Show, Felix approached me.

Oh no. He's going to humiliate me in front of everyone. This is going to be excruciatingly embarrassing.

'All right?' he asked, avoiding any kind of eye contact.

Fiona took this as her cue to butt in. 'Did you really think that just by pretending to like *Star Wars* you'd make him interested in *you*?' she jeered.

Lucy cackled loudly. 'As if!'

I felt myself crumble inside. Petrina rubbed my back gently, glaring back at the slangers.

'Here,' said Felix, holding something under my nose. 'Take this.'

I took the object from his hand and looked at it. *Star Wars Episode IV: A New Hope.*

'You might enjoy it,' he smiled. My insides melted and I hoped that I wasn't about to make a puddle on the floor.

Fiona kissed her teeth loudly as my pale cheeks began to glow an aurora of pink and red. 'Thanks,' I said sheepishly.

Although I planned to watch the film, I ended up spending the evening worrying that Mum had somehow become involved in some kind of sinister cult and Googling them all to see which one it might be. It's well documented that middle-aged men turn to leather and motorbikes when they have their mid-life crisis, but what happens when a woman reaches that vulnerable age? I wasn't sure if this was really such a terrible thing, but when I mentioned it to Petrina she pointed out that a cult would probably need a regular supply of female virgins to sacrifice at the altar. Which put me first in line. I need a boyfriend FAST.

✳ ✳ ✳

From: Blossom Uxley-Michaels   16th Mar 07:02
To: info@poptasticmanagement.com
SUBJECT: SORRY.

Dear Sir/Madam,

I must apologise for my last email. I was angry and I wrote it in haste. Sorry, sorry, sorry.

Please allow me to make it up to you by taking Josh Raven out for dinner. (Nowhere fancy though as I will have to borrow the money from my parents. Unless of course Josh would like to take me out instead. In which case anywhere fancy would be perfect.)

Hope to hear from you soon.

Many thanks,

Blossom Uxley-Michaels

P.S. Could he please bring a signed poster of himself for me? The ones I have of him on my bedroom wall are getting a bit tatty. (Which probably has something to do with the fact that I kiss each poster on the lips before I go to sleep. But not in a weird way or anything untoward.)

✳ ✳ ✳

Today Fiona Tittledown was almost run over by Mr Blackmore and it has been one of the best days EVER. She was having a massive argument with Felix in the staff car park when Mr Blackmore's big black car swung into the parking bay where she was standing. If she hadn't missed Felix's face when she went to punch him and fallen head first into the flowerbed, she would have been dead or seriously injured. The image of Fiona lying in a hospital bed in a coma all tubed-up and dribbling popped gleefully into my head and I desperately tried to make it disappear. I've already got bad karma to pay back after the time I mistook Breeze's pet stick-insect for a twig and sucked it up with our Dyson. I don't want to build a bad karma backlog. (Besides, dead would be better – you can wake up from a coma.) Mr Blackmore was so flustered that he had trouble getting out of the car and ended up falling on his back next to Fiona. It was the best start to a school day that I have ever had!

As a result of her near-death experience, Fiona was jittery and grumpy on-air. Felix cowered in the next room trying his best to keep out of his EX-girlfriend's way! OH YES!!! Fiona took great pleasure in ceremoniously dumping her gorgeous boyfriend live on the radio. Hahahahahahaha! Petrina thinks I should wait a few weeks before I try to make a move, as I don't want Felix to fall into my arms on the rebound. (Although secretly I'd happily settle for a few weeks of rebound love than no love at all.)

END OF WEEK TABLE OF ACHIEVEMENT

SHAME LEVEL PEAK	8 ('fifteen Star Wars films' was on a par with saying testicles instead of tentacles. ARGH!!!)
GUITAR PRACTICE	3 hours 57 minutes
SCHOOL WORK	2½ hours (Petrina is making copies of her revision notes for me. She says they are foolproof.)
PARTY INVITATIONS	0
SNOGS	0 (but now Felix is single, perhaps a snog is on the cards soon!!!)

WEEK 12
ALREADY BONDED!!!

Pete Hartley came round with the finished Camel Toe demo. Petrina, her parents, Walter, Breeze, Andreas, Mum, Dad and I listened in our sitting room as Pete played it in its entirety.

After it had finished, everyone gave us a round of applause and Dad opened the outrageously expensive bottle of Champagne that Pete had brought with him. I had half a glass and felt quite squiffy.

'I'm so proud of you, Blossom,' said Dad, looking happier than I'd seen him for weeks. 'I know how hard you two have worked.'

'Maybe you can focus a bit more on your studies now?' said Mrs Olsen looking at her watch for the millionth time.

'They've got potential,' said Pete. 'Great melodies.'

'Interesting lyrics,' said Andreas winking at Breeze. She looked dead proud.

'I especially liked the song about scary otters,' my sister said, clearly almost choking with admiration. 'The bit that goes – "*He hijacks my thoughts, a blood thirsty otter, The captor of my mind, an uninvited squatter*" – that's just genius.'

I felt my chest swell with pride. I could see that Petrina felt the same.

'Some of the most successful bands in the world write inane lyrics,' said Pete. 'Most people don't give a hoot about the words; they just want to hear a good tune.'

'I care about lyrical content,' said Walter from beneath his fringe. 'It's the soul of the song.'

'Well said, Walter,' said Mum clapping her hands. 'Flying Rapunzel would be nothing without the lyrics. Just a sequence of meaningless chords.'

'I'm not so keen on that one about the weirdo,' said my sister. 'Reminds me of Creepy Dave.'

Petrina's dad stood up and raised his glass. 'A toast,' he said. 'To Camel Toe. May they continue writing . . . er . . . unique songs.'

Everyone held up their glasses. 'To Camel Toe!'

FELIX HAS ASKED ME OUT ON A DATE. Well, sort of . . .

With Fiona still refusing to speak to him, I volunteered to help him out on his lunchtime show (with absolutely NO ulterior motive, ha ha ha!). I was very tactful, making sure that I didn't mention his dim-witted EX-girlfriend at any point, despite feeling desperate to highlight what a humongous quimboid she really is. My delicate handling of the situation resulted in him agreeing to have Camel Toe on his show as guests and promising to play two tracks from our demo. HIGH FIVE! He then asked me to bring it over to his house the following afternoon so that I could play it to him.

In an effort to prepare for my HOT date, I forced myself to watch ALL of *Star Wars*. It took a while to get going, but, once

I'd got past the slow-paced desert bit at the beginning, the action all became rather exciting. At one point, I even found myself feeling slightly attracted to Chewbacca. It's not like I'm into hairy Neanderthal baboons or anything (unlike my sister) – it was his *personality* that I fancied rather than the actual Wookiee race. Chewbacca is brave and loyal, two qualities that are essential in any future partner that I may have. Although I do not think I am becoming a pervert, I have decided against mentioning this to Felix all the same.

The next afternoon, having survived the longest day at school EVER, I agreed to meet Felix by the school gates, so that we could catch the bus back to his house. Petrina came with me to the toilets to help me put on a bit of eyeliner and smoky eye-shadow (not too much – just enough to make them a bit sexy). Then I rushed round to the front of school, where Felix was leaning casually against the gates looking utterly GORGEOUS. My stomach was so full of fluttering butterflies that I felt physically sick and I began to worry that I may throw up in his mouth should he try to kiss me at the end of the date. He smiled and waved as he saw me approach. Then, from out of nowhere, Fiona came running towards him, her enormous norks bouncing up and down and her thick, luscious mane flowing behind like thousands of silky ribbons. She threw her arms around his neck and began kissing him passionately on the lips. He didn't fight her off. My stomach lurched and I stood rooted to the spot. Fiona turned to face me, grinning smugly.

'Hey, Bumface. What you got there?'

I looked down at the memory stick I was holding in my

hand, trying not to wish Fiona into a coma. 'Oh, er . . . it's my band's demo. Felix was going to give it a listen.'

'Oh, *we'd* love to,' she purred. 'How cute. Isn't that cute, Felix?'

Tell her to go away, Felix. Please? I tried sending my voice into his head the way Obi Wan does to Luke Skywalker.

'Er, yeah,' he replied. 'Really cute.'

Fiona beckoned me over with her talon for a fake fingernail. 'Well, come on then,' she said. 'Give it here.'

Don't look away Felix. Look at me. I walked over and reluctantly handed it to her, our eyes locked in mutual hatred.

'What's it called?' she asked.

'Camel Toe – *Poncerama's Revenge.*'

'Ahh. So sweet,' smirked Fiona. 'Well done, you.'

I hate you.

'We'll try to listen to it tonight if we have time,' she continued. 'Felix and I have A LOT of making up to do, don't we, Felix?'

He still looked shell-shocked. 'Um. Right.'

And with that, Fiona Tittledown shoved my demo into her school bag and the two of them wandered off towards the bus stop arm-in-arm.

I felt my heart break into a million pieces.

'Come back to my house,' said Petrina, who had appeared from behind a tree. She linked her arm through mine. 'Walter's coming too.'

'They're a couple of quimboids, Blossom,' said Walter, taking my other arm, having emerged from behind a different tree.

I walked with my two best friends along the high street, dazed and befuddled. I felt so defeated that I didn't even care when I saw The Wizard out of the corner of my eye, leaning against the wall by the yoga centre.

Naturally, I dreaded going into school today. I had braced myself for another day of excruciating humiliation, taunts and whispers, so you can imagine my surprise when Felix came up to me and apologised for his behaviour. He said that after Fiona left his house he'd listened to the demo and really liked what he heard. He was particularly impressed with *Poncerama* featuring Billy Hawkins on backing vocals and *The Man With An Eggy Beard* with Wazzock on lead guitar. I had no idea that Felix and Toby were such huge Steel Dragon fans.

The way I see it, now that I have earned his respect, I am half way to securing his love. We talked a bit about *Star Wars* as well and he didn't seem at all disappointed when I explained that whilst I quite enjoyed the film, it wasn't something I was too crazy about. In fact, Felix said it didn't matter as 'we had already bonded through our love of music'. WE HAD ALREADY BONDED!!! That's almost as good as a proposal of marriage! Only one humongous-norked, quimboid-shaped obstacle standing in my way.

I wonder how much it costs to hire a hitman?

Petrina and I went to the cinema to celebrate surviving yet another week of being weird. My best friend has always had a morbid fascination with the darker side of life and she likes to share her thoughts.

'When I die I want to be buried so that the worms devour

me,' she whispered during *Bite Me – Dusky Dark Part II*. (It was the bit where the troubled but HOT vampire, Nigel, was about to kiss the newly immortal girl, Molly.) 'Then the worms will poo me back out into the soil where the vegetables grow.'

'Shhhhh,' I hissed. 'I can't hear the film.'

'And you can eat me when I've become a carrot,' she continued. 'I'll be part of the grand circle of life.'

'I don't want to eat you, or your poo,' I snapped. 'I want to watch Nigel take off his shirt and look straight into Molly's soul.'

Petrina ignored me. 'I read about a cult somewhere in South America where they sacrifice teens to bury and enrich the earth,' she continued. 'Your dad is into biodynamic farming, isn't he?'

'Yes,' I said feeling irritated. 'But he doesn't use decomposed human bodies as fertiliser.'

'How do you know?'

'Petrina are you suggesting that my parents are going to kill me and turn me into compost?'

Petrina shrugged. 'Just saying,' she said, killing my hot-vampire-Nigel-induced high.

'No!' I protest. 'I don't want to die.'

But the hooded man in the white robe ignores my pleas and picks me up in his arms, slowly carrying me down the aisle.

Rows of identically robed, hooded figures stand either side. The silence is deafening.

At the end of the aisle stands The Wizard with an ENORMOUS snake slithering round his neck. Before him is a black marble table. And a silver sword. It is MASSIVE.

162

The robed man slowly moves towards The Wizard.

'No!' I protest. 'Please don't sacrifice me. Fiona Tittledown would be a much better girl to kill than me. She's much prettier with amazing hair and . . . yeah . . . OK, she might not technically be a virgin, but she'll look much better dead than me. AND her massive norks will make for more compost.'

The Wizard stretches his arms out towards me. He smiles to reveal his razor-sharp fangs. 'Come, my child. It is your time.'

The snake hisses. His revolting forked tongue waggles at me in a very evil way.

The hooded man lays me down on the cold marble table. He steps back and takes off his hood.

'DAD!' I shout. But my father has been brainwashed and looks vacantly into my eyes. I do not know the man before me. He walks back down the aisle. The congregation all remove their hoods. I spot my mum, my sister, Andreas, Petrina, Walter, Fiona, Felix, Mr Blackmore, Paulette, Billy Hawkins . . . they are all there. EVERYONE is there.

'No,' I cry. 'I don't want to die a virgin.'

The Wizard stares at me with his evil, black-magic eyes. 'Now, my pretty. Now you must die. For the sake of the Naked Moon Dance and all things flappy and dangly. YOU MUST DIE.'

Then he leans across me, his pointed fangs looming directly over my neck. I close my eyes tightly and pray that the end will be quick.

'Get back, evil Wizard,' a manly voice shouts from the back of the room.

I open my eyes. Josh Raven is striding down the aisle with a *wooden stake in his hand. 'Let her go, you beast.'*

The Wizard removes the snake from his shoulders, steps away from the table, his arms outstretched, ready to do battle. They have a proper fight. I roll over on to my front to watch. Josh looks HOT. His muscles ripple as he moves. He is GORGEOUS. He pierces The Wizard right in the heart with his stake. The Wizard screams like a girl and then dies in a big bloody puddle. Josh turns to me.

'I love you, Blossom.'

He picks me up in his strong, sexy arms and then carries me out of the Chamber of Sacrifice. I am happy now, content in the knowledge that I will not die a virgin.

END OF WEEK TABLE OF ACHIEVEMENT

SHAME LEVEL PEAK	2 (3 MASSIVE spots on my forehead)
GUITAR PRACTICE	3 hours 41 minutes
SCHOOL WORK	4 hours (should have been more, I know, but those pictures of cats that look like rock stars on twitter are a HILARIOUS and highly addictive distraction)
PARTY INVITATIONS	0
SNOGS	100 (in my fantasies)

Camel Toe have had their first radio airplay, meaning we are officially 'on the map'.

'I'm joined in the studio by two Bridge Mount students who have formed their own band, written their own songs and recently had their first demo album recorded and produced by the legendary producer, Pete Hartley. So please give a warm welcome to Bumface and— er, I mean, Blossom Uxley-Michaels and Petrina-Ola Olsen.'

'Hi, Felix,' I trilled enthusiastically. I'm not sure why, but I feel safe in the studio in a way I don't when I have to stand up and do a reading in front of the class.

'Hi,' said Petrina quietly.

'So, ladies,' said Felix in his über-sexy radio voice. 'We've got to talk about the band's name. Where did you get the inspiration for Camel Toe?'

'Well,' I replied in the professional but friendly voice that I had practised in the shower. 'We wanted something edgy, current and attention-grabbing. We considered The Mooncups and Nina And The Norks but in the end we both felt that Camel Toe was more empowering.'

'Right,' said Felix winking at Toby, who was standing behind wearing headphones. 'So it had nothing to do with the leotard that you wear in Trampoline Club that's about two sizes too small?'

I've actually left Trampoline Club. No more low flying sanitary towels, THANK GOD.

Toby put his hand over his mouth to suppress a giggle.

I was puzzled. 'What do you mean?'

Felix continues. 'So the band could have been called Moose Knuckle or Frontal Wedgie.'

Can you pull a wedgie up your norks???

Through the glass I saw Fiona and Lucy rolling around laughing on the sofa. Walter and Paulette were giving them disapproving looks.

'It's a political feminist statement,' explained Petrina. 'The music industry has turned women into nothing but sexual objects. Well, not any more.'

'Yeah,' I proudly declared. 'It's time to stand up and be proud of our camel toes'.

More laughter.

I glanced at Petrina, who was obviously getting annoyed. 'So I believe you are going to play one of our tracks featuring the vocals of none other than Billy Hawkins from Steel Dragon?'

Felix pulled himself together. 'Yeah, absolutely,' he said. 'So how did this all come about?'

Petrina took the lead this time. 'Blossom's dad is good friends with Pete Hartley, who invited us to record some tracks in his studio.'

'It's REALLY plush,' I butted in. 'Proper real-time glamorous.'

'And while we were there,' Petrina continued, 'we met Steel

Dragon, who were recording an album, and we ended up hanging out with them. Walter got on so well with Wazzock that they exchanged numbers.'

'Really?' said Felix looking very impressed. I saw him turn and wink discreetly at Toby.

'Yep,' I said. 'They text each other all the time.'

'Can you get him in as a guest on the show?' he asked excitedly.

Behind the glass, Walter had turned his back to us.

'Probably,' I said with a smile.

'Cool.'

Toby signalled for Felix to play a track.

'Er . . . OK . . . so we're gonna play one of the tracks off your demo album. This is Camel Toe with *Poncerama* featuring Billy Hawkins on backing vocals.'

It sounded AWESOME and, for the first time ever, Petrina and I felt cool.

Afterwards Toby asked Petrina if she could get his Steel Dragon album signed for him by Billy and Wazzock. Petrina said she'd have to ask Walter, but when she approached him, Walter roared in her face and walked out of the room. Walter has never been any good at expressing his feelings. He roars if he is angry, frightened or upset. I'm not sure which of those emotions the roar was meant to be portraying.

After Felix had played our two songs, Petrina and I were suddenly elevated to celebrity status within the school. People stopped to congratulate us, pat us on the back and ask when they would be able to download a copy of the album. A few of the first years even asked us to sign our autographs on their school bags! (Luckily I've been practising my signature for years.)

We have NEVER been so popular and it feels AMAZING. Fiona and Lucy are naturally not too happy about the attention that Camel Toe are getting, especially from their boyfriends. The sight of Toby putting his arm around Petrina's shoulder in the production room sent Lucy into a five-star on-air temper tantrum that culminated in Walter having to sit on her until she calmed down.

On top of that, my new rock-induced charisma was having the desired effect on Felix, who was now frequently stopping for a 'quick chat' if he passed me in the corridor, much to his mediocre girlfriend's annoyance.

'So did you play one of Pete's guitars?' he asked, catching me off guard as I was closing my locker.

'Yep,' I replied, trying to act casual. 'A custom-made Gibson ES-335.'

Felix swallowed hard.

God I would love to bob for your sexy Adam's Apple.

'Cherry red?' he asked hopefully.

I nodded, my mind still totally on apples.

'Woah.' He trembled as he wiped the palms of his hands on his trousers. Clearly expensive guitars are the biggest aphrodisiac to teenage boys. There and then I vowed, should Camel Toe ever become rich and famous, I would shower Felix with as many sexy guitars as his heart desired (a genuine act of kindness and love from me that could NOT in anyway be misconstrued as a form of blackmail or bribery for Felix's affections).

CHASTE MOON

ALSO KNOWN AS: MOON OF WINDS,
DEATH MOON, MOON WHEN EYES ARE SORE
FROM BRIGHT SNOW, WORM MOON

Perhaps the full moon was to blame for yet another MASSIVE argument between my sister and her boyfriend. I watched from Breeze's bedroom as Andreas screeched up outside in his Aston Martin just as the very same man who Breeze had gawped at in a 'totally sexy way' a few weeks ago was about to walk up our driveway. Creepy Dave must have seen the big Cypriot dressed as Captain Jack Sparrow and scuttled away. My sister stepped outside, dressed as a girl from St Trinian's and the row that ensued on the doorstep was so loud that next door's baby began crying.

'What do you mean I'm having an affair?' scoffed my sister, her blonde pigtails wagging either side of her head like a pair of faithful Golden Retrievers.

Andreas swallowed hard as he glanced at my sister's long bare legs.

'I saw him running away. A mouse of a man!' he yelled.

'I have no idea *what* you are talking about,' said my sister.

'Can't handle a real man, eh?' yelled Andreas, thumping his furry chest with his furry fist.

Breeze folded her arms and rolled her eyes, which seemed to infuriate Andreas even more.

'Who is he?' he shouted. 'Who is the spineless little cretin?'

By this stage, some of the neighbours had appeared in the street, knowing that Breeze and Andreas always put on an entertaining show when they had a public fight. Mr Parkin at number 34 even brought out a camping chair and some popcorn.

'Maybe I *should* find myself a new man. Someone less crass.

Less Neanderthal. Less . . . like a Mediterranean Yeti,' retorted my sister, her flaring nostrils spelling out their own furious Morse code.

Andreas laughed loudly. 'HA! *This* is the model of the perfect man,' he exclaimed, strutting proudly as he ripped off his flouncy white shirt to reveal black chest hair that spread across his stomach, back and apparently further (BLEURGH).

'Do you have some kind of complex that makes you feel inferior to every man who crosses my path?' screeched my sister. 'Or is it just a pitiful case of the green-eyed monster?'

'I know a Jezebel when I see one,' screamed Andreas.

'And I know a pathetic little man when I see one,' screamed my sister.

Andreas placed his clenched fists on his hairy hips. 'There are two kinds of men in the world,' he growled. 'Greek Cypriots – and those who wish they were.'

At this, Breeze smirked then slammed the door shut in his face, which turned purple. He looked around urgently, but couldn't find anything solid on which to take out his frustration that wouldn't either get broken or cause him injury, so instead he repeatedly kicked our lavender bush until he tired himself out and staggered back into his Aston Martin.

Although I have never met or even seen him, for some reason I find myself feeling sorry for Creepy Dave. It's as if there's something about him that resonates deep within me. I suspect we might be cut from the same cloth – faded, black denim in all probability. I hope I'm not in the early stages of developing a psychic ability. That would be THE WORST.

✳ ✳ ✳

When Dad became involved in a fist fight on April 1st, I naturally assumed it was an April Fool's joke. I was wrong.

I'd been listening to music and writing my History essay (An Analysis Of The Role Of Mice In Nazi Germany) in my bedroom when I heard loud voices coming from outside the front of the house. Naturally I assumed Andreas was back and I went into Breeze's room to look out of the window, only to see Dad face to face with The Wizard who was standing with his arms folded.

Dad sort of lurched towards him. I'm not sure if it was a stumble or a planned attack from my father, but The Wizard calmly unfolded his arms and pushed him backwards. Dad faltered and fell onto the grass. The Wizard laughed. Dad scrambled to his feet looking more furious than I have ever seen. I rushed downstairs at the same time as Mum opened the front door. We were just in time to see Dad take a swing at The Wizard, who dodged what *must* have been an unintentional punch and instead landed one right on Dad's nose. My poor father was sent reeling into the side of the camper van.

'Stop it, Merlin,' screamed my mum. 'ENOUGH!'

I rushed over to my dad who was sitting on his bum, nursing a bloody nose.

'Leave him alone!' I shouted. 'That's my dad.'

'I think you'd better go, Merlin,' said Mum in a calmer voice. 'I'll talk to you later.'

The Wizard flexed his fist and walked out of our driveway towards his Land Rover.

Mum and I helped Dad back inside.

'What was that all about?' I asked, knowing that my dad is a pacifist and has never thrown a punch before in his life.

'Not now, Blossom,' said Mum, flashing her fierce yoga eyes. 'I've got to sort out your father. We'll talk about this another time.'

As I turned to shut the door, I noticed a number of the neighbours had come out to see what was going on, including Mr Parkin at number 34, who was in his camping chair again drinking from a flask of hot tea. If we started charging a fee to view our family fiascos, we could make a fortune.

Later that night, Andreas enlisted my help to gain forgiveness from my sister and on the promise that he will sneak Petrina and me into Movie Nights as soon as we turn sixteen. We've already planned to go dressed as Molly Feldman from the *Bite Me* trilogy and a Death Eater. (Petrina doesn't want to show any flesh.)

I brought up a revolting soya milk hot chocolate for Breeze and sat on the end of her bed (eyeing up her bedroom) while she drank it. I pointed out that Andreas has been working hard lately to make his club the success story that it's become and was clearly stressed and over emotional. She eventually relented, so when he shinned up the drainpipe and banged on her bedroom window at three thirty in the morning on his way home from the club, Breeze allowed Andreas to stay for the rest of the night.

The next morning Andreas slipped on my sister's short,

pink towelling robe to make a quick dash to the bathroom just as I was coming out. We collided, knocking the hairbrush I was holding clean out of my hand. Ever the gent, Andreas apologised and bent down to pick it up for me and that's when I saw things I should NOT have seen.

I may not be ready to venture into vegetarianism just yet, but it's safe to say that I will NEVER eat haggis again.

END OF WEEK TABLE OF ACHIEVEMENT

SHAME LEVEL PEAK	9 (NOBODY needs to see Andreas's offal bags.)
GUITAR PRACTICE	5 hours 1 minute
SCHOOL WORK	4½ hours (Petrina's revision notes are BRILLIANT. It totally doesn't matter now that I nodded off all those times in English Literature.)
PARTY INVITATIONS	0
SNOGS	BIG FAT ZERO

When Mum asked Breeze and me to attend a family meeting, we were both puzzled. We've never had an actual, official *family meeting* before.

TOP 10 **BAD** REASONS
FOR OUR FAMILY MEETING

1. Mum is pregnant (bleurgh).

2. We are booked in for group family therapy.

3. We are going to join a weird hippie commune in Arizona.

4. One of them has a terminal illness.

5. They will announce that I am the sacrificial virgin and will die at the altar of The Wizard's cult tonight at midnight.

6. One of them needs a kidney/bone marrow transplant

and I am the only donor that matches.

7. They found out that I am considering getting a Saturday job in McDonalds (but that would mean that one of them has become a psychic mind-reader as I haven't told anyone about my intention).

8. One of them is a psychic mind-reader.

9. They are going to tell me that The Wizard is my real father.

~~10. They are going to tell me that I've been adopted.~~

TOP 10 **GOOD** REASONS
FOR OUR FAMILY MEETING

1. Mum, Dad and Breeze are going travelling for a year and I will be left behind to look after the house.

2. We have won the lottery.

3. Granny Michaels has decided to leave all her money to us when she dies rather than her chosen charity 'Tufty's Helpers: Caring For Disabled Guinea Pigs'.

4. Dad has pulled some strings with Pete Hartley and

arranged a hot date for me with Josh Raven.

5. We are going on holiday somewhere where we won't have to sleep in a freezing cold tent.

6. We are finally entering the modern world and getting a microwave.

7. We are getting rid of the multi-coloured VW camper van and buying a normal family car.

8. They have bought me surprise tickets for Glastonbury this summer. (Josh Raven is headlining.)

9. Pete Hartley has got Camel Toe a HUGE record deal.

10. They are going to tell me that I am adopted.

The kitchen door opened.

'Breeze, Blossom. Sit down, please – your dad and I have something to tell you.'

My sister and I sat at the table wondering what our future held. Breeze gave me a small reassuring smile as we braced ourselves for the bombshell.

'Look, I'm afraid there's no easy way to say this,' said Mum. 'So I'll just tell you both straight. I'm having a relationship with someone else.'

OK, I wasn't expecting that.

My dad looked down at his feet.

I felt a flutter of panic in my chest. 'So you're splitting up?'

Mum shook her head. 'No.'

'Wait up,' said Breeze, sounding a little bit angry. 'You cheat on Dad and he's going to forgive you? Just like that?'

Mum put her hand on Breeze's shoulder. 'It's not as simple as that, Breeze.'

But they are staying together. We're still a family . . . I think . . .

'Please get your hand off me,' snapped my sister, pushing Mum's hand away.

'Is it The Wizard?' I asked.

'If you mean Merlin,' replied Mum, 'then yes.'

I think I'm going to puke.

Dad was still staring down at his feet.

Breeze looked appalled. 'You've been sleeping with a medieval magician?'

'In a way, yes I have,' said Mum, without a shred of regret in her voice. 'And your father knew all about it.'

Whoa! Hang on a minute . . . Back up, here . . . He knew?

Breeze and I turned to look at Dad who slowly lifted his head and nodded.

'It's true,' he said gravely. 'We've always had an open relationship.'

So, I know my parents are about as liberal-minded as people can be, but an open relationship is surely pushing things too far? We don't live in a hippie commune. This is a semi detached 1930s suburban house. With a loft extension.

'So you can sleep with other people?' asked my sister.

'Euugh!' I said, feeling sick to the stomach. 'Pur-lease!'

'Yes,' mumbled Dad. 'We used to be free spirits.'

'We still are,' said Mum proudly.

Dad shook his head as if to rid the hurtful images from his mind. 'I never thought either of us would act on the agreement.'

'But I did,' said Mum. 'And it's not my fault that you can't handle it.'

'I'm not the same person I was twenty years ago,' said Dad.

'So that's why you tried to punch The Wizard,' I said.

'His name is *Merlin*,' interrupted my mum. 'And yes, that's why your dad has been behaving like a jealous teenager.'

I'm a teenager. I can sympathise with Dad. Right now I'd like to smack that pointy-bearded quimboid right in his magical mouth.

'But what about all the weird behaviour?' I wanted answers. And I wanted them NOW.

WEIRD BEHAVIOUR: MUM'S EXPLANATION

THE FREQUENT DISAPPEARING *Merlin is the chairman of The UK Medieval Battle Re-enactment Society. She's been taking part in events with him.*

MUM MISSING THE STORM MOON DANCE *It coincided with the re-enactment of The Battle Of Yore, which she had promised to attend, totally forgetting that it would clash with the full moon.*

PLAYING A LUTE She wanted to take the band in a new direction. (Backwards, obviously.)

THE ENVELOPE THE WIZARD GAVE HER OUTSIDE THE YOGA CENTRE A Valentine's Day card.

THE DRY CLEANING Merlin and mum had to get their costumes dry-cleaned for The Knights Banquet. Mum's dress was covered in fake blood from the last battle re-enactment. Apparently it's 'a bitch to get the stains out. Even on a boil wash'.

THE GOLDEN CHALICE For re-enactments.

THE PENTAGON NECKLACE A gift from The Wizard.

THE SECRECY They didn't want Breeze and me to get upset. And they wanted Dad to get his head around the situation (which clearly he hasn't).

Judging by her rapidly flickering nose craters, my sister was fuming. 'How could you let her do this to you, Dad?

'I'm trying to come to terms with it, Breeze,' he said positively.

But Mum knocked him straight back down. 'You've become the conventional conformist that we always used to laugh at. The boring old fart.'

Dad's eyes dropped.

There was still one more thing I wanted to ask my free-spirited, cheating, adulterous mother. 'But why did you need to start seeing someone else? Why now?'

'Because,' answered Mum, 'our sexual relationship has become stale. Your dad wasn't giving me what I needed any more. I was jaded and hungry for exciting sex, yearning for fulfilment. Then Merlin came along and fulfilled me.'

Oh. My. God. I wished I'd never asked.

Later that evening, Dad spent some time teaching me new chords. He was delighted when I told him that Felix had played *Poncerama* on his show again today. I had actually heard a couple of pupils singing the chorus in the corridor. I'm not going to lie – it gave me a legal high. I was *off my face* on life alone. Dad told me that it was important for me to 'keep my feet on the ground and stay true'. Personally, I think that Dad should be grateful for my new-found celebrity status. It might just save me from going off the rails now that I've discovered I'm from a broken home.

From: Blossom Uxley-Michaels   6th Apr 17:33
To: info@poptasticmanagement.com
SUBJECT: Pride Of Britain

Dear Sir/Madam,

I have recently discovered that I come from a dysfunctional family. My story is emotional to say the least. Firstly, I have had to cope with having woolly, liberal, tie-dye parents for fifteen long years. Then, of course, I have been saddled with the initials B.U.M. until I find someone to marry. (Blossom Raven has a nice ring to it and B.R. would be perfectly normal initials to live with.) I am also due to take my GCSE exams in a few weeks which is an added stress. On top of all this, my mother is involved in a complicated love triangle with my father and a medieval wizard. They are also vegans. As you can imagine, I will probably require counselling at some point in the future. In the meantime, it's the small things that make my world a little brighter.

Josh Raven appearing as a guest on Bridge Mount FM would mean EVERYTHING to me and would make my unhappy life worth living.

Hope to hear from you soon.

Many thanks,

Blossom Uxley-Michaels

P.S. Please don't pity me. Instead you can nominate me for The Pride Of Britain Awards next year. Josh can present me with my award if I win.

I wandered down to the church at the end of our road where Josh Raven's mum was buried. Her name was Gabrielle Raven.

It sounded to me like the name of an archangel. I imagined that she must have been a truly beautiful woman to have borne a son as perfect as Josh. I stood alone by her gravestone, not entirely sure if I was seeking reassurance from an angel or simply hoping that Josh might appear. When I eventually realised that neither was likely to happen, I made my way back home.

During a rainy break time, Felix and Toby came over to our desks and asked if they could join us.

Petrina was so surprised that she snorted two jets of apple juice out of her nostrils. Nobody ever sits with us (apart from Walter, but he doesn't count).

'Er . . . yeah . . . sure,' I said, attempting to be cool.

As the HOT SEXY LOVE GODS sat down at OUR desks, we couldn't fail to notice the stares of disbelief coming from all around. Fiona and Lucy glared furiously at us, wondering why their boyfriends had chosen to sit with the two weirdest girls in the school. But that, my friends, is the power of rock music. Now that we were in a band, Petrina and I had become simply irresistible to the opposite sex. I realised that I was probably looking rather attractive to Mei Miyagi and Kirsty Mackerby too, as rock music is known to transcend sexuality and gender. I'll confess that I found this prospect quite reassuring. It's always good to have a sexuality safety net in case your first preference doesn't work out. I could do a lot worse than either of the Bridge Mount lesbians.

'I listened to your demo all weekend,' said Felix, his long eyelashes fluttering like manly butterflies.

'Really?' I replied, trying to flutter my tiny lashes in an alluring, feminine way.

'Yeah. I like it the more I hear it.'

'Me too,' said Toby. 'It's a real grower.'

'So, any news on getting Billy Hawkins in on my show?' asked Felix.

'Not yet,' I explained. 'I've been pre-occupied. Things at home aren't too good at the moment.'

'Oh,' said Felix.

'My parents' relationship is on the rocks,' I continued. 'It's pretty hard going.'

'Right,' said Felix.

I think he really cares.

'But you'll try to get him in soon, yeah?' asked Toby, looking directly at Petrina. I could feel her melting slowly beside me.

'For sure,' she gasped.

'Cool.'

Petrina and I sat in silence, gawping as they both bit into their chocolate bars.

WOWZOIDS! They even masticate in a sexy way.

Toby looked over his shoulders at the slangers. He winked at Lucy. She smiled back coyly. Fiona pretended to catch the kiss that Felix blew in her direction and put it in her pocket. Behind them I suddenly noticed Walter. He was sitting alone at the teacher's desk, flicking rolled up pieces of torn paper with his fingers into the waste paper bin. His face may have been hidden behind a curtain of lank hair, but I'd never seen him looking so sad.

Proof that popularity pays: we have finally been invited to a real-life party at Matthew Ludlow's house. A proper no-parents-no-jelly-and-ice-cream-just-teenagers-having-fun-with-booze-and-a-DJ-and-sexy-boys kind of party. How cool is that? Matthew Ludlow's parents are heading off to their Spanish villa for a week, leaving his older brother Luke in charge. He was in Breeze's year at school and, from what she's told me, he was always a bit unstable to say the least. Apparently he once rode a motorbike down the school corridor wearing nothing but a slice of square, processed cheese covering his modesty. Breeze insists *that* was the precise moment she changed from vegetarian to vegan.

Luke decided to hold a party on Saturday night and told Matthew that he could invite whomever he wants, so his little brother asked the whole of Year 11. I was beside myself with excitement. A new chapter of my life had begun: *Blossom Uxley-Michaels – The Cool Years.*

I answered the door at around seven that evening to find Sir Lancelot standing on our doorstop, dressed in a white tunic with chainmail sleeves, a hood and a bright red Griffin emblem.

'Good eventide, my lady,' said The Wizard Knight, reaching towards me with his fingers outstretched. Not knowing quite how to respond, I offered my hand in return, which he took and brought gently to his lips.

'Er . . . Mum's just coming,' I said, pulling my hand away and wiping his revolting dribble on my jeans. 'Do you want to come in and wait?'

'Splendid,' he said, stepping inside.

'Who is it, Blossom?' called Dad from the sitting room.

'Ummm . . . it's The Wizard – er – I mean, Sir Lancelot . . . er . . . no . . . it's Merlin.'

Dad slowly emerged from behind the door.

'Hello,' he said quietly.

The Wizard bowed dramatically. 'Good e'en, my lord,' he said, his head hanging low.

'Cut the crap, Merlin,' said my dad in a trembling voice. 'You're shagging my wife. I don't want to hear your false pleasantries.'

This was TOTALLY out of character. Dad's lip was actually quivering with anger. For a moment I thought he might launch into an Elvis Presley impersonation-style attack (blasting The Wizard's earholes with a loud rendition of *Hound Dog*).

'The good lady liketh what she sees.' The Wizard smirked. 'I am the object of her desires. What can a man do?'

'You are pushing me to the edge,' growled Dad.

The Wizard laughed. 'To the edge of the fairy ring?' He held out his arms feyly and skipped round in a circle. 'Where the pacifists are "talking things through"?'

I felt a surge of anger rise up from my gut. 'Shut up, you creepy old man,' I blurted out. 'Why don't you just leave us alone?'

'Blossom!' said Mum sternly, as she swept down the stairs in a long black dress. 'I'd like you to apologise immediately.'

Her date for the evening looked at her adoringly, kissing her hand as she reached the bottom of the stairs. I found it incredibly difficult to feel any sense of remorse as my mum stood before me, dressed as a thirteenth-century nun with The Wizard lurking behind wearing tights and a chainmail head-dress. They looked like a couple of randy swingers on their way to a hideous fetish night. YUCK.

'I don't know what she sees in him, Dad,' I said sadly, as the medieval couple closed the front door behind them. 'He's got a bald head and a pony tail for God's sake.'

'Well, apparently, his wand is *astonishing*,' said Dad sounding defeated. It took me a couple of seconds to realise what he meant. *OH. MY. GOD*. Sometimes I really HATE having liberal-minded parents.

END OF WEEK TABLE OF ACHIEVEMENT

SHAME LEVEL PEAK	3 ("astonishing wand" = DISGUSTING!)
GUITAR PRACTICE	4 hours 58 minutes
SCHOOL WORK	30 minutes (I've more important things to worry about this week, like my dysfunctional family)
PARTY INVITATIONS	**1!!! (YAY!!!)**
SNOGS	0 (not yet...)

THINGS I DID AT MATTHEW LUDLOW'S PARTY THAT I HAVE NEVER DONE BEFORE

1. Got drunk

2. Slow danced

3. Kissed a boy (a PROPER kiss)

4. Crowd surfed

5. Rode through a house on the back of a motorbike with two pieces of processed ham taped to my chest

Matthew Ludlow lives in an enormous house in Yew Walk, the most exclusive, posh, private road in the area. You could fit about ten cars in the driveway. Petrina's mum dropped us off at around eight and the party was already in full swing. There were two DJs – Luke 'Loopy' Ludlow himself, pumping up the guests in the enormous sitting room, and another upstairs in the chill-out room. We surveyed the scene: beautiful, cool people everywhere, most dancing with their hands in the air, a few posed seductively on the designer, animal-print chaise lounges, others rolling ecstatically on luxurious cream shag-pile rugs as if starring in their own MTV video.

Fiona (dressed in the smallest black dress I've ever seen) was attempting to do sexy dancing with Felix (who looked hotter than a thousand burning bras) and Lucy (showing off her mile-long legs in electric-blue skinny jeans) had draped herself territorially across Toby on the sofa, pensively observing the room as she scribbled in a pink, padlocked notebook. Petrina was wearing her usual skirt-woolly-tights-and-cardigan-zipped-up-to-the-neck combo, while I was wearing a slightly-tighter-than-usual King Quiff T-shirt to mark the event as a special occasion.

'Look at all the boys,' said Petrina, her head swaying and her eyes glazed like a charmed snake.

Fiona fixed me with a frosty stare as she gyrated furiously against Felix's leg.

I noticed that despite this supposedly being a party hosted by Luke Ludlow, the guests were mainly Year 11 Bridge Mount students.

'Hey ladies!' said Matthew, throwing his arms around our shoulders, a half-full bottle of lager in his hand. 'Glad you could make it.'

He smelt nice and looked – dare I say it – quite handsome. He'd got a new smart haircut and his spots weren't nearly as bad as I remembered.

'Make yourself at home. There's beer on ice in the bathtub,' he informed us. 'Champagne, wine and spirits in the kitchen and soft drinks on the porch. Get yourselves *in* and get your rocks *off!*' And then the next moment he had disappeared onto the dance floor with his mouth wide open, head thrown back and thumbs held aloft.

'Beer in the bathtub?' I spluttered.

'Champagne in the kitchen?' gasped Petrina.

We looked at each other and then fell about laughing. We were at a real, proper party and we felt cooler than a penguin's bum.

'Well I think I'm off to find the bathroom, then,' I said.

'And I'm heading for the kitchen,' said Petrina.

Fast-forward two hours and three bottles of beer and I found myself with my arms wrapped around Matthew Ludlow's neck in the chill-out room. I wasn't entirely sure of the slow-dancing rules so I just walked round in circles like all the other couples seemed to be doing. Mei and Kirsty were holding hands and gazing adoringly at each other and Max Burcott was dancing with Paulette Dempsey. I saw him slyly slip one hand down onto her bum cheek, but she didn't seem to mind at all. She is so NOT asexual. Matthew smelt quite nice (a bit like a baby covered in spicy hot chocolate), so I was happy to rest my woozy head on his shoulder as we swirled around the dance floor. After about ten minutes we changed direction, but I'd become very dizzy and lost my balance, toppling backwards onto a beanbag and pulling Matthew down on top of me. It was like one of those movie moments where everything slows down and time stands still. He looked right into my eyes and I instinctively knew what was coming next. He kissed me. It felt a bit sluggery having his tongue in my mouth, but his lips were soft and gentle. Overall it was quite a pleasant experience – a seven out of ten. Next thing I knew, Matthew was pulling me to my feet as someone shouted, 'Luke's brought his motorbike into the house!'

Sure enough, Matthew's crazy older brother was driving his huge black Harley Davidson up and down the enormous hallway. I was feeling exhilarated. I was no longer a girl. I was a WOMAN. A real-life, sexual object of desire. A lady who kisses men. With tongues and EVERYTHING.

Fuelled by the three lagers and tumbler of Champagne that someone had just put in my hand, my feeling of elation suddenly escalated. And this is where things get hazy and blurry. Or at least that's what I'm telling people. The truth is I don't really want to remember what happened next. It was like I became someone else for a moment – someone wild, someone crazy, someone NOT me. Although it *was* me. It was definitely me who ended up riding on the back of a Harley Davidson with two pieces of processed ham taped to the front of my bra while everyone clapped and cheered. Yes, that was me. And I know it was me, because I have seen documented evidence on YouTube.

Arrrrrrrrrrrrrrrrrgh.

I don't think there's really any point in explaining what the main topic of conversation was on the Breakfast Show the following Monday of the Easter holidays. Nor is it worth mentioning the constant taunts of 'Pork-tit Bumface' and 'Here comes ham hooters' that I had to endure all day. Petrina said they'd have forgotten about it by the time term starts again. I hope so.

During the show, Fiona asked her best friend in the world why she had been making notes throughout the entire party. Lucy proudly declared that she'd been jotting down observational comedy ideas, as apparently 'there is humour to be found in even the most mundane situations'. Fiona laughed sarcastically, telling her friend that she's 'sailing dangerously close to geeky waters', which sent Lucy into another huge mood. Seriously, I don't understand why those two even hang out together. The only time Petrina and I fight it's over something important, like whether Josh Raven has had cosmetic surgery to give him a bum chin (which he HASN'T – I've studied the old school photos and he has always had a little dimple there. It's just got deeper as he gets older). And even then the longest we haven't spoken is forty-two seconds. (I know this as I held my breath for that duration until Petrina agreed with me that Josh's bum chin was genuine. She said she didn't want to carry the burden of my death with her for life. Wise move.)

Walter saw me snogging Matthew Ludlow on the beanbag. I'll be honest – I didn't even know Walter was at the party. Neither did Petrina.

'Why didn't you tell us you were there?' she asked him as we sat together on the swings in the park.

'You were busy,' said Walter.

'Doing what?'

'Talking to Toby.' Walter's voice was quiet. 'I heard him tell you that you looked "really pretty" right in front of Lucy Perkins.'

Petrina laughed. 'Haha! Yes – that was BRILLIANT. You should have seen her face. She stormed off in a huff and spent the rest of the night sulking and bitching with Fiona.'

'You did though,' said Walter.

'Did what?' asked Petrina.

'Look pretty.' Walter shifted uneasily from foot to foot.

'That's a bit creepy,' Petrina said. 'Watching me without letting me know you were there. You sound like a right old weirdo.'

'But I AM a weirdo,' said Walter his voice slightly raised. 'And I thought you were too.'

'Not any more. Now we get invited to parties.' Petrina puffed her chest out proudly. 'We're in a cool band.'

Walter sneered, 'Really? Do you realise that Blossom doesn't even know what a camel toe is?'

Petrina looked at me as I attempted to push my norks together, but they were annoyingly too small.

'It's your *downstairs* cleavage,' he snapped. 'When a girl wears tight clothing that reveals a little too much . . . a camel toe.'

I thought of my trampoline leotard.

'She knew that,' said Petrina quickly.

'Yes I did,' I agreed, hoping that I sounded convincing. *I HAD NO IDEA.*

Walter looked down and went very quiet for a moment. Then he lifted his head and roared in Petrina's face before climbing off the swing and marching away.

Three days after the party, my first thought upon waking up was: OH. MY. GOD. Matthew Ludlow has given me herpes. I had my first ever cold sore. A sexually transmitted disease at the age of fifteen. The shame. However, eight fretful hours later, I was able to breathe a huge sigh of relief. It wasn't herpes after all. It was just a humongous spot in the corner of my mouth. I'd happily settle for a week of being a spotty face than a lifetime of sexually transmitted cold-sore outbreaks. I'm not going to lie – the Matthew Ludlow situation is going to be awkward. Ever since the kiss, I've been dreading going back to school. He's nice and all that, but I really don't want to go out with him as I think he might be an alcoholic.

My YouTube video has had over 1000 views, so I showed it to my parents myself, before it went proper herpes-style viral. But instead of being shocked and disappointed, Mum was noticeably thrilled with the clip,

'A person's true essence often rises to the surface when they're a little inebriated,' she said. 'I'm seeing a strong statement here, symbolising the power of the female spirit and a blatant campaign for animal rights.'

'Er . . .' Mum had got the wrong end of the stick. 'Breeze told me that Luke Ludlow had once ridden down the school corridor on his motorbike wearing nothing but a piece of cheese covering his goolies. I think I was just doing a slightly squiffy interpretation of that incident.'

Mum smiled, tapping her forehead with her finger. 'That's

what you were thinking up here.' Then she put her hand over her heart, speaking proudly. 'But your subconscious was telling you otherwise. I see a vegan in the making.'

The sudden desire I had right then for a Big Mac was overwhelming. Mum then went on to show me something that I am still trying to erase from my memory. She dragged an enormous VHS recorder out of the attic and played me a home video showing her in her early twenties as Lady Godiva, riding naked on a white horse through a crowded town centre with ALL of her lady parts on public display. Mum explained that Lady Godiva was the first political activist streaker and was the inspiration for her many nude protest demonstrations. She showed me another five or six old films where she is publicly naked with only her blue dreadlocks offering her pale body any kind of warmth. Thank God YouTube hadn't been invented when she was younger – she'd have been an internet sensation. My mother couldn't actually BE any more embarrassing if she tried. Seriously, she'll use any excuse to get her kit off. I wonder if there is such a thing as a nudeaholic?

I thought it was time for a change of tactics with Josh Raven's management so I decided to apply a little bit of pressure.

From: Blossom Uxley-Michaels   15th Apr 16:59
To: info@poptasticmanagement.com
SUBJECT: School Disco

Dear Sir/Madam,

I am writing to invite Josh Raven to be the headlining act at the Bridge Mount school disco on May 27th. Other stunning acts confirmed include DJ Luke 'Loopy' Ludlow and Camel Toe.

What could be more exciting than 711 sweaty teenagers busting their finest moves to Josh Raven's own carefully selected set list? I can only name five things that could possibly be anywhere near as thrilling:

1. Finding life on Mars.
2. Finding out that Santa Claus is actually real.
3. Finding five pounds in your handbag that you didn't know you had.
4. Finding out that you can actually turn water into wine just by believing in Jesus.
5. Finding out that the herpes cold sore on your lip is really only a massive spot.

It's going to be an amazing night – especially for the Year 11s, who will be sitting their GCSEs straight after. I'll be our last night of freedom. PLUS, if he headlines, Josh will get to see my Camel Toe (a name that shows we are edgy, subversive, modern AND have a <u>very good sense of humour</u>).

I know Josh wouldn't want to disappoint his fans. So I will tell them that he will be there.

Many thanks,

Blossom Uxley-Michaels

P.S. There is still time to nominate me for The Pride Of Britain Awards next year. I continue to be emotionally traumatised after discovering that my parents are involved in a sordid three-way sexual relationship.

The pulsing applause vibrates in our ears. Petrina and I stand in the wings, holding hands, our heads bowed in prayer.

'Dear baby Jesus,' I say. 'Thank you for blessing us with our amazing voices and brilliant musical talent. We've been fantastic tonight.'

Petrina nods in agreement, her eyes tightly shut. 'Yes, baby Jesus. And please fill us up with the almighty rock power to propel Camel Toe into awesomeness for the encore.'

'AMEN,' we shout in unison. Then we high five and step out on to the stage. The lights come up and the crowd go CRAZY.

'Hellooooo again WEMBLEY – we're BACK!' I shout.

We both look stunning. We've each got our own stylist and they've made us look HOT. I am wearing six-inch red Jimmy Choos, but I don't walk like a man in drag like I usually do when I wear heels. NO. I walk like a sexy model on a catwalk.

Petrina takes her place behind her silver space-age keyboard. I pick up my Cherry Red Gibson ES-335 guitar and strike a pose by the mic stand. I couldn't look any hotter if I tried.

Petrina plays the instantly recognisable, menacing first chord of The Wizard. The crowd clap and cheer approvingly as we begin.

'The shadow falls, my breath is tight; I feel him waiting.

'Is he a ghost or a crow in flight or is he Satan?'

Petrina and her keyboard then magically lift slowly into the air on the expensive, bespoke hydraulic crane that the record company have paid for. Money is no object on this world tour. Camel Toe is the biggest band in the world. Then, the big gimmick. A hundred-foot giant Wizard appears to drift forwards into the audience. It cost over twenty million pounds to make and operate but who cares? We're not thinking about the starving children in Africa. We're ROCK STARS, BABY!!! (And we'll do a massive charity gig to make up for it anyway.)

I strum and sing at the same time. I can do that now. I'm an expert.

The adulation washes over me like a wave. I hold the mic towards the adoring crowd, cupping my other hand to my ear as they point towards the giant prop chanting in unison:

'It's The Wizard, the dirty Wizard,

The dirty, dirty, dirty, dirty, dirty Wizard.'

There are tears of pride in my eyes. I look at Petrina, dangling seventy feet above my head. I'm glad she did 'the double'. She grins and gives me the thumbs up. We've made it. We are no longer weirdos. We are MEGASTARS.

END OF WEEK TABLE OF ACHIEVEMENT

SHAME LEVEL PEAK	*OFF THE SCALE!!!*
GUITAR PRACTICE	9 hours 41 minutes
REVISION	6 hours (I threw myself into my school work to avoid thinking about the embarrassment of the week's events)
PARTY INVITATIONS	I never want to go to another party again
SNOGS	1 that I can remember, but to be honest, who knows?

Midway through Toby's show, Felix spontaneously put his arm around my shoulder and called me 'babe'. It made me feel all hot and clammy. He was super keen to find out when we could get someone from Steel Dragon in, but I suspect he was also looking to me for a bit comfort and support. There was a rumour buzzing round online that Fiona had been spotted kissing a boy from Cumnor Grove – the posh private boy's school down the road. Of course she denied it, but there was a noticeable tension in the air between her and Felix. I was briefly tempted to tell a small fib to fuel the rumour, but remembering Breeze's pet stick insect, fighting for breath inside the vacuum cleaner kept my bad karma backlog at the forefront of my mind.

Pinning down Walter about Wazzock's guest appearance on Bridge Mount FM was proving to be more difficult than you would imagine. Each time Petrina approached the subject, he ended up annoyed and grumpy.

'So have you tried asking Wazzock yet?' asked Petrina. 'He only needs to come in for twenty minutes or so. Ten minutes on-air with Felix and Toby and then another ten signing autographs.'

'I'm sure he's got better things to do with his life than talking to a couple of idiots on a tin-pot radio station,' snapped Walter.

'Yeah, but have you actually asked him yet?' said Petrina.

'Does it matter?' he said curtly.

'Well, Toby thinks the listeners would really love to hear Wazzock on the radio.'

'So why doesn't Toby ask him?'

'Because Toby doesn't know Wazzock or have his phone number,' said Petrina, trying her best to be reasonable.

'That's because Wazzock doesn't go round dishing out his contact details to total quimboids.'

'Well, how about *you* give me his number and I'll call him myself?' asked Petrina.

Walter's fringe might have masked his icy stare, but Petrina was chilled to the bone all the same.

'OK, OK,' she said holding up her hands. 'Forget I asked.'

Neither of us knows what's come over Walter lately. If he was a girl, I'd probably put it down to his time of the month. But since he's not a girl, it's not that.

I spent a whole day designing the Camel Toe logo. When I showed it to Dad he told me that the Camel Toe humps were 'inspired'. It was our way of sticking two fingers up to the music industry's irresponsible portrayal of women as sexual objects. The Camel Toe logo couldn't be less suggestive or erotic if it tried. It's a positive image for young women that we want to eventually use on our merchandise branding.

I posted the logo up online, so when a group of Year 7 girls came up to me in town, I was expecting the worst. The girl who spoke was wearing lenses so thick they made her brown eyes look like chocolate Oreo biscuits.

'You're Blossom Uxley-Michaels, aren't you?' she said.

'Yes,' I replied, already anticipating the inevitable *Bumface* taunt that all students relish saying for the first time.

'We LOVE Camel Toe,' she said eagerly. 'And we think you are so cool.'

'Yes,' said a girl with a piece of food stuck in her braces. 'You're our inspiration.'

I quickly ran my tongue across my own brace to check that there wasn't any edible debris caught in it. 'Thanks for telling me,' I said proudly. 'And remember – we'll be playing at the school disco.'

'We can't wait,' said Oreo Eyes. 'Can we have your autograph please?'

'Of course. Who shall I write it to?'

I had somehow managed to break free from my oppressive weirdo label. I wasn't just an object of ridicule and spite any more. I was respected and – dare I say it – admired? But, of course, there is always one of my parents ready and willing to knock me back down to Earth should I ever DARE to feel proud of myself.

My (technically challenged) mother somehow uploaded her rediscovered video footage to YouTube and had been proudly showing friends via various social networking sites. This had naturally been shared around and found its way onto Fiona and Lucy's bitchfest blog and as a result, everyone who attends Bridge Mount had seen the film of my naked, blue-dreadlocked mother riding a horse through a busy town centre. I'm not sure I can actually think of anything more humiliating than walking through the park past a group of boys giggling at their smartphones to shouts of, 'Hey, Bumface, your mum's got great tits.' And 'Wahey! I can see that your mum's not a natural blue head then.'

The worst thing of all is that Mum was not even slightly embarrassed. In fact, quite the opposite. She invited both The Wizard and Andreas to view the clips with her on the laptop. In the next room you could hear Dad strumming angrily on his guitar, working on his first concept album that he told me, in secret, is entitled *A Dark Knight Named Death*. Are all parents this dreadful or do I just have the worst luck EVER?

The rumours are still circulating about Fiona and the boy from Cumnor Grove, although she fiercely denies that anything had happened between them. Nevertheless, the atmosphere in the studio was as tense as a barn full of turkeys at Christmas. Felix couldn't even look at her, which meant there was more opportunity for him to notice me . . .

Lucy was midway through an utterly dreadful Mrs Neacher The Rubbish Teacher on-air sketch with Fiona, when Toby leaned over to whisper something into Petrina's ear. I watched her cheeks flush through various tones of pink, before they turned a bright shade of scarlet. When I asked her later what he had said, she replied that she wasn't entirely sure. Before he whispered, Toby had been asking her about Wazzock again.

'Any news from Walter yet?' he said.

'No, but I'm trying my hardest,' Petrina had replied.

Toby winked. 'I know you are.'

Petrina dipped her eyes bashfully.

'I like hanging out with you,' he continued.

And then he bent down close to her and softly murmured something. Petrina says that he'd either whispered 'text me' or 'sex me'. If you say them out loud, they do sound similar, but whichever way I think he really wants her. And Felix wants me too. When I promised to do everything in my power to get Wazzock onto his show, his eyes sparkled as he kissed me gently on the cheek, right in Fiona's view. She threw me eyeball daggers through the glass, but I didn't care. That's the second time he's kissed me this term. If I get a kiss just for good intention, imagine what I'll get if I manage to bring a rock superstar into the studio!!!

END OF WEEK TABLE OF ACHIEVEMENT

SHAME LEVEL PEAK	6 (embarrassing parents are usually a 3, but a naked, horse-riding mother on YouTube is an exception.)
GUITAR PRACTICE	4 hours 23 minutes
REVISION	7 hours (exams are looming)
PARTY INVITATIONS	0
SNOGS	0

WEEK 17
LESBIANS

My general feel-good mood took a dive when Andreas was knocked down by a car. Dad took the phone call from Breeze just after eleven o'clock at night. It took him about five minutes to calm her down so that he could understand what had happened, but it seemed that they'd had an argument outside the club. Andreas stepped back into the road without looking and got hit by a BMW. He was unconscious with a broken leg and suspected head injuries. The next forty-eight hours were crucial. Mum left for the hospital immediately to be with Breeze so Dad and I sat in the kitchen for a while, consoling each other and drinking hot chocolate.

Breeze spent the next day at the hospital refusing to come home until Andreas regained consciousness. She blamed herself – apparently she was deliberately trying to wind Andreas up by making him jealous. (*No surprise there then!*) Petrina came over so that we could attempt to chill out a bit listening to the new Bloody Minx album, away from my family's bubbling panic. In all the drama, Mum forgot to cancel her Medieval Banquet date with The Wizard, so when Petrina opened the front door she found him standing outside dressed up as a nobleman in a long green robe and red velvet cap.

'Oh hi!' she said hesitantly as I remained hiding on the landing like a spineless sea cucumber.

The Wizard took off his hat and bowed low. 'Ah, my good lady.'

'Erm . . . you look . . . er . . . nice,' Petrina mumbled awkwardly.

The Wizard stroked the fur collar of his robe, 'Aye. 'Tis the trim of an otter.'

Did he say 'otter'?

Petrina swallowed hard. 'An . . . otter?'

'Aye. Only royalty are permitted to wear ermine,' said The Wizard.

Oh no, just ermine. They're not otters, are they?

But Petrina didn't appear to have heard as she broke out into a cold sweat and grabbed hold of the doorframe as her legs turned to jelly. 'I can't breath,' she stammered, clutching her chest.

Oblivious to the full-on panic attack that was occurring before him, The Wizard continued. 'Of course as a nobleman, my fur could be that of a fox. But otter is a far superior choice.'

Cowardice be damned - this is a matter of life and death!

I ran down the stairs to find my best friend curled up in a ball on the floor with The Wizard leaning over, holding the fur on his collar towards her saying, 'You can stroke the otter if you like.'

'Stop!' I shouted, putting a protective arm around a stricken Petrina. 'Is that *actually* otter fur?'

'Well, no,' he said sheepishly. 'It's fake fur. I'm vegan. BUT if it *were* real fur then it would be the finest otter fur a man could buy.'

'Will you please stop mentioning otters,' I snapped. 'Petrina suffers from lutraphobia. She's got a genuine phobia of otters.'

'What *really?*'

'You'd better leave,' I said forcefully. 'Mum's not here. She's at the hospital with Breeze.'

The Wizard looked shocked. 'Is everyone OK?'

That simple question was enough to fill my eyes with tears.

'Andreas has been hit by a car,' I replied quietly. 'It's not looking good.'

The Wizard put his hand on my shoulder and looked directly into my eyes. 'Pain is the essence of spiritual growth. Without it, we wither. Go well,' he said.

I watched with anger burning in my belly as he turned and walked back towards his big Land Rover. I only realised that I was crying when two big tears plopped down onto Petrina, who still lay curled up by my feet. I scraped her up off the floor and helped her into the sitting room. Then we huddled together on the sofa in front of the TV.

SEED MOON

ALSO KNOWN AS: GROWING MOON,
AWAKENING MOON, MOON WHEN GEESE
RETURN IN SCATTERED FORMATION,
PINK MOON

The Seed Moon is a phase of new life and healing in times of darkness. Perhaps the full moon had something to do with his recovering, perhaps not, but who cared anyway – Andreas was going to be OK! He woke up starving hungry, complaining of an itchy foot. He still has to stay in hospital for some time yet, but it seems that he's out of the woods. Mum held Dad's hand tightly as Breeze told him of the news on the phone. It was the first time I'd seen them look like a proper couple for ages.

As I pulled my bedroom curtains shut, I noticed them dancing naked under the April Moon. Aware that this was a time of fertility, growth and fruitfulness, I hoped they didn't get any funny ideas about making babies – but it was reassuring to see them so carefree and vibrant together under the stars. I still had to look away sharpish though when they both adopted the Downward Dog position for a spontaneous naked yoga session. I didn't want nightmares.

Returning to school after the Easter break has been a bit uncomfortable, since Mum's YouTube sensation hasn't quite died down yet. To avoid the barrage of taunts, Petrina and I spent most of lunchtime hidden away in the toilets trying to unlock Walter's phone, but we couldn't figure out the password. We had decided to do whatever it took to get hold of Wazzock's number, seeing as Walter had been so reluctant to cooperate. Petrina managed to take the phone from his rucksack without his knowledge during our maths lesson. We felt a bit guilty, but we could see no other option. This was an act of love – to honour the promise that we had made to Felix and Toby. However, our attempts to break the code failed and Petrina snuck the phone back again. We decided to try again another day with our new shortlist of possible passwords that Walter may be using:

POSSIBLE PASSWORDS TO UNLOCK WALTER'S PHONE

1. Wazzock (too recent?)

2. Weirdo (quite possible)

3. Dandruff (too personal?)

4. Moody (does he even realise that he's moody?)

5. Barcodes (his favourite band)

6. Picasso (his cat's name)

7. Camel Toe (possible)

8. Petrina (possible)

9. Blossom (possible)

10. Blunt stylus (his passion)

When we tried again at break time, it turned out to be 'Petrina'. But although we were then able to break into his phone, the name Wazzock didn't appear anywhere in his contact list. He'd obviously put it in under a false name, but with over a hundred and fifty names in there we didn't know where to start. Petrina is completely bewildered as to how he actually knows so many people. She's only got nineteen contacts in her phone. And I've only got ten. I'm trying to convince myself that it's 'quality not quantity' that counts, but when you're fifteen years old it's all about the numbers. How has Weirdo Walter from planet Weirdopia got so many friends? I thought Petrina and I were his only alien comrades.

Matthew Ludlow stuck his tongue in my ear when I was getting a hot chocolate from the vending machine. And I am NOT EVEN JOKING.

'Have you been avoiding me?' he asked, seemingly appearing from nowhere.

YES! Yes I have

'I am not avoiding you.' He'd caught me off-guard. 'Here I am.'

'Only, I haven't seen you around since we . . . you know,' he said, standing uncomfortably close to me. His face was covered in spots. He clearly hasn't given up alcohol yet. I took a step back.

'I've been really busy with the radio station and er – it's been the holidays.'

Matthew took a step towards me again.

I watched the plastic cup fill up with hot water, wishing it would hurry so I could grab it and run.

Please don't ask me out. Please don't ask me out.

'So would you like to go out sometime?' he continued. 'We could go for a pizza or to see a film? Whatever you fancy.'

Oh, balls.

And then, as I paused to figure out how I was going to politely decline his offer, Matthew seemed to take the momentary silence as an invitation to stick his sluggery tongue in my ear. What was he thinking? Bleurrggh.

'What are you doing?' I yelled, wiping my ear with my sleeve.

Matthew looked genuinely hurt. 'But I thought after what happened at the party . . .'

'Nooooo!' I said quickly. 'No, no, nooooo.'

'Oh, right,' he muttered quietly. 'Wrong end of the stick and all that. Yeah. Sorry.'

He turned and walked away, his eyes fixed on his feet. I would have felt bad, but suddenly, right on cue, Felix appeared at the vending machine.

'All right, babe?' he said.

Did he just call me 'babe'? Yes. YES HE DID. Oh, please don't look at my dribbly ear.

I removed my drink from the tray.

'Hi,' I replied, feeling all fuzzy inside.

'So any word about Wazzock yet?'

I casually took a sip from my steaming hot chocolate, burning my top lip in the process. But I didn't flinch.

Stay cool, Blossom, stay cool.

'Almost,' I lied. 'Wazzock will be appearing on your show very soon. I promise.'

'Great. Let me know when you've got a date.' Felix put his coins into the machine slot. 'You know, I think we're going to play another Camel Toe track tomorrow on the show.'

My burned lip was really throbbing now. 'Brilliant,' I said.

Felix nodded. 'Cool.'

Now that I'm considered to be more than just a weirdo, holding a conversation with the sexiest boy in school whilst a blister formed on my burned lip and one of my ears dripped with somebody else's saliva wasn't as bad as you might expect.

For the first time in a while the main subject of school gossip was about someone else: Mei Miyagi, who had been spotted kissing Max Burcott in the staff car park. It seems that Mei just can't make up her mind which way to swing. It makes me wonder if I would ever be able to become a lesbian.

PROS OF BEING A LESBIAN

1. No danger of accidental pregnancy.

2. Instantly doubling my wardrobe.

3. It's cool (and I'm always trying to be cool).

4. I wouldn't have to spend money on birth control or pregnancy tests.

5. I could go to the toilet together with my girlfriend.

6. *No stinky boy socks.*

7. *A girl would understand my love of kittens.*

8. *Girls look better first thing in the morning.*

9. *Girls don't have really hairy backs.*

10. *Girls don't get beer guts.*

CONS OF BEING A LESBIAN

1. *Having to touch her lady parts.*

So that's 10-1 in favour of being a lesbian. Perhaps I will do some non-physical experimenting when I go to university.

Poor Kirsty Mackerby is devastated. She expressed her emotions by throwing herself on the classroom floor and wailing in a Mediterranean style until Mrs Finley led her away to her office to be consoled. Petrina has been looking after Paulette Dempsey who had been going out with Max ever since he groped her bum on the dance floor at Matthew Ludlow's party. Her hurt has caused her to once again publicly announce that she is asexual and will remain so for the rest of her life. As a way of coping, she has thrown herself fully into her Dempsey Love business, deciding to both sponsor the School Disco and produce a new range of 'love-themed'

T-shirts (which she is going to commission Walter to design).

Naturally Fiona and Lucy lapped up the scandal, using it as material for cheap laughs throughout their show, during which Petrina and I were snugly nestled on the sofa in between Toby and Felix, who both seemed to find the topic hilarious, frequently contributing their own jokes to the show via the talkback button. Walter maintained his silence in the studio as he methodically ensured that the show ran as smoothly as possible. I think he's a bit shaken up after having to tell Mei that because of recent events, her agony aunt slot had been cancelled. She went mental, calling Walter a 'freak', a 'weirdo' and then accusing him of being 'sexually repressed'. I'm beginning to think that Mei may be a bit emotionally unstable. If she doesn't get some kind of counselling soon she'll end up a spotty alcoholic like Matthew Ludlow.

END OF WEEK TABLE OF ACHIEVEMENT

SHAME LEVEL PEAK	2 (burned lip and dribbly ear)
GUITAR PRACTICE	6 hours 1 minute
REVISION	7 hours
PARTY INVITATIONS	0
SNOGS	Tongue in ear

WEEK 18
HEY NONNY NONNY

We positioned ourselves at 09.00 behind a bush opposite Walter's house. It felt a bit weird spying on our best friend, especially when we witnessed him getting dressed in his bedroom, but it's the only way we can think of to locate Wazzock. Neither of us could quite believe how fit Walter is with no top on. Eventually, I had to cover Petrina's ogling eyes with my hand as she was sailing a little too close to pervert territory, but it's safe to say that Walter's body is RIPPED! Who'd have thought it!

We followed him as he rode the bus all the way to Park Street where he alighted. Petrina was visibly relieved that he then made his way into the Bravebourne Luxury Hotel, rather than the notorious brothel run by a Madam known locally as Whiplash Tash situated on the opposite side of the road. Petrina claimed that she was simply concerned for his well-being seeing as gonorrhoea can lead to septicaemia.

Hiding behind a parked car, we watched Walter enter the hotel where Wazzock greeted him in reception with a warm, friendly hug. It's a wonder they could actually see each other at all through that hair. Two eyeless aliens from the planet Fringe. They chatted animatedly as they got into the lift, the doors closing behind them. Petrina and I successfully snuck past the receptionist and pursued them up the stairwell. Exhausted and out of breath, we eventually found them on the tenth floor disappearing round a corner, but as we ran to catch them up we were stopped in our tracks by the receptionist and a burly doorman wearing a top hat who then physically escorted us off the premises.

Mission FAILED.

From: Blossom Uxley-Michaels   1st May 15:11
To: info@poptasticmanagement.com
SUBJECT: Headlining

Dear Sir/Madam,

The Bridge Mount school disco is shaping up nicely. I have scheduled Josh Raven at the top of the bill. He can perform as many tracks as he wants. (More than five but fewer than twelve.)

Headlining: Josh Raven
With Support from:
Camel Toe
DJ Luke 'Loopy' Ludlow
Mr Blackmore and Mrs Finley's Smooth Jazz Band

(They insisted on being included on the line up, but they're only playing two songs so don't be too alarmed.)

We don't have a budget to provide a backstage rider, so if Josh wants to request a bald-headed, toothless hooker or a dressing room full of black orchids and magnums of Cristal Champagne then I'm afraid he'll have to sort it out himself. (Just to warn you – he won't actually have a 'dressing room' as such but there is a big broom cupboard that we could clear to make way for a camping chair and a shaving mirror.)

Looking forward to seeing Josh on 27th May.

Many thanks,

Blossom Uxley-Michaels

P.S. If Josh needs somewhere to stay that night because the hotels are all booked up or something, then he's welcome to crash at mine. My sister is almost never home so he can sleep in her bed. (I'll wash the sheets of course.)

When The Wizard invited us to be his guests at a bank holiday Medieval Fayre, I was hoping that we would all say no. However, after much coaxing (and nagging) from Mum, Breeze and I reluctantly agreed to go too. Only Dad stood firm and refused to partake in what would essentially be 'rubbing his face in it'.

Stepping out of our camper van, we were met with a scene

reminiscent of a medieval Glastonbury Festival. We waited next to a minstrel whose party trick was to play two recorders simultaneously with both mouth and nostril. I was secretly impressed and would have quizzed him about his talent, if I hadn't been distracted by the AMAZING hog roast cooking outside the adjacent tent. A nun was brushing on the honey glaze while the pig turned slowly on the spit. The smell was out of this world, so strong and fragrant that it actually caused me to dribble and made my vegan sister dry-retch over a litter-bin.

At that precise moment, a hawk from the falconry swooped majestically above us and managed a perfect bulls-eye poo on Breeze's forehead. Of course I almost wet myself with laughter, but my sister was not at all amused.

'I knew I shouldn't have come,' she shrieked. 'I hate this place.'

'A poo on the head is a sign of good luck,' said Mum (who, incidentally, was dressed as a peasant wench). Breeze rummaged around in her handbag for a tissue, muttering a string of obscenities that made even my annoyingly liberal-minded mother frown.

I tried to offer a little reassurance. 'At least on the plus side, the day can't get any worse.'

Right on cue, my sister raised her head, opened her mouth and shouted, 'OH MY GOD NO!'

I followed her eye line to a young man, who was skulking directly towards her across the main ring on tiptoes. He wore black tights with dark rags hanging like ripped flesh from his overlong limbs. His large grey hat cast a shadow across his pointy face, but I was still able to make out his beady eyes leering in our direction. Imagine a spindly spider crossed with a comedy burglar and you'll get the picture.

'Who is he?' I asked.

'Creepy Dave,' whispered Breeze, as she tried to duck behind me out of view.

Suddenly, as if by magic, The Wizard arrived, dressed as an actual sorcerer. He planted a passionate kiss on Mum's lips.

'I'm not the chairman of The UK Medieval Battle Re-enactment Society for nothing,' boasted The Wizard. 'I've got us the best seats in the house to watch the maypole dance.'

He proudly steered us over towards the Royal Box in the main stand. As we sat down on the plastic golden chairs, we heard a rustling coming from below. Creepy Dave had scuttled across the field and was now standing beneath us, his pointy chin resting on the raised platform floor.

'Hello, Breeze!'

Breeze tried not to make eye contact. 'Are you stalking me?'

Creepy Dave looked shocked. 'I had no idea you'd be here,' he said. The wispy black hairs on his chin were crawling towards my sister's bare toes. Breeze's foot shot back and her flip-flop flew straight into Creepy Dave's face. He handed it back without complaint.

Breeze's rapidly beating nostrils revealed her annoyance. 'So what are you supposed to be then? A minstrel?'

'Nope. I'm a lowly beggar, who has to survive by eating rats and vermin.'

'Lovely,' she said abruptly. 'Great to see you. Ooh, look, I think it's going to start.'

She turned rudely away, leaving Creepy Dave standing with his mouth open for a second longer, as if he were about to say something, before he disappeared quickly into the crowd.

The speakers boomed. 'Fair ladies and gentlefolk. Before the main jousting event, please give a warm welcome to their Royal Highnesses, the King and Princess, who will perform a popular medieval maypole dance especially for you, their loyal subjects.'

The beautiful, elegantly dressed Princess entered the ring, her hand outstretched, delicately resting on that of the King. Behind them a group of about thirteen noblemen and women followed.

'It appears we have a small problem,' said the PA announcer, turning to look at The Wizard as the whole crowd watched. 'One of our noble ladies has been taken ill, which means we are a dancer short. Do we have any volunteers?'

Mum had conveniently nipped to the toilet, so The Wizard turned first to my sister.

'I'd rather eat my own hair,' she snapped.

Then all eyes were on me.

'Please, Blossom,' The Wizard asked softly. 'Your mother would be so proud.'

Obviously I didn't want to get up and do the Hey Nonny Nonny dance in front of thousands of people, but the pressure was on. I looked over at Breeze, who nodded silently.

'OK,' I said grudgingly. 'I'll do it.'

I made my way down into the main ring to enthusiastic cheers from the crowd. A man dressed in purple velvet took my hand and told me to follow his instructions. Before I knew what was going on I was clutching a red ribbon and skipping round a maypole to the sound of a pan flute and drum. In my mind I tried to count the number of life events that could be considered more embarrassing than this. (I finally concluded that there were in fact seventeen – including the time I got trapped in between my parents on the sofa during a documentary about people who have sex with ghosts.)

I linked arms with the man in purple velvet, hopped on one leg alongside a women with a gigantic nork cleavage, intertwined my red ribbon with that of a man dressed in white and twirled in a circle with Fiona Tittledown. WAIT! Rewind . . .

FIONA TITTLEDOWN!!!

Standing, quite startled, before me – dressed as a medieval princess in a gown of green with long flowing sleeves and a tall, pointed headdress – was the coolest girl at Bridge Mount Secondary School.

'What are *you* doing here?' she hissed as we held hands and skipped to the left.

'My mum made me come,' I replied, nodding towards the royal box where my mother was now back in her seat, clearly delighted to watch me making a fool of myself. The dancers changed direction and I found myself jigging to the right with the man in white then looping under the arm of the King, before skipping in a circle once again with Fiona. She pulled me close, pinching the underside of my arm, and whispered firmly in my ear, 'If you tell *anyone* about this I will make your life at school *Hell*. Got that?'

I nodded my understanding as the dance came to an end. I sat on my golden chair rubbing my arm, looking up at Her Royal Highness Princess Fiona receiving her applause from the comfort of her massive plastic throne.

This might not have qualified as the most embarrassing moment of my life, but it was certainly the weirdest.

'So do you think her parents made her do it?' asked Petrina when I told her about my medieval encounter with Fiona. (Obviously when I agreed not to tell anyone, I assumed that meant anyone but Petrina – it's not as if Fiona considers either of us to qualify as actual people.)

'No,' I replied. 'Before she saw me, she was loving every minute of it. The Wizard says she's been a regular participant for the past three years.'

'Wow,' giggled Petrina. 'That's so uncool. Definitely more Weirdo than Winner.'

I genuinely couldn't believe my luck. This was the best ammunition EVER.

The rumour was TRUE. Fiona had been cheating on Felix with a boy from Cumnor Grove. Mei Miyagi spotted them kissing in the park and took a photo as evidence. It was all over every social networking site within thirty seconds. So Felix and Fiona are officially NO MORE. Ha ha ha ha!

During the Breakfast Show, Felix skulked silently around the studio, listening to Fiona using almost every link as an opportunity to slag him off in some way. The amount of anger she was spewing you'd have thought that *she* was the victim, not the other way round. Toby and Petrina both found it all very amusing, giggling with each other, much to the annoyance of Lucy. However, Walter couldn't handle the situation at all, leaving the radio station with his face in his hands muttering 'head freak-out, man' to himself, so it was up to me to try and gain some control over our shambolic radio output. I entered the studio straight after Fiona had finished a link about why boys are more stupid than girls.

'What do you think you're doing?' snapped Fiona, as the heavy door closed behind me. 'Nobody is allowed in the studio while we're broadcasting. Apart from the producer of course.'

'Well, the red light is off and you might have noticed that Walter isn't actually here,' I responded. 'And we promised Mrs Finley that our broadcast content would be responsible and not offensive or provocative.'

Fiona yawned loudly. 'BORING.'

I bit my lip. 'Look Fiona, you two need to start behaving a bit more professionally. The show sounds awkward and messy.'

Fiona flicked her long mane of hair and bared her perfectly straight, shiny white teeth like a rabid dog about to bite. I flicked my tongue along the front of my brace and discovered a long strand of marmalade rind wedged into the front. I pretended to scratch my lip and discretely removed it hoping that nobody had noticed. *God, it's so ANNOYING to be all rindy just as I'm about to have a stand off with a slanger.*

'Shut up, Bumface.' Fiona jabbed her beautifully manicured finger in my direction. 'You might think you're cool now that you're in a band, hanging out with Steel Dragon – who, if I'm totally honest, I think are rubbish – but you're *still* a creepy weirdo and I'm not taking orders from the likes of you.'

'Oh, sorry,' I snapped. 'I forgot I was in the presence of a medieval princess.'

Fiona's lip curled up at one side and started twitching.

Lucy looked at me blankly. 'Eh?'

I couldn't quite figure out if Fiona's expression was that of pure fear or pure anger.

Petrina broke the tension by poking her head round the studio door. 'Everything OK, Blossom?' she asked.

I looked at Fiona who was nervously fiddling with her hair, terrified that her uncool secret was out, but she needn't have worried – my medieval comment had flown straight over Lucy's head.

Lucy giggled into her hands. 'Hey, Fi,' she called to her best friend. 'How do you find a princess?'

'Er . . . I don't know,' Fiona replied anxiously.

'You follow the foot prince!' Lucy doubled up at her own HILARIOUS joke, clutching her stomach tightly. Fiona was so relieved that she fell about laughing too. But they could laugh all they liked – the door had been left wide open for me to make my move on Felix. All I needed was a little help from an elusive rock star named Wazzock.

After the apparent success of our eventful medieval outing, Mum suggested that we invite The Wizard over for dinner.

'Vegan red curry,' said Mum proudly as she set the big pot down in the centre of the table.

'It looks delicious,' said The Wizard, licking his lips. I was alarmed to see that he was wearing triple denim. Denim jeans, denim shirt and denim jacket. I wondered for a moment if he might be wearing denim underwear as well, but the thought made me sick up a bit in my mouth.

'You must have slaved away all day making it,' he said.

So smarmy. If only he could be taught a lesson.

I saw Dad look away as Mum fluttered her eyelashes.

'Ha ha!' she giggled coyly. 'No, it was just something simple I knocked up this evening. Anyone could have done it.'

Oooh. I've had an idea . . . now I know they're under here somewhere . . .

'Don't put yourself down,' said The Wizard, helping himself to a huge spoonful of rice. 'You are an amazing woman. Isn't that right?' he added, looking straight at Dad.

Ah. There we go. Got one.

'Yes,' replied Dad defensively. '*My* wife is amazing.'

'So, Breeze,' The Wizard continued, turning to face my sister sitting opposite. 'How's Andreas doing now?'

Quickly, do it now while he's looking the other way.

'He's doing OK, thanks,' said Breeze. She glanced across at Dad, the guilt of her brief interaction with 'the enemy' clearly visible on her face.

How does your fossilized Breeze bogey vegan curry taste?

'Delicious,' he declared, winking at Mum.

The Wizard put down his spoon and reached across the table to take hold of Breeze's hand. 'It's times like this that you put your life into perspective. You realise what's important and you figure out who you really love.' He looked over at my anguished father and smirked.

Breeze smiled uncomfortably as she withdrew her hand. 'Besides, he's hairier than a Hobbit's arse. Nobody else would have him.'

The Wizard laughed loudly. 'Wow! That's real love.'

As I scooped a spoonful of veggie curry onto my plate, I had an overwhelming urge for a Big Mac. I promised myself that I'd drop into McDonalds tomorrow.

The Wizard looked at me. 'And what about you, blue eyes? Has any lucky young man won your heart yet?'

Dad was becoming visibly agitated. I squirmed a bit.

'Ummm, no.'

'A lucky woman perhaps?'

No boyfriend, so he assumes I'm a lesbian? Idiot.

'She had a big snog with Matthew Ludlow the other week, didn't you, Blossom?' said Breeze.

Arrrrrrrrgggggghhhh! Let's revisit the sexuality debate . . .

'Oooh, did you?' asked my mum excitedly.

'Well, yes,' I said quietly. 'But it was just in the heat of the moment. It didn't mean anything.'

'But how do you know he's not *the one?*' asked The Wizard.

I fidgeted in my seat. 'I just know.'

'So was he a good kisser then?' asked my EMBARRASSING sister.

'I suppose so.'

'He's a lucky boy,' said The Wizard, leering at Mum. 'Like mother, like daughter.'

Dad's expression was one that I had never seen before.

'To the sexiest women I have ever met!' announced The Wizard, holding his glass of wine aloft.

Dad stood up suddenly and his chair toppled backwards onto the quarry tiled kitchen floor.

'Enough!' he shouted.

The Wizard held up his hands. 'Whoa fella. Let's not get into a fisticuffs situation again. Not in front of the good ladies. Show some courtesy.'

'Don't tell me what to do in my own home,' growled Dad, eyes burning beneath a furrowed brow.

'Dad, sit down please,' I begged, tugging at his sleeve.

'No, Blossom,' said Dad angrily. 'Merlin speaks continuously about courtesy like he's some gallant knight of the Round Table, when in reality he's about as chivalrous as a terrorist.'

Merlin stood up. 'I beg to differ. I have treated your wife like the lady she is.'

'And there is my point exactly,' said Dad. 'My *wife*. What kind of gentleman would try to woo a man's wife in his own home, right in front of his children?'

The Wizard aggressively stroked his beard. 'I am *always* a perfect gentleman,' he declared.

'OK, guys,' said Mum calmly. 'Why don't you both sit down?'

Dad ignored her. 'I guess *I'm* not,' he said. 'So maybe you should leave before *I* do something *very* ungentlemanly.'

'A duel, then,' said The Wizard defiantly. 'For the good lady's honour.'

Breeze and I looked at each other in horror.

'Oh, for God's sake,' gasped Mum (although I could tell that she was secretly thrilled by the excitement of having two men fighting over her).

'All right,' said Dad, his eyes fixed on The Wizard's. 'You're on.'

The Wizard maintained eye contact with Dad for a few more seconds before turning to Mum. He took her hand and brought it up towards his lips. 'Thou art the fairest lady.' He kissed her hand softly. 'I will do what it takes to win your heart. To the death if I must, by my troth. Adieu, my good ladies.'

The Wizard withdrew his hand and walked out of the kitchen.

END OF WEEK TABLE OF ACHIEVEMENT

SHAME LEVEL PEAK	6 (Medieval dancing with Fiona Tittldedown was akin to a major physical defect)
GUITAR PRACTICE	4 hrs 14 minutes (Cassiopeia has become an extension of my own body. Like an extra limb or a guitar-shaped bone)
REVISION	3 hours (I know I should have done more but it's been an eventful week)
PARTY INVITATIONS	0
SNOGS	0 (but now Fiona is properly out of the picture, who knows what the future holds?!)

WEEK 19
SUPERSTAR RADIO DJ

Dad was taking his impending duel with The Wizard VERY seriously. It was scheduled to take place next Saturday, at dawn, on the grassy verge in front of the medieval Enville Castle, where legend has it King Ethelred II was tormented nightly by the ghost of a nun who was murdered when she drank a goblet of poisoned wine. Dad was going out for a run every morning before breakfast then lifting heavy logs in the garden after dinner. The two of them were set to do battle with wooden swords for Mum's honour until 'the death'. (I dreaded to think what that means.) Andreas very kindly offered to lend Dad his Braveheart costume, complete with wig, blue face-paint and the actual sword that Mel Gibson held in the promotional posters. Dad has politely refused.

Petrina and I spent yet another weekend staking out the Bravebourne Hotel, too timid to approach Wazzock directly. After lurking around in the car park for an hour and a half, we spotted the distinctive, massive afro of Billy Hawkins, singer of Steel Dragon, arriving at reception, where he was kissed on the lips by a pretty, blonde woman (who we secretly nicknamed Candida due to her excruciatingly skin-tight jeans). About two minutes later who should join them but Walter! Billy greeted him with a huge bear hug and Candida kissed him on the cheek. WOWZOIDS!!! Petrina looked furious. I had to forcibly restrain her from going in after them as they headed towards the lift, reminding her that the last time we were in the hotel the doorman told us 'never to set foot in this place again or we'll call the police'.

We waited outside for another hour until the three of them reappeared. Billy left in a black cab, leaving Candida standing outside the hotel with her arm linked through Walter's. When she kissed him on the cheek and swept his fringe to one side Petrina almost blew our cover, shouting, 'His eyes! She can see his eyes! They're too far away, but I bet they're deep brown.'

'Really?' I replied. 'I always thought they'd be green.'

'No way,' she said with certainty. 'Definitely deep brown. Like Jaffa cakes.'

We watched, astounded as the two of them climbed into a cab together looking for all the world like the coolest, happiest couple in the world.

That evening, when I opened the front door, it took me a couple of moments to place the wiry-looking man who was holding a brown paper bag and standing on my porch.

'Hello,' he said. I finally recognised Creepy Dave. He looked different out of peasant clothes. 'I wonder if Breeze is there?'

His dark hair was parted to the left and he wore a brown corduroy suit, with black pointy shoes. If a cooler man had been dressed this way it might have been considered 'geek chic', but Creepy Dave just looked like a geek.

I was about to call my sister when she whispered (loudly) down from the top of the stairs. 'Tell him I'm not in.'

It was awful. Creepy Dave had clearly heard, but I felt obliged to be loyal to my sibling.

'She's, er . . . gone out,' I lied pathetically.

Creepy Dave smiled sadly and nodded. 'Another time, perhaps.'

His green eyes weren't anywhere near as beady as I remembered. In fact, if anything, I'd describe them as gentle. I watched as he walked away with his head hanging low, like a dog that's just been scolded.

'That was horrible,' I called up to Breeze.

'He's a weirdo,' came the voice from upstairs. 'He's lucky Andreas isn't here right now.'

The sudden twinge of sympathy took me by surprise and left me feeling uncomfortable for the rest of the evening.

Bridge Mount FM is descending into chaos. Fiona Tittledown didn't even bother showing up for the Breakfast Show one morning, leaving Lucy to host with Toby who stepped in at the last minute. The two of them used their hour of airtime to hurl insults at the other's best friend and by the end of the show they were barely speaking. Looks like another relationship is on the rocks. Petrina was thrilled!!! Ha ha ha! BUT we were not at all happy that our radio station was suffering due to the presenter's personal lives. Mrs Finley had already warned Lucy that 'bastard doofus' is not an appropriate phrase to use at eight-thirty in the morning.

As a result, we called an emergency production meeting. Felix, Toby, Petrina, Walter, Paulette and myself all met in Joe's Café after school.

'OK, guys,' said Felix, looking über sexy in his cool shades. 'The Breakfast Show isn't working. What are we gonna do?'

'I say we get rid of the slang— I mean Fiona and Lucy,' said Petrina, quickly correcting herself.

Toby looked uncomfortable. 'I don't want to be the one who tells them.'

Felix nodded in agreement. 'Me neither.'

'I'll happily do it,' I declared. 'I'd be delighted.'

'But who would we get to replace them?' asked Felix. 'I'm busy enough as it is and so is Toby.'

'How about Mei?' suggested Paulette. 'She was great with the listeners' problems. A natural.'

Toby shook his head. 'Na,' he said. 'She's too wild. A loose cannon. We need someone less risky.'

'Blossom and I could do it,' said Petrina. 'It would be fun. And we're not wild or at all risky. What do you think, Blossom?'

I thought about it for a tenth of a second, but it was a no-brainer. 'I'm up for it!'

Toby didn't look convinced. 'But don't you think you might be a little bit too . . . weird?'

Felix took a big swig from his can of Coke and let out an enormous burp that powered out of his mouth for around fifteen long seconds. Toby almost wet himself laughing. 'Ten

235

points for volume and six points for smell,' he declared as he high-fived his best friend.

'Look, I don't mean to be rude,' said Felix when he'd finally managed to compose himself. 'But you two aren't exactly the coolest kids in the school.'

'I think they'd be great,' said Walter defensively. 'They are honest, witty, opinionated *and* intelligent – more than can be said for the two airheads presenting the show at the moment.'

Petrina blushed a little.

'I think it's an excellent idea,' said Paulette.

'OK, then,' said Petrina. 'Let's take a vote.'

And so it was decided that, as of that moment, Petrina and I would be the new hosts of the Bridge Mount FM Breakfast Show.

It took us about thirty minutes to settle in to our first show, but once we'd found our stride Petrina and I discovered that we were actually quite competent radio presenters. We could deliver informative links without fluffing our words, chat about the main topics in the news and our on-air chemistry seemed to work. Don't get me wrong, I'm not saying that we were award-winning standard, but for a first effort we did pretty well. In our after-show debrief, Felix asked us to reveal more of our personalities on air to add 'colour and texture' to the show. For some reason Toby found this utterly hysterical and kept referring to Felix as 'a pretentious moron', which eventually led to a twenty-minute, full-on wrestling match on the studio floor. Petrina and I sat back in our chairs, opened our bags of crisps and relaxed as we watched the two HOTTEST GUYS IN THE

SCHOOL grappling with each other at our feet. Weirdly, neither of us felt dirty or voyeuristically perverted in any way.

Of course, Fiona and Lucy were FURIOUS. They didn't take the news that they had been fired very well at all and assured us that nobody would want to listen to a couple of 'Gothbags' talking rubbish on the radio. For a moment it looked as though Fiona might actually punch me in the face, but she had second thoughts and instead decided to serve me with a verbal warning of 'watch your back, Bumface'. I would say that I wasn't scared by her empty threats, but that would be a lie. Fiona Tittledown is someone that you don't cross. She already had my card marked for discovering her medieval secret. After sacking her from her breakfast show, I was pretty much a dead (wo)man walking.

With Walter suffering from an acute case of Moodyitis, neither Petrina nor I wanted to ask him to design the school disco artwork. Instead, we sat down and knocked up a pretty impressive poster ourselves. Mrs Finley agreed that we could use the office photocopier to print ten copies. Whilst we printed out nine of the agreed ten, we can only pray that she doesn't find out what we decided to photocopy on our tenth go. The machine went totally berserk, spewing out endless A4 prints of our photocopied gurning faces. (Neither of us had the nerve to put our bare norks on the scanner.) In a state of panic, we eventually pulled the plug out and hid the evidence (all two hundred and twenty one pages) in our school bags. Thank God I'd brought my Rescue Remedy to calm us down or who knows what state we'd have been in.

Of course the school was now abuzz with excitement. The prospect of Bridge Mount's best known ex-student returning to his roots was almost too much for everyone to cope with. Only one small problem: Josh Raven hasn't yet confirmed that he will be performing. In fact his management haven't actually responded to a single email that I've sent them. NO PRESSURE THEN!!!

From: Blossom Uxley-Michaels   12th May 16:17
To: info@poptasticmanagement.com
SUBJECT: School Disco

Dear Sir/Madam,

I was hoping that you would be able to confirm my booking of Josh Raven as the Bridge Mount School Disco headlining act on 27th May. I can't offer a fee as I'm afraid I have no budget to work with. However, Josh is welcome to come over before/after the show for dinner. My mum makes a bloody good vegan red curry. It'll 'blow his tits off', but I'd imagine Josh is a man with an iron mouth who can handle his spicy food. In addition, we have plenty of alcohol to quench any rock n' roll thirst that Josh may have following on from the vegan curry – Tia Maria, organic Elderflower wine and Gnat's Piss cider, brewed by the local vicar, are all available upon request.

Josh is scheduled to be on stage at 8.30pm, but his stage call is 7.30pm. We would like to record some interview bits for the Bridge Mount FM Breakfast Show before he performs. Oh and did I mention that the Breakfast Show has had a revamp? It's true – I am now the presenter of the show along with my best friend Petrina. (I hope I don't have a nervous breakdown what with impending exams and living in a dysfunctional, broken home – only joking!!!) So the questions put to Josh will be mature and intelligent – none of that puerile 'what's your favourite colour' rubbish. (Although I did once read that Josh's favourite colour is olive, which coincidentally is my favourite colour too. Could our mutual love of a particular shade of green be a sign of our destined fate to be together? No, not really. I'm only Joshing ha ha ha – if you'll pardon the pun!!)

Can't wait to see Josh on 27th May.

Many thanks,

Blossom Uxley-Michaels

P.S. I also read that Josh paints each of his toenails a different colour. Another coincidence that puts us in the same pod – I like to paint each individual fingernail a different colour, but not in school term time otherwise Mr Blackmore would have a fit. Maybe Josh and I should go the whole hog and start wearing matching olive colour nail polish. Ha ha ha ha!!!!!!!!!!!!!!

After I'd pressed *Send* I worried that I might have sounded a bit hysterical.

Mum was in denial. While Dad was out pounding the streets in preparation for the impending duel at dawn, she spent the evening with Breeze meditating on the sitting room rug.

'Mum,' I whispered as I poked my head around the door. 'I'm worried about Dad.'

Mum's eyes were closed. 'OMMMMMMMM,' she chanted. 'Om is a universal sound. You can join in too, if you like, or you can just enjoy the vibrations. OMMMMMMMM.'

'Mum, I'm worried that Dad might get hurt.'

Mum and Breeze ignored me. 'OMMMMMMMM,' they sang in unison.

Despite being blatantly ignored, I continued to voice my concern. 'I don't think he knows what he's getting into.'

'Cow face pose, I think,' said Mum, hooking one leg over the other and grabbing hold of her own hands behind her back. Breeze's giant nostrils flared as she shadowed her. Their eyes remained closed.

A pulse of anger rippled through me. 'Mum, do you actually realise that your pacifist husband is going to fight your warrior boyfriend in the morning?'

Mum opened her eyes. 'Yes, Blossom, I am well aware that your father is having some kind of mid-life crisis. He'll just have to do whatever he has to do to make peace with himself and if that means proving his masculinity by brawling with Merlin in front of an ancient ruined castle then so be it. Now if you'll excuse me, I need to practise my cow face.'

Dad arrived back from his run out of breath, but fired up. 'I'm ready,' he wheezed, punching the air with both fists. 'I'm going to do whatever it takes to defend the honour of my family.'

'Couldn't you settle the disagreement in a less violent way?' I asked hopefully. 'Like *ip dip sky blue* or *paper scissors stone*?'

Dad put his hands on my shoulders, his blue eyes burning more brightly than I'd seen for a long time. 'This is something I have to do Blossom,' he said gently. 'Have faith.'

And then he kissed my forehead and jogged up to the bathroom.

END OF WEEK TABLE OF ACHIEVEMENT

SHAME LEVEL PEAK	1
GUITAR PRACTICE	6 hrs 16 minutes (I'm trying to get the balance between guitar practice and revision)
REVISION	2 hours (it's difficult to balance)
PARTY INVITATIONS	0
SNOGS	0

WEEK 20
THE WORST FRIENDS

Dad, Breeze and I all piled into the camper van at four-thirty in the morning for the ten-mile drive to Enville Castle. For the first time ever, I prayed that the van wouldn't start, but ironically for the first time ever it started straight away. Mum stayed at home in bed, refusing to engage in the 'testosterone-fuelled squabbling'. As we left the house, Dad said it was probably for the best. 'I fully intend to kick Merlin's face right off and that is not a sight that I want your mother to see.'

We arrived just before dawn, stepping out of the van into the crisp morning air. The ruined castle, silhouetted against the imposing deep purple sky, looked eerily magnificent, sending an icy chill down my spine. We slowly made our way up the hill towards the castle, our feet quickly becoming soaking wet from the dewy grass. I thought about all the blood shed in the countless battles that had been fought there; all the men that had died painful, bloody deaths right where we stood. Breeze shuddered beside me and grabbed hold of my arm.

'I don't like it here,' she whispered.

'Me neither,' I replied quietly. 'It gives me the creeps.'

'You can almost feel the history seeping out of the ground,' said Breeze. 'All those lives lost. All that blood in the soil.'

My teeth began to chatter, a secret Morse code, pleading for somebody to GET ME OUT OF HERE.

'Shhhhhh.' Dad had his fingers to his lips. 'I thought I heard something.'

We all looked around, our fight-or-flight senses on full alert. And then, suddenly, just to the left of Enville Castle, I spotted a human figure.

'Oh my God,' I shrieked.

A ghost!

'What?' yelped Breeze.

'Over there,' I pointed.

Oh God. I'd rather be mugged by a mad man than attacked by an evil ghost.

'I can't see anything.'

I looked again towards the spot where the haunting figure had been standing motionless on the hill, but it had disappeared.

'The light is bad,' Dad said calmly. 'You're seeing things.'

'Yeah, I'm just being silly,' I chuckled nervously. 'It's that story about the poisoned nun. It's got me spooked!'

'Who?' Breeze sounded terrified.

I wish Petrina was here. She'd disbelieve the ghosts away.

'Legend has it King Ethelred II was haunted by the ghost of a nun who was murdered here at the castle when she drank a goblet of poisoned wine,' I explained. I wished I'd never looked it up on Wikipedia.

Dad tried his best to reassure my sister. 'It's just a legend,

Breeze. Like King Arthur and the Loch Ness Monster. Myths and nonsense.'

'I do not like this one bit,' she said sounding a little panicky. 'Let's go back to the van.'

Then I noticed something terrifying. A man was rushing down the hill towards us with a sword raised above his head.

'THE WIZARD!' I shouted.

'This is just all too weird,' said my sister. 'I'm out of here.'

But as Breeze turned to walk away, she managed to lose her footing, slipping on the wet grass.

'Arrrgh!' she screamed. 'I've put my hand in badger poo.'

Dad leaned over her. 'I don't think that's badger poo,' he pondered. 'Looks like deer poo.'

'Who cares what animal laid the poo!' snapped my sister. 'There's a medieval knight about to kill you.'

Dad pulled her back up onto her feet, but by then it was too late. The Wizard Knight was charging straight at my dad; his wooden sword outstretched, his body quivering with excitement.

'In the name of my good lady,' he called. 'I will fight you until the d—'

The Wizard's gallant speech was abruptly cut short by a deafening roar as he found himself being roughly rugby-tackled to the muddy ground. We all watched on in surprise as he landed with a heavy thud and was mounted by a fierce warrior-like figure who had seemingly appeared from nowhere.

'YOU CAN TAKE OUR WIVES,' the Braveheart warrior yelled. 'BUT YOU CAN NEVER TAKE OUR FREEDOM.'

∗ ∗ ∗

After dropping The Wizard off at A&E (where he was treated for a torn lip and loss of his front teeth) and thanking Andreas for turning up to defend his 'future family-in-law', I spent the rest of the afternoon practising on my guitar. Despite everything, with Cassiopeia resting securely in my arms, I felt my life was finally moving forwards. I can strum and sing simultaneously AND instead of instant paralysis, my fourth finger now takes a good five seconds to go into spasm when I attempted a bar chord. I may not be up there with the greatest singer/songwriters of all time, but there is still time for me yet. I'm right at the beginning of a very long musical journey. Petrina's keyboard playing had significantly improved as well, which we were both really pleased about, especially seeing as she suffers from tiny sausage fingers (just like Poncerama) – something we thought may hinder her performance. Thankfully we were wrong.

SCHOOL DISCO SETLIST

1. PONCERAMA – *a lively track already familiar to Bridge Mount students due to being playlisted on the radio station in the run up to the disco. This should warm up the audience.*

2. THE MAN WITH AN EGGY BEARD – *a great track to showcase how well we play live.*

3. SLANGER HOTEL – *we just like the idea of performing this track to Fiona and Lucy, who would never be intelligent enough to figure out that it was all about them*

4. THE WIZARD – *a haunting song with a great sing-a-long chorus to get the crowd going.*

The only thing left to do in preparation is to buy our stage outfits. Then we'll be ready to rock 'n' roll!

The following day, as I was arriving home from a mega McDonaldsathon, I noticed Creepy Dave sitting alone on the wall opposite our house. Upon seeing me he averted his gaze, but did not run away. I was about to approach him when Andreas screeched up in his Aston Martin. He immediately spotted Creepy Dave and sprang out of the car as if he were in some cheesy American cop show, grabbing Creepy Dave roughly by the collar.

'What? Are you some kind of stalker?' he snarled.

Oh. My. God. I'm about to witness a murder.

'N-n-n-no,' stammered Creepy Dave, trying desperately to free himself from the angry Cypriot's grip. Without really thinking, I found myself running to his aid, not sure quite how to defuse the explosive situation.

Andreas's eyes were burning. 'So what do you want, then?'

'Let him go,' I shouted firmly. But they completely ignored me, as if I wasn't there (story of my life).

'I've got something I'd like to give Breeze,' trembled Creepy Dave.

Hello? Can anyone see me? Yoo hoo?

'I bet you have,' whispered Andreas, leaning even closer in towards Creepy Dave's face.

'Don't be so crude,' the rat-like man said bravely. 'I have something of hers that I'd like to return and it's important that I do it in person. She doesn't even know I have it.'

Andreas was getting impatient. 'Give it to me and I'll make sure she gets it.'

'No,' said Creepy Dave, finally managing to pull himself free from Andreas's strong grip. 'I'll come back another time. Perhaps when her pet chimpanzee isn't here to interfere.'

He's going to kill you. Right now. Proper real-time dead.

Andreas's face contorted as he reached out in a blind fury, but it was too late. Creepy Dave was already running far into the distance.

Phew. I had a genuine moment of panic then. What with Camel Toe and the radio station I'd never find time to appear as a prosecution witness at a murder trial.

After months of cold and rain we are officially experiencing a heatwave! The average temperature for May is usually around 18°C but on this particular day the thermometer hit 27°C!! What a scorcher!!! Maybe the heat was to blame for Fiona's act of malice. I know for a FACT that it was she who pulled the plug on our breakfast show that morning. I don't actually have any evidence, but seeing as she had been standing directly opposite the studio, her arms folded with a big smirk on her face the moment we went off air, I was pretty certain she must have been the culprit. Felix marched straight over, telling her to 'grow up', but she just shrugged in mock innocence and blew him a kiss. Felix returned to the studio muttering to himself that he had no idea what he ever saw in her. I know EXACTLY what he saw in her. Two MASSIVE norks.

Felix and Toby sat outside on the playing field with us at break time. The sun was already high in the sky and there was that balmy summery feeling that makes everyone go a bit crazy. I had my guitar with me, so Felix asked me to sing him a song. I played Josh Raven's *Moonlight Stalker* (only four chords). My singing/strumming technique had never sounded better. In the middle of the song Toby (wearing his tiny training shorts) laid his head down on Petrina's lap. She froze. Any kind of physical contact gives her the chills, but combined with the sight of Toby's brown muscular legs, Petrina was bordering on hypothermia. I noticed Walter walk by and thought for a moment that he might stop and join us, but he just continued on his way, head down, looking at his manky shoes. When I finished the song, Felix gave me a round of applause.

'That was brilliant,' he said. 'You're a star in the making.'

I blushed A LOT.

'So any news on your mate Wazzock yet?' he continued.

'Almost,' I lied, trying to impress. 'He's just really busy at the moment, but when he gets a window in his diary he'll be here like a shot.'

Petrina raised her eyebrows at me. I frowned back.

'Cool,' said Toby, still lounging on my best friend's lap. 'He's a real legend.'

'Do you reckon you could get free tickets for us to see Steel Dragon when they play live next month?' asked Felix, edging closer to me so that his shoulder brushed against mine. My cheeks burned even hotter.

'Yes, for sure,' I blurted. 'We could probably get backstage passes too.'

Felix kissed me on the cheek (which was now so hot that I was worried it might melt his lips). 'That would be great, babe,' he said, standing up and offering an extended arm towards his best friend. 'Come on then, Tobe. Let's get out of here.'

I noticed that Petrina was sweating profusely as Toby lifted his head from her lap (although that may have had something to do with the black tights and long sleeved woollen cardigan that she was wearing in the blistering heat).

'See ya!' Toby sang as he shouldered his rucksack.

We watched the two SEX GODS walk towards the school entrance, playfully pushing and punching each other the way that boys do.

'Backstage passes?' said Petrina. 'We haven't even managed to get Wazzock's number yet.'

'There's only one way to do this . . .' I was going to have to confront my oldest friend and rely on our mutual bond of weirdness to help us with our plight.

But Walter was absolutely livid. When we approached him in the classroom, we confessed that we'd followed him to the Bravebourne Hotel and it didn't go down well.

'Why would you do that?' he asked, swinging his record bag over his shoulder.

'Because we wanted to get access to Wazzock,' explained Petrina. 'Toby and Felix are so keen to get him in on the station.'

One look at Walter's expression and I knew that I had made the biggest mistake of my life.

He dropped his bag back onto the floor with a thud. 'So you basically used me?'

Yes. We are horrible, horrible friends.

'Technically speaking, no.' The guilt surged up inside me. 'We haven't actually managed to speak to him yet.'

Walter's hurt rapidly transformed into anger. 'But you went to extraordinary lengths just to spy on me?'

'Only because once we'd cracked your phone password we couldn't find Wazzock's number,' said Petrina defensively. I put my hands over my face.

We've deceived the kindest person we know. We are scum.

'You stole my phone?' exclaimed poor Walter.

'Yeah, but we put it back, didn't we, Blossom?'

I felt awful. We had totally betrayed our best friend. The boy who had rescued me when I'd been tied to the apple tree; who endlessly sketched beautiful portraits of Petrina. Our fellow weirdo. Our protective shield against the rest of the world. The perfect threesome. What had we been thinking?

'I'm so sorry Walter,' I said apologetically. 'We really didn't mean to upset you.'

I was pretty sure that underneath that long, lank fringe his eyes were filling up with tears. His chin was trembling.

But Petrina was on the defensive. 'Look, Walter, I've asked you countless times for Wazzock's number, but you refused to give it to me. In fact, you've been a right moody quimboid lately, huffing and puffing and sulking all over the place.'

'Why can't you see that you can't buy friendship?' barked Walter. 'Those two losers won't give you the time of day once they've got what they want from you.'

Petrina sniffed the air. 'Urgh! What's that smell?' she said. 'Oh, that's right – it's the smell of jealousy.'

Walter sneered. 'I'm not jealous of *them*.'

Petrina folded her arms. 'No, you're jealous of us for finally turning weird into winning.'

Walter's voice was shaky. 'What's happened to you, Petrina?' I suspect it was more of a plea than a question.

'I got cool,' she replied. 'Blossom and I have finally been accepted. We are Winners and you've been left behind.'

Somehow, through his fringe, Walter managed to look at Petrina so intensely that she was forced to avert her eyes. For a moment I thought he was going to roar in her face, but instead he picked his bag up off the floor and walked towards the door. Then he stopped.

Without turning round he quietly whispered, 'I miss you Petrina.'

And then he walked out, leaving Petrina catching flies with her open mouth.

The early summer madness continues as Dad and The Wizard went out for a drink together. It seems they've come to an agreement – Mum will continue to see Merlin, but their rendezvous will be more discreet. However, Mum says that she's gone off him a bit now that he's lost his two top front teeth and consequently developed a lisp. She says it's like having dinner with a balding toddler.

Since winning the ill-fated duel at dawn, Dad has found a new lease of life, something that, according to Breeze, Mum finds extremely attractive. It's as if his triumph has released an irresistible hormone that my mother can't get enough of. Seriously, they are all over each other like a couple of newlyweds. It's REVOLTING. I mean, for God's sake, GET A ROOM (preferably in another house)!

On his way to meet The Wizard, Dad dropped me and Petrina off at Westbury Shopping Mall. We've agreed that black and orange will be our theme colours, so I purchased a new pair of black skinny jeans, Petrina bought an orange mini-skirt (that she will wear over black woollen tights of course) and we will both wear long-sleeved T-shirts emblazoned with the Camel Toe Logo on the front. With our hard-hitting, distinctive branding, Camel Toe is surely destined for world domination!

CAMEL TOE BRANDED MERCHANDISE WISH LIST

1. CARDIGANS (*Petrina insisted on cardigans instead of sweatshirts, which she thinks are too mainstream.*)

2. LONG- AND SHORT-SLEEVED T-SHIRTS WITH 'I LOVE CAMEL TOE' ACROSS THE CHEST

3. KOHL EYELINER (I'm not exactly sure how we could can fit the logo on a pencil, but it's an essential part of our image.)

4. WOOLLY TIGHTS (with the logo discretely placed on the gusset.)

5. TOYS (A little cuddly Camel Toe that could be given away as a free promotion with a McDonald's Happy Meal.)

6. SLIPPERS (Actual Camel Toes.)

7. CONDOMS (Camel Toe is a band that promotes positivity and safety to our fans. You can't get safer than a condom.)

8. HI-VISIBILITY FLUORESCENT WAISTCOATS (Continuing the all-important safety theme, these jackets will be waterproof and flame-resistant and branded with the Camel Toe logo. We may also venture into disposable chemical protection wear, off-shore industry overalls and rape alarms.)

9. PERFUME (I'd imagine the smell of Camel Toe would be the scent of the modern woman.)

10. POST-FEMINIST-IRONIC-BELLY-WARMER KNICKERS

BRANDED WITH THE LOGO ON THE FRONT (*If Emmeline Pankhurst were alive today, she would insist that all her Suffragettes wear them under their petticoats. If THESE knickers fell out the bottom of my trouser leg for the whole world to see I wouldn't mind at all.*)

END OF WEEK TABLE OF ACHIEVEMENT

GUILT LEVEL PEAK	*We have utterly betrayed our dearest friend. I couldn't feel more ashamed of myself.*
GUITAR PRACTICE	*14 hours of solid band rehearsal*
REVISION	*8 hours (panic revision)*
PARTY INVITATIONS	*0*
SNOGS	*0*

WEEK 21
W–E–I–R–D–O–S

'You are trespassing,' the receptionist said sternly. 'You have three seconds to leave. One . . . '

'No, p-p-p-please . . .' I stammered.

'. . . two . . .'

The doorman roughly grabbed hold of our arms.

'. . . three . . . OUT.'

The burly doorman swung us around and began to march us off the premises.

'Hey, wait!' called a familiar voice. 'I know these guys. They're cool. Camel Toe, right?'

My feet were barely touching the floor.

'Yes,' I said weakly, 'We just wanted to ask you a question.'

'Let them go, man,' said Wazzock. 'That's no way to treat ladies. They're my guests. Come on up to my suite, guys.'

The doorman reluctantly released us from his firm grip enabling Petrina and me to strut coolly over to our rockstar friend. OK – not *that* cool. We were hindered by the massive sweat stains on our Steel Dragon *Ladies Love Balls* tour T-shirts.

Wazzock's hotel suite was MEGA HUGE. It was like an MTV crib, with a plush cream sitting room, a cocktail bar, a study, dressing room, a walk-in wardrobe, an en-suite black marble master bathroom and an outside terrace overlooking leafy Manor Park.

Petrina and I found ourselves being swallowed up by an enormous and seemingly very hungry sofa.

'So what's going on?' asked Wazzock, striking a chord on his black Fender Strat.

'We just wanted to ask if you would like to come on to our school radio station as a guest next week,' I replied.

Wazzock lifted his red bandana and scratched his head. 'No way, man,' he said from underneath his fringe. 'I don't do interviews.'

Candida, who had introduced herself formally as Trudy, the band's PR woman, rolled her big blue eyes. 'It's true. He's a pain in the arse,' she said. 'He may give it the old rock-god arrogance on stage, but in reality he's the shyest man in the world. In fact, I'm amazed he's even talking to you right now.'

'Yeah, but these guys know Walter,' said Wazzock. 'Blossom and *Petrina.*' He and Candida exchanged a knowing look.

She seemed surprised. 'Petrina! Right!' she smiled, revealing a set of perfect pearly white teeth. 'I love Walter!'

Petrina scowled. 'He's our best friend. Except we've sort of fallen out with him a little bit.'

'I can't imagine Walter falling out with anyone,' chirped Candida. 'He's so sweet.'

'Yeah, well you don't know him like I do,' Petrina snapped back aggressively. (I think she might have had a touch of PMS.)

Candida shifted awkwardly on her leather seat. 'Apparently not.'

'Is there any way I can persuade you to come on the station?' I asked hopefully.

Wazzock shook his head. 'Uh-uh,' he said. 'Not unless you knock me unconscious with a baseball bat, bundle me into a van, tie me onto the studio chair and torture me with a cat o'nine tails until I can take no more.'

Petrina looked at me. 'Can we do that?'

I shook my head in defeat. We'd let Toby and Felix down and it was beginning to dawn on me that I was possibly about to let the entire school down, too . . .

The moment we played Josh Raven's *Moonlight Stalker* on the Monday breakfast show the corridors began buzzing with excitement. You could almost reach out and touch the anticipation with your finger.

'I can't believe he's really coming in to our school,' squealed Paulette, handing me a hot chocolate from the vending machine as I pulled off my headphones. 'He's so hot.'

I am going to look like the biggest fool. Queen Quimboid of Quimland.

'Aren't you asexual?' asked Felix cheekily. 'I'm surprised he floats your boat.'

'I mean his *music* is hot,' she replied quickly. 'His chiselled jaw and ripped muscles do nothing for me AT ALL.'

'Well, I think he's the sexiest man on the planet,' I said, staring directly at the second sexiest man on the planet.

Felix flashed his gorgeous smile. 'Bridge Mount is fast becoming the A-List celebrity hang out,' he beamed, casually dropping his arm around my neck. 'Josh Raven, Wazzock . . . who's it gonna be next?'

Petrina looked at me from the other side of the studio and mouthed 'tell him'.

Can't I just remain in denial? It's much nicer than reality.

'Umm . . . Felix . . .' I said hesitantly. 'There's something I need to tell you.'

Felix ignored me, pulling out a stack of CDs from his rucksack. 'I've got all six Steel Dragon albums here, plus a few rare E.P.s and limited-edition vinyl singles. To have them signed by Wazzock will be a dream come true.'

Does anyone have a spare sandpit for me to bury my head in?

'Yeah, well . . . you see there's a bit of a problem,' I continued.

'I've got a Steel Dragon tour T-shirt that I'd like him to sign,' said Toby, adjusting one of the guest microphones. 'I might even get him to sign my leg so that I can get it tattooed on permanently.'

A blob of drool plopped onto the mixing desk. Petrina quickly wiped it away with her sleeve, hoping that nobody had noticed.

Felix seemed to approve. 'That's a cool idea,' he said. 'I might get one too.'

I'm afraid I had to wipe the corner of my mouth as well.

'How about the four of us go and get a coffee after school today?'

A DOUBLE DATE?! OH. MY. GOD.

Petrina clapped her hands excitedly. 'That would be great,' she chirped.

259

OK. They're in a great mood. Should soften the blow. I'll do it now . . .

'Yeah, we'd love to,' I agreed. 'So, the thing is . . . we asked Wazzock if he would come in to the station, but he said no. He doesn't do interviews. He's actually really shy, you know.'

Felix and Toby looked at each other.

That wasn't so bad.

Moonlight Stalker was coming to an end, so I pulled on my headphones in preparation for my next link. 'Joe's Café after school, then?'

'Er, actually I don't think I can make it after all,' said Felix. 'I've just remembered that my mum wants me to ummm . . . put the bins out.'

'Me too,' said Toby quickly. 'I've got to play golf.'

'I didn't know you played golf,' said Petrina.

'Ummm, yeah,' muttered Toby. 'I'm handicapped. A one hundred bogey, under par.'

It was clear to us that Felix and Toby were heartbroken at the news. In fact, they were so upset they didn't speak to us for the rest of the day. To be honest, I don't blame them. It's my fault entirely and I am shouldering the guilt to prove it. I set them up for an inevitable fall, knowing exactly how much disappointment really can hurt. I should have known better.

I had made a promise to the school that I seemed unlikely to fulfil. Wazzock wasn't going to perform and it looked as if Josh Raven wouldn't either. Who was I trying to kid? I'd got caught up in the moment, promising an evening of rock 'n' roll coolness with no guarantee that I'd be able to pull it off. But, despite my impending public humiliation, I wanted to ensure that Camel Toe put on a brilliant show.

Having rehearsed every single day for the past couple of weeks, we knew we sounded good, but we wanted Walter's honest opinion on our live act. Thing is, he won't talk to us at school and isn't answering his phone or returning any of our messages. When Petrina spoke to his mum she said that she'd hardly seen him over the past few weeks as he'd either been locked in his room or hanging out with Wazzock. Our friend had clearly dropped us and we couldn't really blame him.

'Hey, Bumface,' sneered a voice behind me in the corridor. 'We're all waiting for an epic fail on Friday. Don't you go letting us down!'

I turned round and saw Fiona Tittledown and her gang of slangers bent double with laughter.

'Just ignore them,' said Petrina, linking her arm through mine. 'Everything is going to be fine.'

I felt panicky. 'But what if Josh Raven doesn't turn up? What if I forget how to strum and sing at the same time? What if I look like a fool?'

'It's going to be all right,' she said calmly as she stroked my arm. 'You'll see.'

Fiona's piercing voice echoed down the corridor again. 'Who does she think she is?' she scoffed. 'Best friend to the stars? HA! Wazzock doesn't want anything to do with her. As if someone as famous as Josh Raven is going to show up upon *her* request!'

'Poor, deluded Bumface,' jeered Lucy Perkins. 'Don't forget, she honestly thinks she stands a chance with Felix. Hilarious!'

Fiona doubled up in hysterics. 'Well you can't blame the girl for aspiring to be as cool as moi!'

The peel of malicious laughter rang through my ears, vibrating vigorously through my body until I felt physically sick.

'That's right, Fiona,' I turned and spat uncontrollably. 'Because it's *really* so very cool to spend your free time dressed as a princess, while old men in stripey tights dance around you shouting "whither is the privy?"'

The colour drained from Fiona's face as her puzzled cronies turned to face her.

'Eh?' mumbled Lucy.

'What Blossom is trying to say,' said Petrina gleefully. 'Is that your super-cool friend is partial to a bit of medieval re-enactment on a regular basis.'

Lucy looked utterly appalled as Fiona buried her face in her hands.

'Not so cool now,' I said with a wry smile. 'You minging, plume-plucked harpy!'

Petrina gave me a swift high five as Lucy and her buddies bombarded a shell-shocked Fiona with stream of cruel taunts. But our tiny victory was short lived.

I rested my head against Petrina's shoulder. 'If Josh Raven doesn't show up on Friday I will be the most hated girl in the school.'

'Don't be silly,' said Petrina, but the sour smell of public humiliation had already wafted into my nostrils. I breathed it in deeply, my lungs filling to capacity with the impending shame.

At the end of the corridor a comfortably familiar figure leaned against the wall, legs crossed, record bag slumped on the floor. Walter glanced at us through his fringe as we approached him. I smiled, looking for a sign of reassurance, but he just picked up his bag and disappeared around the corner.

'Ignore him,' said Petrina sagely. 'He's a right old mardy chops.'

She did a good job of faking her annoyance, but I could see straight through her pretence. Her eyes lingered sadly on the spot where he had been standing.

From: Blossom Uxley-Michaels   24th May 16:21
To: info@poptasticmanagement.com
SUBJECT: Friday

Dear Sir/Madam,

Will Josh Raven be attending the Bridge Mount School Disco?
Have you even read a single email that I have sent you?

Yours hopefully,

Blossom Uxley-Michaels

🐫	Very important request for Josh Raven	7th Jan	16:45
🐫	URGENT – Josh Raven needed VERY URGENTLY.	12th Jan	17:03
🐫	Requesting Josh Raven's presence	21st Jan	08:10
🐫	JOSH RAVEN WANTED NOW	25th Feb	12:54
🐫	ANNOYED!!!	8th Mar	18:12
🐫	SORRY.	16th Mar	07:02
🐫	Pride of Britain	6th Apr	17:33
🐫	School Disco	15th Apr	16:59
🐫	Headlining	1st May	15:11
🐫	School Disco	12th May	16:17
🐫	Friday	24th May	16:21
🅟	Your enquiry	24th May	16:22

Dear Blossom,

Yes

Best wishes,
Poptastic Management

Poptastic★
management

Currently listening to *Want You To Want Me Because I Want You (A Lot)* by Josh Raven

Poptastic Management is a division of Poptastic World Media Group Ltd. All Poptastic logos are copyrighted trademarks and not to be reused for third party promotional purposes unless permission has been granted. (Permission will not be granted.) The contents of this email are confidential and intended for the recipient only. If you have received this email in error, please eradicate it from your records. Immediately.

🌿 DO YOU HAVE TO PRINT THIS EMAIL? REALLY?
Please consider trees and small animals before printing this email.

Yes? YES? What did *that* mean? *Yes* we have read your emails? *Yes* Josh Raven will be attending the Bridge Mount School Disco? *Yes* is the opposite of no? Yes sir, yes sir, three bags full? WHAT DID IT MEAN?

Arrrrrrrrrrrrrgggggggggghhhhhhhh!

Looking out of Breeze's window that evening (whilst secretly returning a vest I'd borrowed), I saw Creepy Dave once again sitting on the wall opposite our house. I was curious to find out why he was so keen to meet my sister and what was in the brown paper bag that he so desperately wanted to give her. He looked a little embarrassed when I crossed the road and sat down by his side.

'Hey,' I offered as an ice-breaker.

'Hey,' he replied softly.

We sat in awkward silence for a few moments, staring blindly at the horizon, looking for a way to bring on the big thaw. I took a deep breath and turned to face him, noticing at once how pretty his bright green eyes were, especially set against the three-piece, olive tweed suit that he wore.

'Andreas didn't scare you off, then?' I asked.

'Nah,' he replied with a smile.

'Seen kittens with more rage, huh?'

Creepy Dave laughed warmly and the ice began to melt.

'So what's the deal with Breeze anyway?' I continued. 'She's got big feet, flappy ears and, quite frankly, she smells.'

Creepy Dave's expression suddenly became serious. 'She was perfect at school,' he said.

Are we actually talking about the same person?

'I kind of hoped that, if I got to know her, a bit of her coolness might rub off on me.'

'But Breeze was a misfit too,' I pointed out. 'Literally too cool for school.'

'Yeah, but she was happy to be the lone sheep.'

Just like Walter.

'I, on the other hand, desperately wanted to be accepted.' Creepy Dave looked away, stifling a small cough into his fist.

You totally fancied her.

'On the last day of term, right after our exams had finished,' he continued, 'I followed Breeze onto the bus as she made her way home. The bus route went in the opposite direction to my house, but I wanted to just be near her one last time. I took the seat directly behind her and saw she was engrossed in the final pages of a dog-eared novel. She finished the book just before the bus pulled into her stop, stuffing it carelessly into her rucksack. Then as she got up out of her seat the bus jolted and the book fell onto the floor. I picked it up, fully intending to hand it straight back, but the doors closed shut as I called Breeze's name.'

He held up the brown paper bag. 'This book made me realise that Breeze was as weird as me. I wasn't alone. Now I want to return it and say thank you.'

Now this sounds like a book that I really NEED to read. I wonder what it's called. . . Weirdos vs Quimboids – The Feud that Keeps on Giving *perhaps?*

'What's the name of the book?' I asked.

Dave hugged the paper bag close to his chest. '*The Outsiders* by S.E. Hinton.'

He looked towards the sky where the pinks and purples were merging like watercolours with the auburns and golds. 'I treasured this book as if it was the most precious thing in the world,' he said.

'It sounds very special,' I whispered.

Dave stood up and placed the brown paper bag containing the book in my hand. 'Please return this to Breeze. And tell her thank you. She really made a difference.'

He gave me a knowing smile that I understood instantly and then headed off into his own glorious sunset. I watched him until he turned the corner of my street and disappeared out of view.

Breeze, who'd been hiding by the front curtains, went very quiet when explained the reason for Dave's persistence. She took the book and ran upstairs to her room, where she spent the rest of the evening.

HARE MOON

ALSO KNOWN AS: BRIGHT MOON,
GRASS MOON, MOON WHEN LEAVES ARE
GREEN, FLOWER MOON

The curtains lift. I am standing on the stage before the entire school with Cassiopeia resting in my hands. I am a superstar under the single spotlight that shines down upon me. In the front row I see Wazzock and Josh Raven. They are here to watch me. The crowd waits expectantly as I prepare to perform Poncerama. I strum the first chord and open my mouth to sing . . .

A moment of panic as no sound comes out. I strike the chord a second time, but again the words do not emerge. No matter how hard I try, I cannot seem to sing and strum simultaneously.

The crowd begins to boo. Josh and Wazzock are shaking their heads in disappointment. I feel the humiliation rising within me. Fiona and Lucy are pointing. They are laughing. Felix and Toby begin to laugh too. Gradually everyone in the assembly hall is laughing and jeering at me.

'She's naked!' laughs Josh Raven. 'And her norks are tiny!'

Echoes of laughter ring round the room as I look down at my unclothed body. I try to hide myself behind my metallic blue Yamaha Pacifica, but it's only a small guitar. A well-expensive, cherry red Gibson ES-335 would have concealed my modesty far more effectively.

I'll be honest – scheduling Mr Blackmore and Mrs Finley's Smooth Jazz Band as the warm-up act for the School Disco was probably not the best decision ever made. Watching the headmaster tinkling almost orgasmically on the ivories, while Mrs Finley gyrated her plump hips slowly in time to the rhythm of her saxophone was possibly the most disturbing sight anyone from Bridge Mount had ever seen. It makes me shudder just thinking about it.

Thankfully Luke Ludlow's DJ set that followed created a kind of remedial disco, enabling the traumatised pupils to dance any distressing images out of their memories. Someone who has already undergone a course of therapy, but clearly requires more is Luke's younger brother, who appears to be sticking to his alcoholic ways. Matthew managed to smuggle in three bottles of vodka, one of which he emptied into the jugs of orange squash that had been laid out for thirsty dancers on a trestle table. As a direct result, by seven-fifteen most of the first years were either crying in a corner or attempting to stage dive into an audience that parted like the Red Sea as they jumped.

The Dempsey Love branding was visible on every available surface in the hall, where Paulette had set up a stall selling her own original T-shirts (designed by the über-talented Walter). Judging by the amount of pupils brandishing logos such as *I'M CUPID'S BOSS* and *IMMORTAL ASEXUALITY* across their chests, she was doing a roaring trade. Paulette herself was dressed in a power-suit with shoulder pads wide enough to take out an entire American football team.

Clutching the last Poptastic Management email in my hand, I studied the words, desperate to glean some meaning from it. But when Josh Raven didn't turn up for his scheduled stage call at seven-thirty, I felt an impending, heavy sense of doom.

'I'm going to look such an idiot, Petrina,' I wailed as we stood in the wings, waiting to perform. 'I'm Bumface. I've been ridiculed all my life and now it's about to get even worse.

Everyone will hate me.'

I'm even beginning to hate myself.

Petrina looked at her watch. 'There's still time yet,' she said calmly. 'You never know, he might show up.'

I shook my head. 'I'll officially be labelled the biggest weirdo to come out of Bridge Mount EVER.'

'Have you actually looked out there?' asked Petrina, pointing towards the excited audience. 'They might just be weirder than us.'

I peeped out from behind the curtain where Max Burcott was strutting around flapping his elbows like a chicken. It took me a few moments to realise (with horror) that he was actually performing one of his signature dance moves. Staring at him with hateful eyes was Kirsty Mackerby, who was wearing a set of multi-coloured flashing rabbit ears. Lucy Perkins stood at the snack table, deep in concentration as she carefully crushed a handful of Quavers with her fist, before pouring the crumbs into a glass of Coke (which she then drank). That's almost on a grossness par with Breeze's bogey collection. But not quite.

Beside me Petrina was scanning the crowd of students.

'I'd have thought Walter would be here to show some support,' she said.

I shook my head. 'We've been horrible to him. He feels hurt and used and, quite frankly, who could blame him?'

Petrina pretended to be blasé. 'Oh, he'll get over it,' she said unconvincingly.

'Why are you being so cold towards him?'

Petrina quickly looked away. *Is she crying?*

'We're not cool enough for him now that he's best friends with a pop star,' she said bitterly.

'All right?' asked a voice from behind me.

I turned round to find Felix standing there, looking hotter than the devil's bum, which I'd imagine is very hot indeed.

'I just wanted to wish you good luck,' he muttered in his soft sexy whisper. 'And to give you this.' To my surprise, his outstretched hand was holding a present. Yes, it was wrapped up in a crumpled mishmash of sellotape and Christmas wrapping paper, but he'd clearly gone to some effort.

I eagerly tore open the gift. Inside was *Star Wars Episode V: The Empire Strikes Back,* the second film and the fifth chapter in the series.

I would have preferred a box of chocolates or some cake, but I don't want to seem ungrateful.

'Is this the one with the goblin?' I asked.

Felix raised his eyebrows. 'Yoda? Yes it is.'

I closed my eyelids and for a split second, imagined pressing my lips against his, but when I opened my eyes, Felix had gone. Back to join his sluggery-lipped girlfriend, I suppose.

Just then, the loud, pulsing music faded out and Luke Ludlow's voice bellowed out of the speakers. 'OK, guys, it's time for more live music now. Two girls already making a name for themselves in the music industry, having recorded with the likes of the legendary Pete Hartley and Steel Dragon. Ladies and gentlemen, I give you . . . CAMEL TOE!!!'

Petrina and I gave each other a well-wishing hug and

walked out onto the stage to take our positions, soaking up the rapturous applause from the excited audience. Fiona Tittledown was standing right in front of the stage glaring at us with hatred. She still wasn't on speaking terms with Lucy, who was knocking back another plastic cup of crispy Coke. I picked up Cassiopeia and, under the glare of the bright spotlight, spoke nervously into the microphone.

'Hello Bridge Mount! We're Camel Toe!'

This was it. Was it to be the triumph we had been waiting for or the car crash the slangers predicted?

Petrina began the instantly recognisable opening chords of *Poncerama* and we were off.

It was a feeling like none other: a feeling of elation, adrenaline, happiness and purpose all rolled into one. *Poncerama* had received so much airplay on Bridge Mount FM that everyone in the audience knew most, or all, of the lyrics. To hear the words that I had written being sung back at me was mind-blowingly satisfying.

> *'Poncerama oooh, Poncerama ooooh,*
> *It's no wonder that nobody really likes you.'*

In amongst the faces I spotted Lucy, Felix, Toby, Kirsty, Matthew, Paulette, Mei and Max all pounding the air with their fists, chanting the chorus as if it was their own personal anthem. Even Fiona was involuntarily mumbling along with the lyrics. In that instant, my beloved Camel Toe had kicked down all the social boundaries that divided Bridge Mount Secondary School into Winners, outcasts, jocks and boffins. We were a room full of weirdos singing together, united by music. I glanced across at Petrina to acknowledge our special moment, but her eyes did not return my gaze. She was searching the audience, looking for the missing piece that would make the moment perfect. But Walter was nowhere to be seen.

The song came to an end and, before we'd even fully soaked up the adulation, we launched straight into *The Man With An Eggy Beard*. We were hyped. This was our angry song, where we could really let rip. Our anxiety, insecurity, sadness, fear and frustration came flooding out in front of an equally emotionally-charged audience. They cheered and pogoed as if they were in the front row of the Pyramid Stage at Glastonbury. It was AWESOME!!!

And then something special happened. Something totally unexpected. Something utterly BRILLIANT. Just as we arrived at the middle eight section, somebody else began to play the super fiddly guitar solo that I'd secretly been dreading. The mystery guitarist had magical fingers, plucking the strings the way only the most skilful musicians can. Petrina and I were stunned. As were the audience, who went quiet as they searched around the stage for the phantom guitarist. Slowly, from the darkness of the wings, emerged a man in black, his trademark red bandana pulled low over his fringe and his shiny Fender Strat slung loosely over his shoulder. The audience gasped, then went crazy as the realisation hit them. Wazzock, lead guitarist from Steel Dragon, was on *their* stage – the exact place where Mr Blackmore bored them on a weekly basis with his righteous sermons on morality, values and why hoodies are the root of all evil. I saw Fiona Tittledown standing motionless in amongst a sea of jumping teenagers; Toby and Felix ecstatically embracing each other in astonishment, as if they were witnessing a real life miracle occurring before their very eyes.

Right then, Petrina and I were propelled into the outer stratosphere of coolness. We were living Coolians from the Planet Cool, as Wazzock played on stage with us until the very last note of our song.

When he'd finished, the normally shy INTERNATIONAL ROCK STAR stepped to the front of the stage, taking hold of my microphone.

'Hi, guys,' he mumbled quietly. 'Good to see you. I'm here as a favour to a very dear friend of mine.'

Petrina's eyes were searching the crowd.

'A cool guy asked me to help him finish a song he'd written for a girl who's very special to him.'

Who does Walter fancy? Oh God. Not me. Oh please no . . . That would be like snogging my brother – if I had one. YUCK.

Wazzock spun round to face my oblivious best friend. 'Petrina-Ola Olsen.'

Phew. That would have been soooooo awkward . . . Oh!

'Poohead,' he continued, as the muffled, suppressed sound of giggles echoed across the school hall. 'This song has been written for you by Walter, who would like to share a secret with you. He wants you to know that his middle name is Edward. Walter Edward Ecclestone.'

Petrina's face was beginning to glow like a beacon. Wazzock took a plectrum from his pocket and began softly playing a simple, heart-melting love song, with a melody sweet enough to charm the honey-bees. He started to sing.

'I'm leaving today with you,
In my mind, that's all I want to do.
When you're near everything gets slow,
Two outsiders with no place to go.
Meet me at old Joe's Café,
Take my hand, we'll run away.'

Petrina's knees buckled as Walter's lyrics nuzzled their way under her skin, forcing her to grab hold of her keyboard for support. At the back of the audience, through her tears, she noticed the familiar figure of her dear friend leaning heavily against the wall, his head down, eyes obscured by his fringe as always.

My heart fluttered as I realised what was happening between my two best friends. How could I not have noticed before? It was so obvious; it was so . . . so . . . perfect. At the front of the stage, caught up in the romance of the moment, Fiona Tittledown had violently rammed her tongue down Felix's throat, occasionally glancing in my direction to ensure that I knew my place. But her territorial display was wasted on me. For whatever reason, I just didn't seem to care. I was consumed by the thrill of the moment, letting Wazzock's gruff, but surprisingly fragile, voice wash over me.

'I'm just like you,
I'm the WEE to your POO.
You're just like me,
I'm the POO to your WEE'.

Throughout the room students were swaying in time to the hypnotically beautiful melody, enchanted by its gentle simplicity. Paulette Dempsey was clearly enjoying the touch of Max Burcott's hands on her bum as they whirled round in their slow dance spiral of lust, her declaration of asexuality on hold once again. Kirsty Mackerby had been reduced to a giggling frenzy after Mei Miyagi impishly whispered something into her ear. Mrs Finley and Mr Blackmore were moving swiftly through the audience, confiscating any illicit lighters that anyone dared to hold aloft, and an inebriated Matthew Ludlow sent drinks crashing to the ground after Wazzock's soothing guitar lulled him to sleep, causing him to lose his balance and topple backwards on to the trestle table.

'I'm dancing tonight with you,
Kiss your face, that's all I want to do.
When you're near I can take the pain,
It doesn't hurt when they call us names.
Meet me at old Joe's Café,
Take my hand, we'll run away.'

Petrina had already pushed halfway through Wazzock's captivated audience before I'd even noticed that she'd left the stage. She stopped in front of Walter, who was still gazing down at his dirty baseball boots at the back of the hall. Becoming aware of her presence, he lifted his head and Petrina gently swept his fringe to one side. For the very first time, she was able to look into Walter's almond-shaped eyes. Petrina smiled – I saw she'd been right all along. They were a deep brown colour. She tenderly kissed his lips and she mouthed 'I'm sorry,' before resting her forehead against his.

> *'I'm just like you,*
> *I'm the WEE to your POO.*
> *You're just like me,*
> *I'm the POO to your WEE'.*

I left Wazzock to receive his applause alone, taking the opportunity to look outside for any sign of Josh Raven. Of course he wasn't there. Maybe it was time I accepted once and for all that he wasn't coming. Walter might have been able to sweet-talk an international megastar, but why would Josh even acknowledge the request of Braceface Bumface Pork-tit Ham Hooters?

Once again, Petrina and I took up our places on stage and continued to play the last two songs of our set, with Walter jigging happily from foot to foot in the wings. The final chord of *The Wizard* marked the end of Camel Toe's debut performance. We took our bow and left the stage.

'He's not coming, Petrina,' I said dejectedly. 'I've let everyone down.'

'Are you kidding?' she replied. 'Wazzock performed here at Bridge Mount. We are the coolest kids in school.'

I shook my head. 'We're not cool, Petrina. We never have been and we never will be. Let's face it – we're always going to be weirdos.'

'Yeah,' said Walter, putting his arms around our shoulders. 'But we're the coolest weirdos in town!'

I'm a nobody. A daydreamer with an over-active imagination. This is my reality check. THIS IS WHO I AM.

Walter and Petrina fell about with laughter, but were stopped suddenly in their tracks when chants of 'We want Josh Raven,' began to resonate loudly through the school hall. I felt the colour drain from my face and a rush of fear well up in the pit of my stomach.

'It's OK,' said Petrina kindly. 'I'll tell them.'

And she bravely walked back out onto the stage to break the news that would crush the heart of every girl (and gay guy) in the school. Walter was about to follow when something caught his attention. He walked towards the window, leaving his girlfriend to submit herself to the torrent of abuse that would undoubtedly follow. I felt like the biggest quimboid to EVER walk the earth.

'WOWZOIDS!' shrieked Walter, his face pressed up against the glass.

'Don't be so melodramatic, Walter,' I said wearily. 'Petrina's been called plenty of names over the years. They can't say anything that she hasn't heard already. Poohead, Corpse-breathed Viking, Four-eyed speccy arse – water off a duck's back. Anyway, it's *me* they're all going to hate.'

Walter looked impatient. 'Shut up for a minute and come here.'

I sighed deeply and slouched across to the window where a huge black car and a transit van had pulled up outside the school gates. The passenger door of the black car opened.

'NO WAY!!!' I screamed, jogging frantically on the spot with excitement. 'Tell Petrina, Walter. Tell her *now!*'

As Walter ran across to the stage, I rushed round to the fire exit that opened directly into the staff car park. And there, as if starring in one of his own moody music videos (without the rain), was Josh Raven. Standing by the gates, wearing heavy charcoal guy-liner, skinny black jeans and a tight olive green T-shirt that showed off his RIPPED body, he looked proper real-time HOT. My heart pounded in my chest. I'd waited for this moment for a long time.

'Josh?' I shouted, cupping my hands around my mouth.

Josh waved his hand dramatically above his head. 'Blossom?' he called back. 'I'm so sorry I'm late, darling. Who knew a penazzle would take so long?'

WHAT is a penazzle . . . ? Oh!

And then, like Mr Gay from number 69 Gay Road, Gaytown in Gayland, he *minced* across the car park towards me, hips wiggling like a long-distance walker. OH. MY. GOD. He was more camp than Dad's VW van.

'Oh, look at your Camel Toe', he trilled, pointing at the logo on my chest. 'So cute!'

I thought of the testosterone-fuelled music videos that

I'd watched countless times on YouTube – Josh's RIPPED bare torso, his cute bum, the kissing beautiful women in the rain – and realised that I'd been duped.

But it still didn't stop him from being sexy.

I wonder if I could turn him?

Josh ran his hand through his luscious dark curly head of hair and linked his arm through mine. 'See that old fire escape over there?' he said as we hurriedly walked along. 'That's where I lost my virginity to Barry Palmer when I was in the sixth form. Put me off hairy backs for life.'

NO. I definitely couldn't turn him. And Barry Palmer? Really? Josh could do so much better.

'So you were really popular at school, then?' I asked.

'Everyone thought I was a bit of a weirdo,' he replied. 'It wasn't the most fun I've ever had. But who's laughing now?' He raised his perfectly plucked eyebrows at me knowingly.

'How did you get so cool?'

Josh smiled warmly and tapped his rock solid pec. 'I was always cool in here,' he reached out towards me. 'And as long as you are cool with yourself, then you're cool in there.'

Wowzoids! He almost touched my nork. I LOVE HIM.

'Now, lead the way to my adoring fans,' he purred as I composed myself and steered him into the school.

Mr Blackmore was stepping out of the door to see what was going on when we bumped straight into him.

'Hello, Josh,' he said surprisingly calmly. Josh was not only an A-List celebrity, but also a notoriously difficult ex-pupil. 'Punctual as ever, I see.'

'Adrian!' screeched Josh, flinging his arms around his old headmaster. 'You look a heck of a lot better than when I last saw you.'

'Yes, well, let's not talk about that, now,' Mr Blackmore replied swiftly. 'You need to get yourself on stage before a riot breaks out. Chop, chop.'

He held the door open for us allowing us to pass.

'I bet that was a bit strange for you,' I whispered. 'You can't have seen him for years.'

'On the contrary, darling,' chirruped Josh. 'I see him almost every month. He's one of the regulars at the Sailor Boy Club in Soho. He looks surprisingly dishy in a pair of hot pants.'

I swallowed down the tiny bit of sick that had risen into my mouth as a disturbing image appeared in my mind that I fear will stay with me for a very long time.

The sound of rowdy, impatient students rang through the corridors as we approached the stage.

'Oooh, who's the hotty?' he asked, winking at Walter who was silently lurking in the wings.

'He's taken I'm afraid.' I smiled. *By my best friend!*

'The cute ones always are,' said Josh with a cheeky grin.

Watching Josh Raven perform a magical rendition of *Moonlight Stalker*, with Petrina, Walter and Wazzock standing by my side, I felt, for the first time I could remember, that I belonged. We'd achieved something great, but we were part of something much, much greater. Some may call us Weirdos; a bunch of misfits who look different; the outsiders who don't fit in. But if that means we're simply individuals following our own paths, being true to ourselves under no false pretence, then we will wear that label with pride. W-E-I-R-D-O-S. A non-exclusive group open to anyone who has strayed from the flock.

When I arrived home after the school disco, I was filled with a sense of hope and enlightenment. Was *I* really the biggest misfit in the Uxley-Michaels household? I considered Andreas's blue-painted face and tartan kilt when he dressed as Braveheart, Dad's eco-warrior dreadlocks and bum tattoo, Mum wearing her medieval nun outfit and Breeze in her St Trinian's school uniform. I was about to declare myself as the true outsider of the family, but then I remembered the whole 'pork-tit' incident and realised that we are all as strange as each other.

The May Hare Moon was shining brightly, lighting up the dusky sky. It is said that the flowers grow at night during this time, dancing in honour of the full moon.

I was feeling vibrant and in bloom, so when my parents monthly ritual was over and they'd gone up to bed, I snuck outside into the garden to perform my own naked moon salutation, alongside the dancing flowers. Without an MP3 player sounding out a beat, the rhythm of suburban life became my music: the wind whistling in the trees; the distant hum of traffic; the jet rumbling across the night sky and the disgusting cries from the randy foxes mating in the garden two doors down. I'll be honest – it wasn't for me. All that cold air blowing around about my lady parts left me feeling vulnerable and exposed and I couldn't get inside fast enough. So, as a token gesture to the magnificent full moon, I busted a few of my best dance moves and ran back into the house before any of the neighbours spotted me. I mean, I wouldn't want anyone to think I was a weirdo, would I?!

ACKNOWLEDGEMENTS

No gushy lovey dovey stuff from me. Just a straight forward MASSIVE thank you to the biggest bunch of weirdos I know:

Non, Liz, Robert and all at Catnip. Pip and all at Bounce. Sophie and all at MBA Literary Agents. Vicky and her magic artwork. And finally my lovely Goddaughter Ella. Thank you all. You are proper real time AWESOME.

ABOUT THE AUTHOR

Natasha was born on the summer solstice and shares a birthday with Prince William which makes her part hippie and part royalty in equal doses (and that is an actual scientific fact). After school, she skipped university to try her luck as a runner on feature films and pop videos before a programme controller lured her into the magical world of radio. She spent the next twelve years having THE BEST FUN EVER hosting shows on Xfm and BBC Radio 6 Music.

Natasha has appeared on TV shows such as Richard and Judy, presented radio shows with comedians such as Jimmy Carr, interviewed loads of international celebrities, including Dave Grohl from Foo Fighters and Chris Martin from Coldplay but none of them liked her enough to want to be her friend – possibly because she's just as weird as the characters she writes about . . .

Natasha now lives in Croydon with her husband Jim, sons Oscar and Wilfie and two Glastonbury cats, Derek and Mavis, and Enid, her chocolate Labrador rescue dog.

You can find out more about Natasha at:
<u>www.natashadesborough.co.uk</u>